THE MIRRORED PRINCESS
THE CASTARA SERIES

S C LICATA

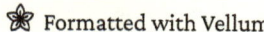 Formatted with Vellum

To my husband who loved and supported me every step of the way
and The Finer Things Literary Club.
I couldn't have done it without all of you.

THE WORLD

VARETHRIEL

THE SACRED LAND

F CASTARA

IGNARIA

AERONIA

SKYBORN
CHAPEL

AQUARIA

HOMESTEAD

TERRANIA

SOLEVARA

CONTENTS

PROLOGUE

As tradition would dictate, the king, the high priestess, and the kingdom's two best herbalists—one for the mother and one for the babe-—were all present as the Fae queen labored to bring the heir apparent into the Fae world of Castara.

After an especially brutal birth, the new prince entered the world just as the full moon crested the night sky, marking the imminent change of reign upon the prince reaching his majority.

Exhausted from the pain, the queen collapsed and tuned out all the noise other than the wails of her new son. Her murmured words, stifled by the chaos of the room, went unheard as a tear slid down her cheek. The priestess and the herbalist for the new babe moved to the side of the room to begin the birthing rituals. The king, pulled between his queen and his newly birthed son, ultimately went to her side upon noticing her distress.

"He looks healthy," he whispered into her ear while he

stroked her hair, his attention remaining on his son who was being fussed over.

"It isn't done," she said as she turned her face away, hiding the tears that streaked down her face.

The king's eyebrows furrowed as he shifted his focus to her and then to the other herbalist, who had gone unnaturally still next to them, color draining from her face.

"What's wrong?" he demanded, coming to his full Fae height. The tips of his ears quivered.

"I-I don't..." The herbalist's wide eyes shot to the other herbalist, who left the babe and hurried over to them. The second herbalist began applying pressure to the queen's abdomen, her features becoming increasingly more alarmed.

The king questioned the two in front of him. "Has the princess been born? Should we get the herbalists from the other room?"

"It isn't done," the queen repeated quietly to no one in particular, shaking her head, eyes squeezed tight.

Everyone froze for one more breath before she cried out in agony, sending the room into greater pandemonium. The high priestess, who swaddled the new prince in her arms, watched as everyone else tried to fix whatever was ailing the queen.

Through her suffering, the queen's broken words rip through the confusion. "There will be another!"

Shock washed over everyone's faces, but there was no time to dissect her words since a second babe was in fact coming.

A quarter past the rise of the moon, a second son was born into the Vaylor family. The first known set of Fae twins.

CHAPTER
ONE
NISSA

S lamming the door to my flat, I drop my bag, wipe the water droplets from my face, and shove my wet hair off my shoulders. My head leaned back against the door, I pull the wind deep into my lungs and rub the dull ache in my chest.

With the elemental energy depleting and the synthetic options failing, rootwalking has become almost impossible over long distances. I was supposed to be at the heart of the Two Kingdoms hours ago. Normally I would never complain about minimizing my time in Castara's capital, Solevara, but I've missed a fitting. Which guarantees that I'll have to listen to a lecture from my mother about the importance of all the ridiculous responsibilities that revolve around me being in the Elite City.

Despite her thoughts on it, I *can* wear one of my many elaborate dresses collecting dust in the closets at her austere residence. I doubt anyone would remember all the dresses *I've* worn here over the years.

I look out the window as the wind whistles through the

cracks in my door. A sigh leaves my chest. Goddess, what I would give to not be paraded around and forced to smile for one more day. Maybe this storm will turn into one of the Goddess's destructive tantrums. Then I won't have to worry about a dress at all.

If tonight's Beltane festival is canceled, I could have stayed at the Homestead with my plants another day. Instead, I'm alone in this one-bedroom flat, counting down the moments until I can go home.

Too bad Gaia rarely attacks the actual kingdom. She prefers to hit us where it hurts us the most—in the elemental lands.

Come on, Gaia, be in a mood. It's what you do best.

My lips quirk. I turn towards the small cupboard and begin digging through the vials and jars as the thought of the weekend theatrics builds the ache in my chest. I understand that I'm part of the only two sets of twins ever born to the Fae and that our presence is an encouragement during the fertility holiday. But—

A sharp pain lances through me as lightning fills the room. I knock over a number of glass containers and double over in pain. My knuckles turn white on the edge of the cabinet door as thunder rattles the flowerpots at my back.

After a few slow, deep breaths, the pain eases just enough for me to resume searching through the dried herbs, tinctures, and teas. Something to ease the ache of anxiety from simply being here.

With shaking hands, I set the kettle on and mix chamomile, lavender, blue vervain, and motherwort into a mug. I try to will away the pain until the kettle boils and turn towards my plants, hoping for a distraction.

Communing with my natural energy will help. Like most Earth Fae, plants and herbs have calmed me since I was a child. As I've gotten older, the idea of helping something grow from a tiny seed into a magnificent healing plant is my chief source of joy.

One hand pressed to my aching chest, I lean down to inspect each petal and leaf before checking the dried roots and flowers I left hanging upside down. The watering system I've set up appears to be working properly. I could ask my mother or sister to see to my plants, but considering neither of them has ever once stepped foot in this flat, I'm confident that not a single one would still be alive. The intricate system is the only way I make Solevara feel at least slightly like a home away from home.

Typically, I'm only here once a year for a few days during the festival. This visit is different. I'll be stuck here for weeks, until our birthdate and the new king's coronation. My twin sister, Nova, will be the new queen. I've been summoned to attend. Not that anyone outside of my mother will care whether I'm here or not. And even her desire for my presence is purely for appearances.

I rub my nagging chest and turn to the whistling kettle. Pouring the hot liquid over my mixture, I watch the steam swirl into the air and take a deep breath of the sweet floral scent. My mother's lack of interest in me doesn't bother me as much anymore, but Nova's indifference still hurts.

The Fae are always fascinated to see the almost identical twins. Our eyes are all that separates us. Otherwise, we're a perfect match with our brown wavy hair, heart-shaped faces, and button noses. Nova has a little more curve to her compared to my hard edges, but it's barely noticeable when we're dressed up, which she always is. They don't realize that my twin and I are basically strangers.

Squeezing those eyes closed, I shake away the thought of my estranged sister. I have enough to deal with being here. I don't need to torture myself. I'm here—as required. I'll put on

5

a few pretty dresses, show up, and then I'll go back to the Homestead the moment they say they don't need me anymore. Forget everyone here until the next time I'm required. Just like they forget about me.

Bringing the tea to my lips, I slowly blow before taking a long sip of the concoction, welcoming the heat that radiates from my gut through my body.

My small room lights up from a flash of the storm outside. Gripping the warm mug in both hands, I make my way to the back window and look up the hill to the vine-covered limestone castle. Fae fire shines in a high window through the dark storm, calling to me like a beacon. As the waterfall beneath it overflows from the torrential downpour, another arc of lightning reaches down from the sky. The destructive power strikes dangerously close to the slate tiles and copper-tipped ridges that adorn the castle's roof.

Unexpectedly, the air is violently ripped from my lungs. A wave of pain seizes me. I collapse to my knees. My tea and pieces of my mug splatter across the floor as I use both hands to hold myself up.

An audible gasp escapes when my bond with Nova is wrenched to the front of my chest. The sensation ripples through me, like someone just rearranged my insides while attempting to break through my breastbone from the inside out. The wind rushes from my chest as the strings that connect me to my twin are pulled taut, ready to snap.

The bond has become almost undetectable over the last few years with how distant we have become, but this... I've never felt anything like this between us.

I claw at my chest like there's a physical connection reaching from my body towards Nova. A physical tether that I can gain purchase over to lessen this pressure pulling from me.

A broken sob leaves my throat. Each muscle in my body shakes and locks into place.

The edges of my vision begin to fade to black right before tension inevitably snaps one of the strings. I'm yanked back into reality with a bloodcurdling scream that I barely register as my own.

My mouth hangs open in a silent wail. The only breaths I'm able to pull in are short gasps as each string to Nova is slowly and painfully fractured apart. With a single, frail connection left to my twin, a stabbing sensation shoots through my back.

My body finally gives out. *If this is death, at least the pain will stop.*

I BLINK awake as a hand strokes my cheek. The room has darkened around me and sky-blue eyes—Nova's eyes—stare down at me. *Identical in every way other than those eyes.* My lavender irises are the only way to tell us apart.

"Oh Nissa..." The whisper comes through a choked sob.

The voice has me scanning the rest of the face. My eyebrows come together when I see the tears slide over fine age lines.

"Mother," I croak through my tight vocal cords. The worst of the pain has receded, but phantom pains still radiate through my empty chest. Taking shallow breaths, I lay my hands over my heart. *I don't feel the bond, at all.*

"I'm here," my mother murmurs.

I glance around my flat, my confused mind grappling to understand. I swallow thickly as I put the pieces together. Whatever just happened, I survived it... but Nova didn't.

My mother helps lift me off the floor and prop me against

the wall edging my narrow bed. Numbness branches through me, easing the impact when she collapses down on the mattress beside me and studies my face, unaware of the pain she just caused to shoot through me. I can see the uncertainty as she tries to form her next words, but I don't need her to tell me.

"It's Nova," I offer to ease her discomfort at having to break the news.

She withers into my lap, her tears turning my sage dress dark green where they fall. "Oh, Nissa... My Nova! My Nova is gone," she wails into the fabric.

I stroke her hair and take slow, deep breaths, adjusting to the hole now dug into my chest. Nova and I have grown apart, but we always had that bond intertwining us on a biological level. If I'm honest, that was the *only* connection we had left.

The more hysterical my mother grows, the more uncomfortable I become. She hasn't been this physically affectionate towards me since I was sent away to the Homestead when I was a child. Nova is—*was*—the favored daughter. *The Daughter of Gaia.* In fact, this is the first time I have been asked to stay longer than a few days for Beltane. And it wasn't from a true desire to have me here.

"What will I do without her?" Her words are muffled.

The pain is still taking its toll on my body. It makes it hard to form a response, so I just close my eyes and rub comforting circles on her back as she sobs. I no longer hear the storm raging outside the thin walls.

"What happened?" I finally ask, my head leaned back against the wall.

Her crying slows, and after a moment I feel her sit up. I open my eyes, and she's smoothing her twisted bun back to her typical perfection.

"I don't know..." Tears still fill her eyes. She shakes her head and gulps back a sob. "The Guardians came after the

8

storm slowed. They didn't have details when they told me. Only that she was..." She squeezes her eyes shut and buries her face in her hands.

"They didn't tell you anything?" I balk.

As she shakes her head into her hands with a whimper, I rub the ache in my chest. Fae don't just die. We are essentially a force of nature. It's why Gaia, our goddess, is referred to as Mother Nature by the humans.

"The Vaylors should have sent someone other than the Guardians to tell you," I seeth.

We sit in uncomfortable silence until she looks up at me, her wet eyes now thinning. "How did *you* know?"

I wish it surprised me. She is actually questioning if I am a part of whatever happened to my twin, when she is the one who found me passed out on the floor.

I huff out a disbelieving laugh. "The bond, Mother," I offer dryly. Her concern for my well-being seems to have passed, so I don't feel the need to explain about the pain.

She stares at me with suspicion swirling in her eyes for a few more breaths. "The storm destroyed the festival grounds..." Her voice slows, and she seems to gather herself. "But the gala will still be held tomorrow night. I'll have them send your dress."

"You can't be serious." My jaw drops. "The Vaylors still expect us to attend the gala?" They want us to get dressed up right after my sister's death and celebrate just like any other year?

My mother stands. The closed-off woman I know reappears before my eyes. Smoothing her dress, she rises to full height and lifts her chin. "You know what day it is and why it's important for us to be there."

The tremble in her voice is barely noticeable anymore.

TWO

NISSA

W e approach the large gothic doors to the ballroom and wait for our ostentatious introduction. This is a formality that I'm accustomed to but have always hated. At least in the past I was able to enter behind Nova and slip off to the side. Today there is no Nova to hide behind, just my mother and me.

I take in the elaborate carvings at the heart of the wooden doors. An engraved intertwined sun and moon representing Gaia. Rays of her power stretch out to the four corners, pointing to each of the elements—fire, wind, earth, water. I snort at the irony as a pair of human servants split the image in two, using all their effort to pry the huge doors apart, the hinges groaning.

The uniformed male Fae stationed inside dips his head in respect at my mother and me. "Madam Navarro. Princess Nissa."

Princess?

I jerk my head towards him. My lungs ache as my dress fights against the air I've inhaled. I *have* to have misheard. I've only left my flat once since my mother's visit. I don't know how many in court have been informed of Nova's death. He must have mistook me for her.

But he didn't say *her* name. He said *mine*...

My heart is pounding in my ears, and I'm not sure I can take another breath. He ushers us forward, looking confused as he notes my shocked face. Like he has no idea that his introduction just stopped my whole world

"Daughter of Gaia, Princess... Nissa Navarro," he announces to the ballroom. This time he says my name like a proclamation, giving me no way to deny that I heard him correctly.

How in the worlds hadn't I realized that my twin's death would mean they would expect me to replace her?

Of course. It makes sense. These are the same Fae who've only ever seen me as some backup that they could hide away until they needed me. *And now they need me.*

But somehow, I still didn't see it coming.

The Vaylors were the ones who sent me away. I was never trained for this role, and now they expect me to step in as the Daughter or Gaia, the Princess of Castara. This has to be some kind of sick joke. It's only weeks until our majority birthdate and the coronation. They can't seriously expect me to replace Nova and become the *queen.*

My heart pounds, my magic stirring at my finger tips, and I instinctively rub the empty ache that's still pulsing in the center of my chest.

It isn't that I don't think I could do the job of queen. It isn't hard to smile and be a pretty party planning accessory at the king's side. Nova was eager to become whomever they needed her to be. Blowing in whatever direction they needed her to on a given day.

But I've never wanted this life.

It may have taken me a while to realize it, but sending me away from the Elite City may be the only positive thing the Vaylors and my mother ever did for me. I'm thankful I grew up doing something useful, away from the petty pursuits that spread like a blight among the same Fae in the ballroom in front of me. Gossip and complaining grow like weeds among the Elite, even as their powers are growing weaker and weaker every day. But with all their chatter, no one is asking why the Goddess is attacking our power source. No one is talking about anything of significance. No one is asking why the *true* Daughter of Gaia is dead.

I don't realize my feet are still rooted in the doorway until my mother's hand pushes against my lower back. I stumble into the ballroom barely catching my footing on the polished floor before I embarrass myself. The entire Elite are watching, all eyes on me.

I'm not ten steps into the room before they pounce like starved animals after their next kill. But I have no desire to be one of their meals. Fae, who've only ever looked my way when they mistook me for Nova, are congratulating me on becoming their new princess. Fawning over me, acting as if this is some achievement that I've been working towards my whole life.

The truth: this role is being forced on me purely because of the day I was born—and *my sister's death.*

Which I still have no details on.

I guess it was no different for Nova. Only chosen by the day she was born. Except for the fact that she wanted this life, and as the first born was *actually* chosen by the Goddess. I wasn't.

With each undeserved accolade thrown my way, the corset of my dress grows tighter. My lungs fight against the constricting boning in the bodice. The dress is too tight, almost making me wish for a fleeting moment that I had made that fitting yesterday.

Would that have changed anything? Would Nova still be alive?

I tug at the waist of the absurd monstrosity of a dress that the Royal Guardians dropped off at my mother's house. If they are going to push me into a dress that contradicts every aspect of my personality and style, they could at least have brought it to my place.

The overly large brown faux flowers that dot the fabric look half dead. When magic flowed freely in our lands these fabric florals would have bloomed through the night, changing the color and aesthetic of the outfit completely. But with the current state, elemental magic can't, and shouldn't, be used on such mundane things. Leaving me in this half dead garment.

The only positive attribute is the mushroom-style skirt with its absurd number of tulle layers in different shades of brown. While I would never be caught in this silhouette under normal circumstances, I'm thankful for the mountains of billowing fabric. They puff out so far that at least it keeps everyone a few twigs away. Nevertheless, I'm concerned that my lack of oxygen combined with the weight of the skirt could cause me to collapse at any moment.

I've barely registered anything that the female in front of me has said before she grips her forearms and looks to the floor, offering the Earth Fae respect. "Stone and soil steady your steps, your Highness." She hurries off and the next couple approaches, eager to have their turn at me.

I'm trying to focus on what they're saying, but their words start to sound as if they're speaking to me from underground. I blink repeatedly, trying to make out what is being said but it's to no avail. My mother's glare narrows in on me as I sway in my heels like an unsecured vine in the wind. *How mortified would she be if I stepped right out of them to ground myself on the black walnut flooring?*

My magic flares in my veins as it dawns on me—she knew this was coming and said nothing. Alira Navarro, always the face of grace and composure, just like Nova. She could have warned me, in my flat or when I came to pick up this ridiculous monstrosity of a dress. Instead, I'm standing here, in a full panic, trying to keep a smile pinned on my face and my magic buried away.

My eyes dart frantically, looking for something—anything—to give me an excuse to escape. I scan the room. As usual the gala is a spectacle for the senses, like every royal event I've been forced to attend over the years.

The massive white wisteria tree coming out of the center of the bar has a kaleidoscope of bottles surrounding the base. Elemental mixologists are busy creating a plethora of energy-infused experiences for the guests. I watch one pick up a bottle burning orange with sparkling embers and pour it into an orb filled with smoke before handing it over to a Fire Fae. Another pours a thick stream of sap from a caramel-colored bottle into a leaf-lined glass, topping it with a nasturtium. It isn't my favorite earth experience, but I'd take anything that could dull the anxiety unfurling through me.

It's clear that many of the Elite have already consumed numerous experiences. Everyone seems to be blissfully spinning and swirling across the dance floor or laughing loudly as they mingle in front of the massive fireplace. A huge fae fire is glowing in the hearth. They must have added the human-made liquid fire to have a blaze so large.

Everyone's nonchalant attitude only sends me spiraling deeper. Obviously, they know about Nova's death. They just announced to the entire room—including me—that I am now the princess. Yet no one is grieving or discussing whatever happened to her. As if she never existed at all.

Maybe they're all just too afraid to admit she's gone. Death is so rare. No one wants to acknowledge that we aren't immortal, especially when we're losing more of our elemental powers daily from Gaia's storms.

And now I'm supposed to become Queen of these Fae.

No one here has ever noticed me before tonight. And despite the room being completely full, no one seems to notice now that my whole world has been unearthed. I feel utterly alone in this crowded ballroom. Yet again I'm abandoned by Nova, who's left me to fend for myself.

A tingling starts in my fingers. At first I think it is my magic, doing its best to break through my attempt at suppression. But when it begins to move up my hands and all the voices fade into one buzzing drone, I realize I'm wrong. I sway. I'm way too lightheaded for these uncomfortable high heels.

Just as I'm sure that I'm about to pass out, I hear the calming voice in my head.

Breathe, Nissa. You can do this.

My body, over which I've been progressively losing all control, responds immediately to the command. I feel the cool rush of air bloom in my lungs. The small group around me turns in my direction at the audible intake. My mother's eyes are wide in anticipation of what she's sure is the inappropriateness about to come out of my mouth.

Smile. Say excuse me. Walk away. Breathe.

Without question, I follow the directions again echoing through my mind and turn to escape through the doors I just entered.

As I take the first step, I'm met by two distinct sets of eyes staring me down. As if my senses weren't off-kilter enough with the announcement, now I'm face to face with *them.*

The announcement of their names breaks through the fog. "Prince Caspien Vaylor and Cillian Vaylor."

The Princes of Castara. And the only other set of Fae twins.

Caspien is soon to be crowned as king. With me being announced as the Daughter of Gaia, I'm supposed to be his future queen. That's bad enough.

But my eyes are fixed on the other prince—Cillian.

And that familiar lazy, arrogant gaze is unexpectedly fixed back on me.

THREE

NISSA

E very Fae knows the story of the origins of Castara and Vaylor, our first king.

Thousands of years ago, when Apollyon betrayed the human's god, Elohim, a war broke out between the two. Asteria, the Goddess of the Stars, and Gaia, the Mother of Earth, condemned the demon god's actions and assisted Elohim in banishing Apollyon and his vampires to their own world of Alhena. The goddesses' betrayal enraged Apollyon so much he swore retaliation. So, to protect their people, Asteria and Gaia left the human world for new homes. Each created their own divinely designed world, each made to amplify the energy and powers of their peoples.

Pollara for the witches, and Castara for the Fae.

Gaia built out the Fae world, Castara, with two kingdoms ruled by one king. The Two Kingdoms—Solevara and Varethiel —each surrounded by elemental lands. The lands – Terrania, Aquaria, Ignaria, and Aeronia– were created to forever feed our energy, providing the Fae with immense power and protection.

Gaia placed our first king, Vaylor, on the throne and decreed that his queen would not fall pregnant until it was time for a new king to be raised up to rule. Prophecy and history show that on each prince's date of birth, a female baby – the Daughter of Gaia – would also be born, providing a betrothed for the prince. Prince and Princess were to be trained side by side and would replace the current monarchs on their majority birthdate. The same day that they would come into their magic.

When Queen Isolde was preparing to give birth to the next king, our goddess decided to shake things up a bit. Instead of one son being born to the royal Vaylors, there were two. And instead of one female baby, there was Nova and me.

The Fae's first two sets of twins. Both born on the same day.

In the following weeks, the High Priestess of Castara consulted the Goddess Gaia to determine what this could mean for the new generation of royals. The priestess's answer was one I have always been thankful for. Caspien and Nova were the first born, so they were who Gaia intended to rule. Cillian would be second-in-command, and I was there to assist Nova in anything she needed.

Well, at least until they decided it would be easier just to send me to the outskirts of Solevara to live at the Homestead, my family's farm before we were born.

But no one foresaw this. No one expected the Daughter of Gaia to die just weeks away from becoming the queen.

Leaving me, the *forgotten* daughter to fill her shoes.

A sharp breath fills my lungs as Caspien and Cillian approach. Unlike my entrance, the crowd falls back instead of pushing forward, heads dipping towards the floor. I guess I don't have the same reverence and fear of the princes as the rest of the room. I've been around them often enough during my required yearly visits.

Nevertheless, I don't truly know them. Not any more. And I have had no desire to.

After I was sent away, it was clear that Nova didn't want me anywhere near Caspien, her betrothed, and Cillian has ignored me for years. So just like my sister, the two males in front of me are essentially strangers. Strangers that are held on a pedestal just because of their birthright and birthdate.

Unfortunately, it seems they're now about to become a big part of my life. For a moment, I consider continuing my exit and brushing past them out the door. Instead, I pull my shoulders back, taking them in with my new reality.

Both Caspien and Cillian are on the taller side, even for Fae, giving them an intimidating presence. Even from across the room, their elemental energies are permeating the air. No one could question how powerful these males are, despite most Fae's powers waning and the full extent of the twins' powers suppressed until their birthdate in a few weeks.

I wonder if they've even been affected by the destruction in the elemental lands.

The Goddess obviously created the Vaylor twins to appeal to every female in the Two Kingdoms. As usual, Caspien is put together and polished, his face clean-shaven and his midnight hair slicked back. Thick with packed muscle, he strides forward, his deep crimson suit and black shirt tailored to fit him flawlessly. The clothing accentuates his dark features and represents the element of a Fire Fae.

And Cillian is... well, Cillian is frustratingly perfect. I have no doubt he's just as strong as his brother, but he has more of a long, lean body. Wide-shouldered and narrow-hipped, to me, he always looks ready to cleave into the water. Which makes sense for a Water Fae.

Tonight he has a scruffy-jaw look that is annoyingly tempting. I take in how his light brown hair is slightly rumpled from his habit of running his hands through it and the way his dark navy suit compliments his ocean-blue eyes. They're brighter than normal, with a hint of a sparkle like sunlight shining off rippling water.

I shift uneasily as he moves closer and continues to stare at me.

The Goddess really should have pulled it back a little on these two. But they're Vaylors—the ruling family—and the royal heart stones hanging on each of their chests identify them as such. The chosen family of Castara. The two stones dance with their elements over their hearts, burning fire and swirling water.

"You look stunning tonight," Caspien says in greeting to me, the deep timber of his voice as warm as Fae fire. "You look just like her..." he adds, shaking his head slightly.

His expression is tinged with sadness and something else I can't place. I don't know him well enough to decipher how he intended the words, but it leaves a sour taste in my mouth. His betrothed—*my sister*—just died.

Nova and I were identical in many ways— but outside of how we look, my twin and I could not be more different. Not that anyone would know that since all they ever saw when they looked at me was Princess Nova's sister. The thought of Caspien replacing her with me trails an icy finger down my spine.

"Very original," I mutter. It's the best I can manage. "You would think being a twin yourself you could come up with something a little more creative."

Cillian's low chuckle pulls my attention towards him. "Something funny?" I demand.

"Not at all, Nis." His lip quirks up at the corner. His eyebrows make a quick jump, his eyes swimming with stifled amusement. "It's a nice dress."

"Don't call me that." I narrow my eyes on him. "And you don't have to rub it in." I throw my arms out, letting them fall into the massive pile of tulle heaped unflatteringly around my waist. "I didn't pick this thing."

Caspien's mouth thins as he takes us in. The playfulness on Cillian's face drops off.

Goddess, I wish I was back at the Homestead, and it's barely been an hour since I've been announced as the princess.

Cillian and I were friends when we were younglings. Best friends. *More than best friends.* Until we weren't.

I used to look forward to visiting Solevara for Beltane each year. Cillian and I would send wisps to each other, counting down the days, filling me with the same child-like anticipation as waiting for my seedlings to break through the soil. Until that excitement withered and died. His wisp stopped coming and he stopped responding to mine. And the next time I visited it was clear why.

I may not have had time to process being the princess yet, but what I do know is that he doesn't get to treat me like tree fungus for years and now suddenly act like we're friends when it suits him.

I was able to handle it when I was paraded around for a couple days and sent back home, but now... We're going to have to set boundaries.

I open my mouth to tell him exactly what I think when someone links their arm in mine and begins to pull me away. Instinctively I pull back until I realize who's by my side.

Queen Isolde Vaylor.

Like her son Caspien, she's a Fire Fae. Short brown hair

hangs in soft waves framing her face. If I didn't know that the seamstresses had been banned from weaving magic into the dresses I would have thought this was alive with fire. The ebony fabric of her dress flows down her body like liquid, making the fire in her eyes glow. We're both on the shorter side, but she holds herself like she is the tallest woman in the room.

I instinctively straighten my shoulders as she pulls me along. Every head turns our way as we pass, each Fae subtly taking notice of her.

Isolde has always kept her distance during my visits to the Elite City. Almost like I was one of the servants, which was fine with me since she's kind of terrifying. It's clear where her sons get their superior attitudes. A spark always remembers the fire that gave birth to it.

To the rest of the room, we probably appear like perfectly normal acquaintances, linking arms, sharing a quiet conversation. But she squeezes my bicep with her other hand, making sure I continue to walk with her. There will undoubtedly be a reminder of her blood-red manicured fingernails when she lets go.

Gliding us away from her sons and through the room, she gracefully smiles and nods at the Elite, while she talks under her breath to me.

"Princess," she says, voice low, "I regret that you have to be pulled into this so quickly. But it could not be helped." Her tone leaves no room for question or challenge. "With such a direct attack on Solevara, the Fae are unsettled. The loss of your sister is regrettable. But when we announce the *incident* to the rest of the kingdom, we must avoid panic. Especially with the coronation so near."

I open my mouth to ask the details of what happened to

Nova, but her fingers tighten even further, effectively cutting off my words.

"As the royal family, we must assure the Two Kingdoms that this loss will cause no problems. Gaia's will is clear. You are your sister's twin. Therefore, you are one of the Daughters of Gaia and will now be announced as such. This will pacify all fears. It is your job to put your feelings aside and simply smile."

One of the Daughters of Gaia. Yes, I was born the same day as the Prince but they have never considered me as such. Nova was the decided Daughter, *the* Princess. I snort at their new opinion of me and she shoots me a sharp look.

Gaia can be quite volatile. When she's happy there's great peace through Castara, but when she isn't... she makes it known. I don't actually remember much of that peace. The destruction of the elemental lands started when I was just a child. Attacks on the very lands that she created to provide us with power, essentially cutting us off from our natural source of energy.

Everyone has their opinion on why the Goddess is weakening the world she blessed. Many of the theories are more murmurs of concern about the royal family being unable to fix whatever has upset Gaia. I can only imagine how much yesterday's storm increased those concerns. *And Nova's death...*

Queen Isolde's appraising eyes move from my toes to my face with a disapproving curl of her upper lip. As if I didn't already hate how this dress makes me look, she just set it in stone.

"Be sure to stand up straight. It will give the Fae in the room more confidence in you."

I realize she has led me to the stage, and she is ascending the steps towards King Kiel.

A moment later, the king makes the official announcement about Nova's death. When he motions to me, his solemn expression is replaced with a benevolent smile. His declaration telling everyone I'm the Daughter of Gaia. The Princess of Castara.

Then the wisps go to work, sending word through each element to every Fae in the Two Kingdoms.

And all I can think is- *this isn't how I imagined joining the Vaylor family.*

CHAPTER
FOUR
NISSA

A noise uproots me from sleep, and I groan as the events of the last two days shatter the bliss of my sleep. I lay in bed, scrubbing my hands over my face as I try to blink away what is left of my dream.

BANG BANG BANG

All I want is to close my eyes and slip back into a place where I can pretend that this is nothing but a horrible nightmare and that I can return to my normal life. Instead, the two Guardians stationed outside of my flat seem to think I need to rise with the sun.

BANG BANG BANG

I throw my legs over the edge of the bed and pad through the small space to my front door. I jerk the door open, ready to let them have a piece of my mind, but the words evaporate the moment my startled eyes land on a human—my best friend.

I push my way past the Guardians blocking Ophelia from me and throw myself at her so hard I almost knock her off her feet.

"Okay, okay. I understand. You're glad to see me." Wriggling free, she tosses back her braid of striking auburn hair and winks an amber eyes at the two Guardians. "Thanks."

They're watching us closely. The humans in Castara are all manual laborers or servants. The majority of Fae see them as inferior. Fae and human friends are unheard of. I'm shocked they even knocked to let me know Ophe was here. Then, she's rather good at convincing the opposite sex to do what she wants.

Grabbing her wrist, I pull her into my flat and slam the door closed in their curious faces. The last thing I need is more attention on me or to put her in any danger.

As soon as she's inside, she says, "I was already planning an escape to come for the memorial later today, but when the wisps were sent out with the news, I sped things up." She searches my face. "How are you holding up?"

I collapse back onto my rumpled mattress, "What do you think?" I ask, throwing my arm over my face.

"Oh no, no, no. You don't get to hide from me that easily. I can't believe you didn't send a wisp to tell me yourself. You pollinator! Abandoning me as soon as you're a royal." The teasing is back in her voice. "Or am I not allowed to call you that now that you're"—she whispers like it's a secret—"*the princess?*"

"Yep, pretty sure it's treason or something," I grumble back at her.

She throws a pillow at my head. "Do you even know the definition of treason?"

I smile a real smile for the first time since I left the Homestead. Her presence alone lightens the pressure in my chest. When they sent me away from the Elite City years ago, they brought in Ophe's family to take care of me. Her father already helped with our lands on the Homestead and her mother now took care of me. I was raised next to Ophe. We became more like sisters than Nova and I ever were.

I sit up, pulling the pillow into my lap, squeezing it. "I'm glad you came, but you didn't have to. I'm sure your father won't be happy about it."

"Pfft, don't worry about him. I'll tell him my presence was commanded by"—she pauses dramatically—"the *Princess of the Castara!*"

I make a face. "Call me a pollinator all you want, just don't call me *that.*"

She just grins back at me. Ophe doesn't have on her usual makeup, so the scar that runs down her cheek is on full display. She hates it because it clearly marks her as a human without healing powers. Personally I think it makes her even more stunning than she already is.

Before Ophe, I'd never seen a scar on anyone, and I constantly brought it up. I quickly realized she was never going to tell me how she got it and gave up asking. From then on, I took up defending her when others took note of it. We bonded after that.

"Okay, enough with the loving stares," she says, batting a hand at me. "I'm here, I'm amazing." She tosses her braid over her shoulder. "Now, spill. I need to hear all the details."

"Where should I start? How Nova is dead, and no one is telling us anything." I rub my chest unconsciously, the phantom pain still present. "How I was blindsided by the announcement that I'm the new princess, like she never even existed. Or maybe about my uncomfortable run in with the twins."

"The hot twins! Always start with the hot Fae. Have I taught you nothing?" Ophe has always been male crazy. My disinterest baffles her.

"Be serious." I throw the pillow back at her. "I'm supposed

to be the queen, Ophe. Me! The one they couldn't even bother to let live in the same city with them is supposed to rule Castara. And be what, *with Caspien-* bonded mates? How in the worlds does that even make sense?"

An everlasting connection is supposed to happen between the king and queen on coronation day. But a shiver runs through me at just the thought of being with my sister's betrothed.

"Okay, I hear you. And bear with me here." Ophe puts her hands up in mock surrender when I shoot her a glare. "*But...* where is the bad? Caspien is unnaturally attractive, even for a Fae, and you are going to be a kick-ass queen. I know they've always made you feel like less than Nova. And I am *so* sorry about Nova..." Her eyes soften. "But, Nis, you are seriously amazing. You have a mind of your own and could really do some good here. And again, extremely hot mate!"

"Oh, well, when you put it like that, bring on the wedding bells." I roll my eyes, but some of the tension in my chest eases hearing her confidence in me.

Ophe is way more casual than me when it comes to relationships, or hookups in her case. Fae or human, she doesn't discriminate. It isn't that I'm a prude— But every male I showed interest in just saw me as a way to the royal family.

Caspien is just using me in a different way. He needs his "princess" to become king.

She turns a little more serious. "You'll feel the mate bond soon. That always happens when the new Fae king and queen are crowned. I've read the histories. After that, I'm sure you'll get your happily ever after, Nis."

Very few Fae are divinely blessed with the Goddess's mate bond. On coronation day, which is also the new king and queen's majority birthdates, it's a sign of Gaia's divine will when the new monarchs feel the bond.

"The bond isn't some magic that makes you think you love someone." I throw my hands up, in frustration. "Mates are supposed to be *made* for each other, the perfect half to the other. You can't just switch them out for someone else last minute. Even if they are twins." It comes out in a rush as panic returns.

Ophe watches me with wide eyes. As if she can read my thoughts, "And you saw Cillian?"

My heart buries itself deep in my chest at her implication. She knows how I felt about Cillian. She heard the plans that we made the last time we spoke as younglings. And she held me when I cried after he moved on without a word to me.

"The Vaylors think they need me." I try my best to sound calmer as I voice the thought that's been spinning through my mind since Isolde dug her fingernails into my arm and told me just to smile. "But what if they don't? Maybe without Nova, Caspien can just become king and find someone else to love and make *her* queen. Someone who isn't me."

"Well, shit." She leans back with me, thankfully overlooking the fact that I ignored her question.

We lay there in silence for a few minutes, both staring at the cracked ceiling. "They still haven't told you what happened?"

"No and other than Isolde mentioning 'an incident' to me, it was like Nova never existed. Any time I tried to bring it up at the gala, she cut me off and changed the subject, or introduced me to some other Elite."

We fall into companionable silence again, making me miss my life at the Homestead even more.

"I don't want to do this, Ophe," I confess, my voice more tentative than I'd like.

The admission grows in the air between us. I'm worried she's not going to acknowledge it as the moment stretches on.

Maybe I don't even want her to. It is a selfish, impossible thought. Nova's unyielding devotion to the crown over everything else always infuriated me, but no one could ever accuse her of being selfish...

Ophe reaches over, entwining our fingers together. "You wouldn't be able to come back home," she says, sounding defeated. "But maybe you could leave..."

Rain begins pelting the window of my tiny room. The perfect sunny weather hasn't returned since Nova's death, but until now the storms had passed.

"Or maybe you should give Caspien a chance ," she rushes out, like she believes the weather is some omen of disapproval. "Maybe the Goddess has a plan here."

The Vaylors have never wanted me, and I definitely don't want to be one of them. There has to be a way around this.

I sigh. "The Goddess's plan died with Nova."

FIVE

NISSA

O phe and I spend the rest of the morning ignoring the fact that my entire life has been turned upside down. But that feeling in my chest continues to get worse despite my best friend being there.

Ultimately, I decide to take her advice and approach Caspien after the memorial this afternoon. I can share my concerns before doing anything drastic. Maybe he feels the same way about all of this as I do. After all, his mate is the one who died. I can't imagine he's thrilled to have some lookalike shoved at him.

I change into a flowy white dress with draped straps and floral lace that peeks out from the neckline. It's nothing like the stiff white satin shroud my mother had sent for me to wear. Thankfully, Ophe brought me a grief dress from home. An elder returning to their element, or the rare case of an accidental death, is the only time Fae don't exclusively wear their elemental colors. Instead, we wear white, the presence of all colors, uniting all elements in honor of the deceased.

Ophe and I travel to the Skyborn Chapel separately at the insistence of the Guardians. *For my safety.*

Entering through the open archway, I take in the stunning Temple of the Wind Elementals. The thin beams that make up the "ceiling" are covered in a gossamer fabric that's rippling in the wind, creating a beautiful living pattern. The windows that line the walls are glassless, allowing a gentle breeze to flow across the space. I close my eyes, taking in the comforting melody that fills the room.

"Nissa, darling!" My mother's grief-laced wail echoes across the chapel over the chimes that are responding to their calling.

My eyes snap open, and she throws herself at me. Every muscle in my body tenses as all eyes in the room turn to take us in.

"Nova would be so thankful that you are here for her," she says with another wail, drawing even more attention.

I mentally roll my eyes at the theatrics as she clutches me tighter. I know she's actually upset to have lost her favorite, but this affection for me is all for show. A performance. I wiggle my arms free, adding space between us.

Leaning around her, I scan the seats for Ophe. One of the few human guests, she's sitting in the back row of the chapel alone with the servants. I spot her just as my mother grips my wrist and begins to drag me towards the front. When I subtly pull my arm back, bringing us to a stop, she wheels on me so fast I stumble back a step. She takes a chilling step towards me, leaning in close so no one else sees her expression. Her white dress makes her blue eyes look like ice.

My confidence slips, but I stand my ground. "I'm going to sit with Ophe."

In a single blink, disdain replaces the grief. "You will join us at the front for the procession like the mourning sister and *princess* that you are. It's time you grow up and stop playing with the *help*," she hisses under her breath.

I grind my teeth together to stop a retort, noting the expectant eyes drinking us in. A few are looking in Ophe's direction, following the path of where I was looking before. The Elite are waiting on any morsel of drama they can find, and I'm not about to hand them my friend.

I shoot her an apologetic look. When she waves me off, I follow my mother to the front of the room. Hands curled into fists, I move towards the dais with my head held high. Nova would have entered quietly, head down. Ever the image of elegance and grace.

But I'm not Nova and never will be.

Colorful petals, and light blue wind wisps dance around our ankles as we walk down the aisle. The wisps seem happy to have visitors in their sanctuary.

The Vaylor family is standing at the end of the nave, right in front of the dais that opens up to the cliffside. Caspien steps forward as we break through the hordes of Fae who have come to express their sympathy.

"I'm so sorry about Nova." He envelopes me in a hug. Unlike my mother's, his embrace almost feels sincere, as if it was actually meant for me, not one for those around us, starving for royal attention.

Pulling back, he places his hands on my upper arms and looks down into my eyes. "Are you feeling better today?"

I'm not sure if he is referring to my new role or the death of my sister. But the intensity in his obsidian eyes has my stomach churning, and I instinctively step out of his hold.

King Kiel is flanking him on one side. Cillian is on the other, observing us. All three are dressed in formal mourning whites. Their colored heart stones shine even brighter against the starkness of their white shirts. Kiel loses interest in us quickly, returning his attention to the fawning subjects around him. But I have to force my gaze away from Cillian's steady stare.

Breathe, Nissa. You can do this.

"I'm fine," I tell Caspien, giving him a slight nod. My cheeks warm as I realize that my noncommittal answer is actually true. I can hear the soft crying of mourners at my back, yet I haven't so much as shed a tear for my own twin sister.

Caspien's eyes soften, and he places a hand on my hip. He squeezes softly in reassurance, like he can see my thoughts written all over my face. A smile of sympathy lifts the corners of his lips.

Still sensing Cillian's attention, I send a cursory glance in his direction and find his eyes on his brother's hand at my hip. Unconsciously, I take a step back, then curse myself for being an idiot. Sure, when I was young and naive, I imagined Cillian and I would end up together, but I know better now. And I got over that delusion long ago.

"Well, I'm here if you need anything at all," Caspien offers, his usual self-assurance slipping when I move away.

The hurt on his face settles deep in my chest. He's mourning his beloved, I remind myself. We both have to make the best out of this incredibly messed-up situation. Caspien has been nothing but kind since the announcement. He loved my sister.

Unfortunately, that's all I can see when I look at him. I can't imagine a world where I forget that he was Nova's betrothed. Her mate, not mine. Maybe he'll feel the same way about this switch.

"Could we talk privately later?" I suggest. I'm doing my best to keep my eyes firmly on the eldest twin.

"That sounds good." Caspien's face breaks out into a

relieved smile. He steps back into the procession and motions me into the space between him and his brother.

Taking my place, I can feel Cillian's eyes burning into me, but I refuse to return his stare. Instead, I look up at Caspien as he addresses the next Fae that approaches him. He was made for this. The ease with which he talks to the Elite makes that evident. Just like Nova, he has sacrificed his life for the kingdom. Born and trained to do whatever is necessary for Castara.

The High Priestess's voice fills the space. "By the grace of the Goddess, please be seated."

I glance to the back of the room where I wish I could hide with Ophe. When she gives me two thumbs up, her eyebrows jumping up and down suggestively, I swallow back a choked laugh.

All mirth evaporates as Isolde appears at my side. "Princess. I assume you will be ready for the Royal Guardians tomorrow," she says as she guides me towards the front row with the rest of the royals.

I blink at her multiple times. As we settle into our levitating seats, I search my brain. "I'm sorry, what am I supposed to be ready for?"

"Did you not receive my correspondence? It should have been hand-delivered this morning," she says, tone annoyed. Her sharp eyes swing to the back of the room to the rows of royal servants. As if she's about to summon one for a reprimand.

My mother leans around me. "No worries, my Queen," she whispers. "The letter was delivered to my home this morning. Nissa will be packed and ready for the Guardians to move her into the castle at the first light of day." Her eyes bore into me for compliance.

Thankfully, the High Priestess in her white mourning robe walks up on the dais at that exact moment, since my brain isn't able to form any type of acceptable response. Nova moved into the castle around the last Beltane, and I suppose with her death they're wanting to take extra precautions with me. Which doesn't make me feel any better about the idea of moving in. In fact, it does the opposite.

I am going to be on lock-down tomorrow morning. My life will no longer be my own. I'll have to hand over the little freedom I have left to the Vaylor family and the Goddess's will.

My breaths are shallow, but I do my best not to focus on the future.

The wisps continue their antics flying up and down the aisles, gliding under the floating seats, shocking Fae as they pass between their legs. I briefly wonder how long the seats will remain suspended with the wind failing.

We all look up when a loud screech announces the arrival of a flock of dryrds. The colorful, scaled creatures dig their talons into perches around the space. Everyone watches the beautiful mini dragon hybrids in awe. Most have disappeared as their homelands have been destroyed. This is the most I've ever seen in one place.

Even Halcya, the High Priestess, seems distracted by the display of respect as the rare creatures peer down at all of us. After a moment, she recovers and begins the last rite. Praising my twin for her flawless life as the Daughter of Gaia, she lists off Nova's positive attributes.

All the opposite of me.

I shift in my seat, my heart pounding in my ears, at the confirmation that I'm not cut out for this life.

Halcya's voice drones in the background as I look down the aisle and find Cillian watching me. His face looks unexpectedly concerned when our gaze meets. He tilts his head in look of enquiry, as if asking if I'm okay.

Not long ago I thought I was. But now I truly don't know.

How in the worlds can I be expected to give up my whole life. My twin did just that for the Vaylors, and she's dead. Those same royals banished me away, only to pull me back now when it benefits them.

Many of the red-rimmed eyes that stare up at the high priestess are those of the same Elite who drank and danced at last night's gala without a care. The realization that my mother isn't the only Fae putting on a show turns my stomach.

Is this what Nova's life was reduced to? The selfless princess, who gave up her whole life, *including the relationship with her twin sister,* for these Fae, who never really cared about her.

If they can all be this selfish, why can't I?

My chest tightens. My head is swimming with the realization that this will be my life. Or lack thereof. I won't have a life. I will have to be who they want me to be.

Until they don't need me. Yet again. What if Caspien doesn't need me to become king? Or what if he falls in love with some other female when the bond isn't there? Will they send me away again after they get what they need from me?

Movement around the room pulls my attention back to the ceremony. Everyone in the nave reaches for the symbols of their elements for the final ritual. We raise them into the air to represent Nova's return to her element in death. There's a mix of floating water droplets, feathers, leaves, and fire.

"Nova is at peace in her element, continuing to support the Fae through the wind. Just as she would wish." Halcya raises her own white feather and looks to the sky. "In honor of Nova, we offer the Goddess these gifts."

Quiet fills the room. Even the dryrds and wisps go unnaturally still. After multiple moments pass, with nothing, the whispering begins. The dryrds take flight. Some hands lower.

Many Fae still hold up their element, waiting for Gaia to take them. Waiting for the memorial to be complete.

That ache in my chest shifts. *No*, it cracks in half. The guilt of not wanting this... the fear of only being wanted for my birthdate. The sadness from Nova's life being cut so short... It all breaks apart, replaced with all out rage.

Not only did the Goddess allow this to happen, but now she disrespects Nova in the greatest way by not taking the memorial offerings! *Her chosen!*

How dare she not show up and show respect to the princess that she chose to rule this world! What, out of a temper tantrum? Gaia already howled and roared with that destructive storm when Nova was dying. Another attack on our world. But this is another level. Could the Goddess really be so selfish?

Nova didn't choose to die—she chose to devote her life to Gaia's calling. And Gaia can't even show up now.

Well then, I don't have to show up either. I'm done. I'm done with all of this. Forget talking to Caspien. If Gaia is all-powerful, then she doesn't need me. The Goddess can make whoever she wants the king on her own.

Obviously, we're all just interchangeable to her. And I won't be another pawn that can be discarded at a moment's notice.

Through my anger, I see Halcya's throat bob as she swallows and lowers her feather. Her eyes are wide, looking to the Vaylors for a breath, before her sultry calm returns. "Gaia does not follow our time and *will* show up according to her will. Please place your elemental component in the basin at the front of the dais."

Two humans appear. They struggle to lift an engraved basin and place it at Halcya's feet. Everyone stands. The Vaylors lead the way, depositing their elements.

When it's my turn, I pause. "This is for Nova," I whisper to the Goddess. "Not for you," I add, eyes hard with my rage.

The moment the leaf enters the bowl, a low pulsing pain radiates through the back of my head. Cillian's eyes track me as I make my way to my mother.

"I need a moment," I lie. Then I walk straight out of the Skyborn Chapel, around a wall until I'm out of sight of the Guardian already on my heels.

Now is my only chance out. An instant later, I press my hand to a tree and disappear into the root system. It doesn't take me far before I hit dead roots, damaged in the storms. Forced to re-materialize, I find another system and rootwalk again.

Appear. Disappear. I rootwalk as fast as I can manage until I'm close to my flat.

I need to get to a portal.

CHAPTER
SIX

NISSA

T keep chanting *"now or never, now or never"* over and over in my head as I shove the bare minimum of my belongings into a small bag. If I focus on anything else, I know I'll hesitate. I can't think about leaving Ophe and her family. I can't think about the fact that I won't know anyone in this new modern world.

I squeeze my eyes shut and shake my head. *Now or never. Now* or I'll be locked in that castle forever. *Now* or I'll lose my voice, my personality. *Now* or I'll become a silent queen to a male that is most likely not my mate.

It has to be *now*.

Since our pantheon of gods oversees the Fae, witch, and vampire worlds, my best chance not to be found is the human world. Rumor is that the human god separated from ours when the other species left their land. All I know is that their god supposedly stays out of our Gods' affairs.

Ophe went with her family to visit the human world about five years ago. I was so fascinated about the idea of another world, one where no one knew me, I annoyed her endlessly with all my questions.

Unfortunately, I remember her telling me that there were Guardians patrolling near the human portal on the Fae side. Maybe they were only there for the scheduled trip, to ensure it went smoothly. I can only hope the Guardians aren't a constant presence at the portals. I guess I'll find out.

Each portal is positioned in a different elemental land. The human world's portal is in the Earth Fae's sanctuary—Terrania. It was once commonplace for Fae to visit their elemental lands, but I only recall coming here a single time as a child before the royal family deemed the elemental lands too unsafe from the years of storms battering them.

The deeper I walk into my element, the more the air feels electrified, buzzing around me. Despite the fact that fae don't come into their powers until they hit their majority, I have had small bursts of power for as long as I can remember. Something that very few know.

My heart breaks with each step, my magic alive and itching to heal the brokenness that surrounds me. I've heard descriptions of the damage the Goddess has inflicted on all the different elemental lands. But to see the destruction in person is devastating.

The gorgeous trees that should be towering overhead are little more than shattered remnants of their past life. Our Goddess has torn through the area, splintering and snapping the magnificent redwoods and smaller varieties of trees, stripping the few that remain of their bark, leaving them exposed.

I do my best to keep my footsteps light, but with the ground covered with dead foliage, it's difficult to be quiet, even for an Earth Fae. I watch the area for any Guardians stationed here, but see no sign.

I sit down on a fallen tree that I've just climbed over and listen for any movement. Maybe the Guardians were pulled when access here was restricted. Or they could all be watching over the city during Nova's memorial. Watching the royals. Watching *me*.

I take a deep breath as I run my hands over the soft, spongy moss. Maybe I'm in the wrong place altogether.

The sun is peeking around the clouds and shines easily through the fragmented canopy. I close my eyes and tilt my head up to let the sun warm my face, the smell of nature filling my lungs. The magic here may be diminished, but goddess, what remains has my magic singing. My chest feels lighter as my natural element rejuvenates every cell of my depleted, exhausted body.

This is the first time the sun has fully come out since Nova's death. Maybe this is a good sign, evidence that our Goddess supports me leaving. My lips twitch up at the thought. Maybe Gaia is on my side for the first time in my life.

As soon as my body adjusts to the calm of nature surrounding me, a twig snaps. My eyes spring open, and I find Cillian casually leaned against a tree in front of me. He's still in his white mourning clothes from the memorial, but he's lost the jacket and the sleeves of his shirt are rolled up over his toned forearms. I hate how attractive he is.

His head tilts, his steady gaze taking me in. I don't know how he snuck up on me in the dry brush. The ferns and moss are barely peeking through the dead undergrowth.

"The weather seems to be improving..." he states as he studies the sun streaking my face.

I exhale the wind that's caught in my chest. I sit up a little straighter as his eyes drop to the small satchel of my things that I've placed next to my feet. Cillian being here is just as bad as running into a Guardian.

"Did you follow me?" I demand, narrowing my eyes on him.

No comment on the satchel. Maybe he didn't notice it.

"A guy can't creep around the woods for the fun of it, Lila?" He flippantly throws out the nickname that he began using during the last Beltane festival that we spent together years ago.

An unwanted ache fills my chest. Pain that I pretend has passed. But if I'm honest, it still resurfaces at the most inconvenient times. Like now, as a memory of us laying together in the garden a few hours into the gala. Our friendship had finally blossomed into more and I couldn't have been happier. Even when my mother scolded me for the dirt on my dress at the end of the night. I just smiled through the lecture. The feel of his lips still on mine.

He had come looking for me that night and found me sprawled under a tree making buds on a vine bloom one at a time in the moonlight. I had not told him about my shows of magic yet. Ophe was the only one that knew. I still remember the huge smile on his face as he called me Lila for the first time.

Cillian saw *me*, and I loved it. *I loved him* – and the name he gave me. Regardless of the fact that the flower buds had not actually been a *lila*. He only ever used the name in private, and at the time it felt like our little secret. A few months after that year's Beltane gala he stopped reaching out. He stopped paying any attention to me. I haven't heard it in years and now it just feels soiled.

I definitely don't need his attention on me now. "Don't call me that," I snap out.

"If I can't call you Nis and I can't call you Lila, what am I supposed to call you? I know the last thing you want is to be called is *princess*." His face shows no emotion, but he drawls my new title like it tastes bad on his tongue.

"Maybe my real name? You lost the right to use anything more familiar when *you* decided to end things between us." I try to match his indifference. Instead, it comes out more wounded than anything else.

"You only visited once a year," he says, popping up a shoulder. "Did you expect me to send you a wisp every day?"

"Decided I wasn't worth your time anymore?" I arch a brow.

"It wasn't like that." He casually scans the broken wilderness, his bland tone fueling my anger.

"Great. Thanks for the explanation." Jaw tight, I stand. "I'll let you continue your creeping alone." Walking back the way I came, praying he doesn't ask about my small satchel. I've hiked it over my shoulder. I can't afford to leave it behind, and I'm not going to stick around until he gets suspicious.

"You're going in the wrong direction."

I freeze a few steps in front of him, swallowing. My heartbeat thumps in my chest. He eyes the strap over my shoulder, knowingly. *Of course he knows. He's always been able to read me.* And why else would I be out in the middle of the elemental lands?

"I believe she was closer to the portal." He states pulling his eyes back up to my face.

My brow scrunch. "She...?" I ask, gulping so hard I'm sure if the wind hadn't started blowing the dead limbs, he'd actually hear me swallow.

"Nova. That's why you're here, right? To see where she died..." His voice trails off, and his gaze goes to my satchel again, an eyebrow lifting.

The color drains from my face. I should be trying to cover my shock, but I've never been good at hiding my emotions.

He takes a step towards me, his head tilting. I match the step, retreating.

"You didn't know," he says.

"No... yes—" *Shit,* he just gave me a reason to be here. "I mean, I heard the incident happened here, but it's a whole different thing than confirming it. No one will tell me anything."

His face is impassive as he mulls over my lie. I know I should do more to distract him from why I'm truly here, but this small piece of information is too much to take in.

"Do you know what happened?" I can't stop scanning the area, but instead of looking for the portal, now I'm searching for any trace of my sister. Flexing my hand open, I reached out my magic to the forest, hoping it will offer even the slightest hint about what happened to my twin.

His eyes soften, and I get a glimpse of the boy from my childhood. Before everything fell apart. His throat bobs as if he's deciding if he's going to answer, the male notch there reminding me that he's no longer a boy.

"Come on." He abruptly turns and starts walking. "I understand them wanting to keep the details quiet so the kingdom doesn't panic, but you're her sister...." He quickly glances back to see me hurrying to catch up.

For the first time since my twin bond with Nova snapped, I think I may get some answers.

"They believe a small group of rebel humans broke through the portal while Nova was here. She was outnumbered, and the Guardians didn't get here in time. I was told it happened somewhere over there."

Nova's death wasn't an accident. It was an attack.

My brain doesn't know how to process all of the questions swirling through it. "Humans attacked her...?" I shake my head, trying to clear it. "Did she suffer?" I scan the area for signs of violence.

I had no idea humans were so volatile. Vampires, sure. But then, I don't really keep up with intra-world politics.

"I don't know." He comes to a stop a branch ahead of me, near a clearing and points to the left.

My eyes linger on the spot. But nothing stands out, nothing calls to me. Shouldn't the place where my twin, my other half, died feel different? Shouldn't I be able to tell that she was here? This is where Nova's body and spirit went back to join the Goddess, and I can't feel her. Had we grown that far apart?

Ahead, remnants of a stone archway are visible through the crumbled rock of a cliffside. I can just make out stairs that climb the cliff before they disappear directly into the rock face. *The human world portal.*

My heart stops. I realize I'm standing halfway between the location where Nova died, leaving her legacy for me to carry on. And halfway to my escape, away from this royal life that killed her and moved on like she never existed. I'm literally standing between the two lives that I'm faced with. Be the queen that Nova was destined to be—or *run*.

I clinch the skirt of my dress in my hands. My mind is screaming for me to race for the portal, the exit from this life I'm being caged into by a Goddess who doesn't care.

"Are you okay?" Cillian's voice rips through my thoughts, grounding me back to the moment. His eyes trail down to my clenched fists.

I immediately release the fabric and smooth the wrinkles. Once I would have done anything to have his eyes on me, but right now, he is seeing right through me, and nothing good can come from that.

"Why was she here?" My voice comes out husky.

Emotion oddly similar to concern flashes across his face before he looks back to the clearing. "I don't know."

I study the last area that my sister existed in her physical form before the element reclaimed her body. "And you said the Guardians didn't get here in time. Why weren't they with her?"

"She came alone."

My eyes go wide. Nova was the rule follower. That was one of the issues we had. She wouldn't even push back enough to find a moment to spend with me on my visits.

He hesitates, eyeing me. "I was hoping to figure out why she was here. That's actually why I'm out here. Any ideas?"

A humorless laugh leaves my throat. "If anyone would know, it would be your family. I barely knew her." My frustration builds. What in the worlds, in this elemental land, at this portal, could be important enough to have Nova stepping out of the rules.

Cillian begins to walk the clearing, as if looking for clues on the forest floor. "Barely knew her..." he mumbles under his breath, shaking his head, "but you're just alike."

The comparison shouldn't hurt. It shouldn't tear at my heart the way it does.

"Of course. We looked alike, so we were basically the same person, right?" I roll my eyes in disgust, not trying to hide it from him. "So glad you can see so much depth in people beyond their looks."

The irony of it leaves my chest in a bitter laugh.

He's the one Fae who I ever felt saw me as someone other than Nova's sister. And now he's telling me I am no different than her.

He's wrong. Nova would never run. The thought of my twin leaving this life that she gave everything for, would be insane. It would be selfish. And anyway, she always wanted this, did everything to be who they wanted her to be.

So, why else would Nova be out here? A dozen reasons race through my mind, most ruled out immediately. These aren't her elemental lands, and I doubt she got here by accident. Did she meet someone? Did someone bring her out here?

My brow furrows as the facts continue to bring me back to two things: Nova would never run, and she was attacked.

"You know what I meant, Lil—" Cillian cuts himself off, clearly irritated at my warning look. "Fine, no nicknames. But obviously you're *different*." He takes a step closer, running both hands through his already messy hair. "I just meant that you're apparently both stupid enough to come out into Terrania *alone*."

As if calling me *stupid* is better?

He closes his eyes, fingers still threaded through his brown locks, and pulls at the roots. The shirt stretching across his chest in response and I swallow at the tight fabric.

"Nothing can happen to you." His lids open, ocean-blue eyes locking on mine with a new intensity. Goddess, he is gorgeous.

My heart rate kicks up. Does he finally realize I'm trying to leave? "Right, because all of you need me. I was disposable before, but now I matter."

He lets out a frustrated growl. "You weren't fucking disposable."

"Could have fooled me," I mumble, putting space between us as I seek out any signs of my twin. I still come up with nothing. I can't tell that anyone was here before this moment, much less that there was a full attack and murder.

A loud crash fills the space behind us. Before I can turn to see what happened, Cillian is between me and the noise. From where I'm positioned behind him, I can see the straining muscles and rapid pulse in his neck.

I peek over his shoulder, looking for the enemy that he's poised to defend against. A small dryrd is flying up over the trees. A trail of scorched leaves floats down behind it to a heap of newly incinerated limbs on the ground. His little black body and the iridescent blue lining his wings shimmer in the sun as he flees his destruction.

An unexpected giggle bubbles out of me at the harmlessness of our attacker. Cillian looks back over his shoulder at me as his coiled body slowly releases. I quickly cover my mouth and stifle another laugh at his serious expression. He watches me for a second before his serious features are broken by a ghost of a smile.

He clears his throat as he steps away, the serious look back. "We should get back. This area isn't safe."

"Clearly. See you at the castle tomorrow." My shoulders are hunched as I continue to look for any signs of anyone else here recently.

I know if I don't use the portal now, then it will be much harder once they move me into the castle. But I can't leave without figuring out why Nova was here. We may not have been close, but she was still my twin. My other half. If she was running, something devastating must have happened. And she didn't feel like she could reach out to me. Or if someone lured her out here, then I need to figure out who. We may have failed each other for years, but I won't let her down now.

"I'll take you back. I want to make sure you make it safely." His footsteps follow behind me.

"I don't need you to ensure my safety. Thanks, though," I respond, dismissing him as I trek through the brush.

"You kind of do. But beyond that, I can see how exhausted you are." He hesitates before adding, "Unless you have no plans to return..." His words fall off as he gives me a pointed look before looking to the portal.

Annoyance washes over me. He's proof of how difficult escape will be if I go back. But I have 5 weeks until the coronation.That should be plenty of time to figure out what happened to Nova and figure out a way out. Then I'm gone.

I hate that he can still read me. But the twin-bond breaking has left my energy depleted, barely able to get here. Especially with how many times I had to change root systems.

Every element has their own form of travel-—rootwalking, mistwalking, smokewalking, and breezewalking. It's the only magic Gaia grants the fae before they hit their majority. In the past, Earth Fae could travel anywhere in one pass. But as the trees and plants have died off, rootwalking is interrupted every time we hit a dead or dying root. Breezewalking has also become unreliable, whenever Gaia decides to stop the breeze midair.

Water and fire are the only elementals that aren't having issues, since they can pull water and natural electricity from the air whenever they wish. At least for now.

I'd hoped to glean enough energy from the lands to shift into the roots, but the little remaining power here isn't enough. I could rootwalk back to the city, but the thought of that long trek has my bones feeling weighed down with how often I would need to remateralize.

"It doesn't make you weak to accept help, Nissa."

As much as I don't like him using nicknames, my true name feels like a slap in the face. It makes the fact that we're essentially strangers all the more real, and I hate myself for not liking it.

When I don't respond, I hear him slowly approaching me from behind, like I'm some wounded animal. I'm not. He long ago lost the ability to hurt me.

He eliminates the little space between us, and I can feel his heat behind me for a moment. The wind catches in my chest as he gingerly places his hand on my hip. Slowly he slides his fingers across my stomach, pulling me back into his chest. I try to breathe past how natural his touch feels.

"Just what every female wants to hear—how tired she looks." I laugh weakly as my magic reacts to him holding me. We haven't touched since that night in the garden, and I instantly feel stronger in his arms. But that's not all I feel. His touch is like a brand on my skin even through my dress.

"Have you ever mistwalked?" His breath brushes across my ear. His voice is low and full of something I can't place.

"No." It comes out more breathy than I intended. I swallow at the sensations that are firing though my body.

"Your body will warm before you feel a tingling sensation. Then we'll begin to move. If you get dizzy, just close your eyes."

I exhale the wind I've been holding, welcoming any explanation for the magic suddenly swirling through my body. Warmth fills me, and the air I expelled is quickly pulled back into my lungs as he starts circling his thumb on my stomach. My muscles contract involuntarily. I'm suddenly overcome with a new level of heat. I shudder as the tingling starts.

His chest vibrates as he laughs at my reaction, his breath teasing the shell of my pointed ear. My limbs begin to feel as if they're light as air. I squeeze my eyes shut at the overstimulation. I cross my arms over my midsection, gripping his arm that sits across my stomach and his hand on my upper arm for support.

Moments later my feet hit the ground again. His hold on me tightens, making sure I don't fall forward as I reacclimate. I slowly open my eyes to the front of my flat. Jerking out of his hold, I can finally breathe again, even though my head remains in the clouds from the mistwalking.

When I face him, he is already starting to disappear into water vapor. "Bye, Lila. See you at the castle."

I realize when I close the door that I never told Cillian where I live.

CHAPTER
SEVEN
NISSA

My mind runs rampant through the night with endless scenarios that would send my sister into Terrania. I need answers as soon as possible so I can get out of here.

The next morning, I walk out of my flat to the two grumpy Guardians who finally found me last night after my trip to the portal. I give them a sly smile as I lock up and pull my hood back over my head to begin the short journey to my mother's residence.

It took them hours to find me after the memorial and they were less than pleased when they did locate me. I take a deep breath, savoring the sliver of freedom I have walking the streets for a little longer. Even if these two brutes are following close behind.

The sun is rising, and the beautiful pink and orange sky tints the alley as I make my way over the cobblestones. I run my hands through the vines that grow up the building walls making sure I don't inadvertently make anything bloom in front of the Guardians. I brush the soft leaves with my fingertips, and keep my head down, sticking to side streets to avoid being noticed.

I've never gone out much in Solevara beyond the required events while visiting. I hated being recognized—or really, mistaken for Nova. But now there would be no mistaking it. If people recognize me, they'll know who I am.

And the last thing I want is attention.

I exhale as I take the last corner with only a few glances my way. At the end of a wide boulevard, I press my hand to a door, activating the lock to my mother's lavish home. As I enter, I call out to her. Relief fills my chest when she doesn't answer.

The royal family provided my family with this house the moment Nova and I were born. Moving us all from the Homestead into the Elite City to have access to the best herbalists, teachers, trainers. Anything the twin Fae girls would need— bringing us under the Vaylors' wing early. They had trained, not just Nova and me, but the whole family on how to be regal.

I still have a room at this house, but it never felt the same after my father left. I couldn't handle my mother. I had gone from one of his "little princesses" to "the" princess and *me*. I was always in the way. Pushing for too much time with Nova. Making her look bad by just existing. Or just being a bad influence on her in general.

Entering the foyer, I hang my hooded cape over the elaborate coat rack positioned by the door. The house feels empty. Not in the "no one is home" sense but the lack of personality. It's filled with expensive furniture and decorated professionally, but there are no family likenesses, no mementos. No life. Not since my father left.

He was always so much fun, chasing us down the halls, spinning my mother around in grand dances that we'd been taught for the galas. She would cook on the nights the servants were sent away. Laughter had filled these rooms once upon a time.

The last memory I have of my father was him fighting with my mother about sending me away. It sounded like he'd disagreed with the decision, and when it came time for me to go, he gave me a hug and walked out of the front door. I returned for the next Beltane festival, excited to spend the weekend with my family. *And Cillian.* But instead, my father was gone, and Nova was busy at the castle.

My mother simply said he couldn't do it anymore. A light had gone out in her eyes, and from then on, she kept her distance. She never outright said it, but I could tell she blamed me.

After that there was little laughter, and definitely no fun.

I couldn't get away from this house, and the ghosts that haunt me every time I walk through these doors, fast enough. It was a relief for everyone when I got my own place. The instant I was old enough, I got my flat. And my mother didn't protest.

I shake off the memories and make my way up the curved staircase and down the austere hall to the end where our rooms are. Instead of entering the familiar door to the right, I open the door on the left and ease inside.

Nova's pristine room is decorated in an array of blues and whites with large windows spanning the back wall. An unsettling feeling washes over me as stale air weighs down around me. I don't think I've ever been in her room when the windows weren't wide open to let her element blow through. Tears prick the backs of my eyes.

As much as I wish the tears were of sadness, it's frustration that courses through me.

Nova and I had grown so far apart. She'd chosen the Vaylors over her own family. I understood her obligation as the princess, but she was never able to stand up to them for our relationship. Never able to put time aside when I visited, never reached out when I was gone. Being in this house just reminds me that, as much as our father did, she abandoned me, and that hurt as much as being sent away did.

But I'm not going to walk away from her. Not until I know what happened.

Unfortunately looking around this room gives me no insight on where to start my search. I move to the small table beside Nova's bed and slide open the drawer. Rummage through books on etiquette and random ribbons and trinkets.

The contents validate my suspicions that she was little more than her role as the princess. I'd always hoped she had happiness beyond Caspien and who this world expected her to be. *Nothing.*

I spent the next hour going through her dresser and closet before moving on to check under the bed. I'm so caught up in my search that I almost don't hear the footsteps. My head jerks up, smacking the wooden slats beneath the mattress. The bedroom door creaks open, me still prostrate on the floor.

"What in the worlds are you doing?" my mother's confused voice carries to my ears.

I slowly pull myself out from under the bed, turning to look up at her. "I was looking for something," I state simply as I rub the bump on the back of my head.

"Something?" Her eyebrows pull together as she glances around the room. Thankfully I placed everything back where I found it as I searched.

"Uh, yeah. I let Nova borrow... a necklace. I was just looking for it." I don't know why I feel like I can't just ask her what she knows. But honestly, I feel like she would cover up the truth if it helped the royal family.

Squinting at me, she takes one more look around the room.

"Right. Well, she moved most of that stuff to her room in the castle."

My eyes go wide, and I scramble up from the floor. This room was a dead end, and I knew it. But this gives me a renewed hope. I hurry towards the door and give her a tight hug over both of her arms. The shock is evident the moment I wrap around her. I break the contact as quickly as it starts. "Thanks. I've got to get back and pack."

She lingers in the doorway, staring into Nova's room until I'm at the top of the stairs. "Nissa."

My stomach churns. I twist back to face her, hand on the railing, eager to escape.

"Be careful." There is no emotion on her face, as if she's said nothing at all. But the warning hangs thick in the air down the long hallway.

"Be careful...?" I slowly repeat, my eyebrows raised in question.

"Digging into the past can be dangerous. Just be careful."

I bob my head a few times, and contrary to the speed of my heartbeat, I slowly descend the stairs.

Warnings from my mother are nothing new, but they are normally about preserving my reputation for the sake of the royal name. This feels different. This is ominous.

CHAPTER
EIGHT
NISSA

As I exit the residence, I find a group of Guardians have joined the two that followed me here. I sigh at their presence, noting that they had come *here* to move my things to the Castle. As I guide them back to my flat a sense of dread fills my stomach. *I have missed my chance to run.*

My lack of sleep makes me a complete delight to deal with as the Guardians haul my meager luggage to the castle. It's a quick transition since most of my belongings are still at the Homestead.

Isolde and a Guardian are waiting to greet me when I enter the castle. Each Guardian receives a small inception tattoo along their collarbone upon completing their training. As they move up in the ranks the iridescent mark of the Royal Guardians is extended up their necks.

The Wind Fae in front of me, that I've seen with Cillian during past visits, has a tattoo that reaches all the way to the tip of his ear. It marks him as one of the highest-ranking Guardians I've ever seen. He has an air of importance—or maybe arrogance is a better description—since he refuses to meet my eyes.

I follow the queen when she silently motions me forward down a hallway. The Guardian stays a step behind us as she leads me down a long corridor of doors that open to sitting areas with desks and other casual meeting spaces. Peeking inside, each is decorated specifically to match an element of the different types of Fae.

Isolde leads me into her personal study—a dimly lit cave of a room with a fae fire in the hearth and a burning centerpiece surrounded by dark sofas. The Guardian pulls the door closed behind us. A desk sits off to the side with images and symbols of fire burned into the wood. The burgundy walls and black curtains give the room a dark ambiance, especially with the flickering light reflecting off the metal shelving.

The Guardian takes a stance next to the door and places his hands behind his back, facing straight ahead, looking at nothing in particular.

Isolde, who is watching me with pressed lips, gestures for me to take a seat on one of the black, carved basalt chairs, and she takes up the one opposite me. She studies me silently for a moment, taking me in. Her back is straight as a board as she sits at the edge of the uncomfortable chair, hands folded in her lap. The stark difference in our postures has me fidgeting before I chastise myself for letting her belittle me without saying a word.

If she's going to drag me here before I can even get to my room, *after* uprooting my whole life, she can be the one who talks first.

After completing whatever judgement is going through her mind, she finally clears her throat. "Princess, I want to introduce you to Niko." Her eyes slowly slide to the male at my back.

He walks over to us to stand next to the queen. The mark of

the Royal Guardians on his neck shimmers in the flames from the fae fire. His sun-kissed hair has a windswept look that frames his face with natural waves, and his eyes are a unique pale blue.

"Niko is the Lord Commander of the Guardians. He is here to go over standard protection protocol and brief you on the incident with the former princess."

Incident. I know better now. I do my best to not show my disgust at her lack of emotion. Niko's eyes remain on the wall behind me.

"Niko," she snipes.

"Princess Nissa." He dips his head. When he raises it again, he finally meets my eyes. What I took as arrogance and indifference is something else. His eyes are tired, and his throat bobs as his gaze snaps away from mine.

"Moving forward you will have security with you at all times," he informs me. "You are not to leave the property without multiple escorts. Communication with anyone outside of the castle walls will need to be approved."

My jaw drops. "You have to be kidding. You're going to monitor who I speak to?" I sit up straighter. Any sympathy I had for this exhausted-looking male evaporates in the flames of this room as the last bud of freedom I may have had slips through my fingers.

"The..." He hesitates and gives a quick glance at me then Isolde before he again fixes his gaze on the very interesting— and plain—wall behind me. "The incident with your sister is forcing us to take additional precautions to keep you safe."

"And what exactly *did* happen to Nova?" I snap back.

He tilts his head side to side, stretching his neck before saying, "Princess Nova Navarro exited the property with two Guardians to return to her mother's home at approximately—"

I cut him off. "If I wanted to read some official report, I

would request it." *Can I request it?* I'm standing now. I know what Cillian told me outside of the portal, but I want to hear their version. "What happened? Who killed her?"

Weary eyes slowly lower to meet mine. For one slow blink, Niko's eyes close. *Guilt?*

When he reopens them, he is less formal, compassionate even- "Princess Nova left your mother's house soon after she arrived. She exited through the windows in her room at the back of the home."

I almost snort. Nothing about that place was a home. Not since our father left.

"So someone could have taken her?" I challenge.

"There was no sign of forced entry or a struggle." He hesitates, then adds, "We later tracked her to the portal to the human world, where she was attacked and killed."

"By humans?" I can't hide my derision at the story.

"That is what we believe." He nods.

"Believe?" I bite out the word. "Because you weren't there. No Guardians were there to protect her."

"Correct." He tilts his chin up slightly but I can see my words cause some type of pain.

"That part is being handled," the queen states blandly, expression bored.

"And does anyone know why my sister was there?" I ask my attention still on him. "Why would she go to the portal?"

"I cannot comment on that." he states with an apology tinting his tone.

"And was she with anyone else?" I push forward. I see Isolde look in his direction from the corner of my eye.

"I cannot comment on that," his words going more brisk and to the point.

"Why would humans from the portal want to kill her? I didn't think we had much to do with their world."

His eyes cut to Isolde and then back to the wall. "I cannot—"

"Comment on that." I deliberately step into his line of vision. "So you know nothing?"

"We're continuing to investigate. Some information is privileged for the safety of the kingdom." He has slipped back into his wooden demeanor that started this conversation.

I don't expect to learn any more from him. "Right. So can I go now?" I turn towards Isolde.

"Yes, the seamstress is waiting for us."

My shoulders drop, but I don't argue. I didn't learn anything beyond what Cillian already told me, and I'm tired of the lack of answers. I'll find them on my own. If I'm "privileged" enough for them.

As Isolde leads me through the castle, she fills me in on the lessons I will begin immediately. With a plan to start first thing in the morning, she leaves me with a human female holding a cloth measuring tape.

If I had more of my clothes here, I would be offended that they were pushing a new wardrobe on me so quickly. If Nova and I shared the same element, I fully believe they would shove me into her wardrobe, since they seem to think we're interchangeable. But Nova almost exclusively wore impractical, elaborate gowns. And with the seamstress inquiring about my preferences, I have a seed of hope that I will actually like my new clothes.

The rest of the day is spent having every leaf of my body measured before being handed off to two females who have a gleam in their eyes as they give me a once over. Makeup and hair products sit behind them like an arsenal ready to attack.

As the sun is setting, I am finally led to a dark green room with wooden accents where they put all my stuff. I take in the beauty as the servant shuts the door behind them. Leaving me alone for the first time since I walked into the castle this morning. I sit down on the massive bed, but I'm afraid to lie back in case I mess up all the hard work they just completed.

Thankfully my hair is the same, just styled better than I could ever do myself. But my makeup is over the top—similar to what Nova did every day.

My fingers trace the vines that hold the bed and the beautiful stone-colored bedding above the floor. There's no doubt this room is a step up from my flat.

I drum my toes against the cold flooring and scrunch my nose, realizing it isn't natural wood. Whoever designed this room did a stunning job but clearly wasn't an Earth Fae with the ability to ground. I walk over to the live wall and run my hand along the moss-covered stone. Small plants are peeking out between the cracks in the rocks. Thankfully I brought some of my favorite plants with me, because this won't be enough.

While it is beautiful, being closed in this room makes me want to climb the walls. The sooner I can get out of this life, the better. But I need answers before I can do that.

AFTER BEING RELEASED from the second day of lessons, I stick my head into the hall and creep out of my room. I tiptoe through the corridor, heading back in the direction of the offices I saw the day I moved in. Yesterday's search of Nova's bedroom was fruitless so I'm hoping her study has more than the pretty dresses to search through.

After one wrong turn, I'm able to find the right area and subtly begin glancing into open doorways. Most have been left ajar, but a few at the end of the hall remain closed. I pass Isolde's private study, then gently attempt to open two doors, first listening for any voices inside. Both are locked, and I move further down the hall. One of the last doors pushes open easily when I turn the knob.

The delicate scent of white jasmine surrounds me. The smell I will always associate with my sister. I hurry into Nova's study—more of a dressing room, really—and ease the door shut. One of the windows that cover the wall is still cracked open, blowing the floor-to-ceiling gossamer curtains in the wind she loved so much. The fresh air swirls around the room, making me feel closer to my sister than I have since the bond was broken.

As I look around the room, my heart sinks a little in my chest. While I can feel her presence here, the space has few personal touches beyond the typical décor for a Wind Fae. Nothing screams "Nova." Nothing tells me more about the sister I knew so little about. The space is bland, void of personality. Just like they had raised her to be—present but not heard. My shoulders drop as I realize it's unlikely that I'll find anything useful about my twin in this room.

I run my fingers through number windchimes and wind instruments in the corner of the room. I walk over to the changing area in the corner with its full-length mirror and small vanity.

Carefully sliding each drawer open, I find meticulously organized jewelry, makeup, and fragrant oils. I trace the outlines of a few of the magnificent jewels set in every type of metal you could imagine. There's jewelry to match every possible Wind-elemental color, the perfect accessory for any dress.

Closing the last drawer, I take a deep breath and head to the elegant inlaid wooden desk. Everything there is equally organized. Slim books about past queens, etiquette, and royal events. Folders with calendars and menus.

When I reach the bottom drawer, there's a light-blue

leather-bound notebook hidden under a stack of new ones. The leather is soft and worn, the binding cracked from use. A flicker of hope for answers blooms inside of me.

But when I try to open the pages, the book fights against me. *Locked.* Though nothing appears to be holding it shut. I flip the book over in my hand, studying it. Again, I try to pry at the cover, attempting to pull it apart to no avail.

Frustrated, I set the book atop the desk and finish digging through the drawers. When nothing else stands out, I push to stand, my hand flat on top of the worn leather cover. A strong draft blows through the cracked window, and a tingle of magic shoots up my wrist. I fall back into the chair and lift the book, my eyebrows drawn together.

This time when I tug on the cover, it lifts with ease. The magic holding it shut either wasn't strong enough to differentiate between Nova and me, or she had spelled it so I could open it as well. *Wouldn't she have taken something precious enough to lock with her if she was running? Was she leaving it for me?*

I quickly flip through the pages as I lean back into the floating high-backed chair behind the desk. Nova's entries are all written in beautiful swirling calligraphy but are nothing but notes upon notes about her lessons and what failings she felt she needed to work on. Or she was told she needed to work on.

I scan a few more pages before growing impatient with all the criticism I read. Thumbing further into the book, I skim page after page. My eyes finally catch on an entry where the words are scribbled messily, absent of her normal fine script.

I pause, reading the rush of thoughts so out of character that Nova couldn't even stop to correct her mistakes on the page. A confrontation with Caspien after finding a female leaving his room.

Any frustration I had with my sister splinters, leaving the

fracture raw and aching. Each beat of my heart feels as if it rubs against my chest painfully. This must be it. The reason she was leaving. She had devoted her life to be the person they asked her to be, and to this male, the person Gaia "blessed" her with. Just for them to still tear her apart after so many years, and for him to betray her so grievously.

The door to the study swings open, hitting the wall heavily, halting me in rereading the passage. A petite girl stumbles in with a pile of boxes so high I can't even see her face. When she lowers them, I see her rounded ears. A human servant. Her eyes lock on me and all color drains from her cheeks.

She quickly bows her head towards the floor. "Princess Nissa, I apologize. I'll come back later." She sets the tottering boxes on the floor and starts to retreat.

"Wait, what are you here to do?" I ask, eyes on the stack of boxes.

"I was asked to clean out this room." She stands straight as a board, formality coating each word.

Of course they would clean out Nova's stuff—she isn't coming back. But it still feels like an invasion of her privacy. Which is ridiculous as I sit here holding open her private journal in my lap.

"Did you know my sister well?" I ease the cover shut.

"I'm Dahlia, her personal maid, your Highness," the girl says, offering little.

"Can you tell me about her before she died? Was she upset about something?"

A quick glance up at me. Then her focus returns to the floor. "She was acting normal the last time I saw her. Then, she was last seen alive at your mother's estate, not here."

I nod to myself at the confirmation of what Niko briefed me on. "Were Prince Caspien and she happy?" I probe, curious about others' perspectives on their relationship.

The maid's eyes fall on the notebook. I immediately place my hands flat over the book.

"As happy as you would expect." She gestures at my lap. "Prince Caspien had become less inconspicuous, which frustrated the princess, but she wasn't really surprised by it."

My eyebrows must have jumped all the way to my hairline. "So the cheating was ongoing?" I asked, confessing my personal invasion of Nova's privacy.

It was the girl's turn to look surprised. "Of course, Princess. They had an agreement. But your sister knew it would all work out once the divine mate bond connected them."

My mind is struggling to keep up, trying to take in what she's saying and reconcile it with the journal entry. It did add up. Nova's journal expressed her hurt, but she focused more on Caspien's lack of discretion than the actual act of cheating on her.

"Was my sister seeing anyone else?" Maybe she was running to be with him.

"No, your Highness. Princess Nova was devoted to her role, waiting for Prince Caspien to love her. But he never looked at her like Prince Cillian looks at you."

I blink at her. *What, like he wants nothing to do with me?* I almost snort. My bafflement must show.

The girl gives me a sheepish look. "I apologize if I overstepped. I shouldn't have said anything." A blush pinkens her cheeks. "It's just Princess Nova always said the prince was only pretending to like those parasite princesses."

It's the term the servants use for the females who shamelessly flirt with the princes for personal gain. The same females that Cillian moved on from me with. But apparently Caspien liked to have his fun with them too. "Caspien or Cillian?" I'm getting confused.

"Prince Cillian. She said his interest in those other females fled like the wind as soon as you left." The girl's voice is filled with whimsy, a small smile gracing her face.

I realize I'm gaping at her when she starts to shift between her feet. The only words I can find slip out. "Prince Cillian has barely spoken to me for years." And my sister definitely never shared any of these thoughts with me.

Not that I've tried to approach him either. In fact, we always do our best to avoid each other during my annual visits now.

For half a second, I remember the sweet, studious young male I once knew. The boy who wanted to spend time with me, not because of who I was but because he was interested in *me*, not "Princess Nova's sister." I shake my head slightly as if I could literally remove the thought from my head. It's a ridiculous thought. Cillian said it himself in the woods, *"You're just alike..."*

And it's Cillian. He ended our relationship. Not me.

"I'm betrothed to his brother." The words feel wrong coming out of my mouth. I don't even realize I've said it aloud until Dahlia quickly nods at me, her rigid posture returning, her eyes dropping back to the floor.

Guilt floods me for making her feel chastised when I don't actually plan on following through with the betrothal.

"My apologies, Princess. I didn't mean to imply-—" Stopping mid-sentence, she bends at the waist, then straightens, and backs out of the room. "Do you need anything else before I go?" she asks as she wrings her hands together.

It takes me a moment to come out of the rabbit warren that she just sent my mind down. "Do you know why my sister would have been in Terrania, near the portal to the human world?"

Her brow knits. "She was by the human portal when she died?"

"Yes." I'm a little surprised she didn't know, with how the rumor mill operates among the servants.

She slowly brings her eyes back to mine. "I, um..., I don't understand. Princess Nova had no reason to be near the portal as far as I know. You should be able to ask the security team though. They would have an official reason for her request to visit."

"The humans attacked her while she was *alone* at the portal, Dahlia."

Her mouth drops open.

I press on. "Have you heard anything from other humans here, ones with connections in the human world? Why the humans would want to kill the next in line to be the Fae queen?"

The sweet pink that graced her cheeks earlier has changed to a full red. She takes a small step towards me before freezing, her hands slightly raised. "Please, I promise humans here are no risk to you," she says, words quiet but frantic.

"Dahlia," I cut her off. She's young but seems even younger because of her height. "I'm not upset with the humans here. I just want to know why my sister was killed. And what sent her to the human portal to begin with."

Her eyes gleam with unshed tears. I hate to have upset her with my questions. But Ophe is the only other human I could ask, and her ties there ended after her family's last visit.

"We're forbidden from speaking about politics if we visit home," she says. "The glamour over us prevents it. And your side of the portals are spelled to notify the Guardians if any species other than a Fae tries to enter from our world. If someone made it through the portal and was able to kill Princess Nova before the Guardians made it to her..." She shakes her head, "I just don't know how that's possible."

The *'if'* isn't lost on me. It spikes my curiosity even more.

Standing, I thank her and pause as I skirt past her at the door, the journal tucked tight to my side. Mind spinning, I say, "Please keep this conversation between us."

She gives a firm nod. *I hope I can trust her.*

I still don't have answers for why Nova would have been there. Honestly, now I'm wondering if she was even at the portal when it happened. Did they lie to me? *Did Cillian lie to me?*

Is he keeping secrets? I have no reason to trust him beyond instinct.

In the hallway, I'm about to head to my room to finish looking through Nova's journal when I hear his deep voice down the corridor on my left. I know I should go right—

My feet don't seem to agree.

CHAPTER
NINE
NISSA

L ight spills out into the hall. I can't make out what was just said so I creep closer. The deep timber I hear is undeniably Cillian's voice. I would recognize it anywhere. But I freeze when an airy feminine voice responds to whatever it is he said.

The female sounds familiar but I can't place her until I peer through the crack in the door. My eyes find Cillian first, seated behind a massive glass desk filled with water, little fish following the path of his hand just below the crystal top. He snares my gaze, unable to pull it away, until I hear her voice again.

"What a hard day it has been for all of us. Praise to the Goddess that you reached out. What comfort can I offer you tonight?" I find the high priestess through the thin slit and my upper lip pulls back in disgust at her seductive words.

She is almost unrecognizable from the female I saw at my sister's memorial. Her attire and accessories represent each of the four elements, but the dress barely covers her important parts, rising even high in her seated position. Her thick pouty lips are painted a vibrant red and curl into a sultry smile directed straight at the prince.

I hate how my stomach twisted as I searched his face for a response. Jealousy blooming like a poisonous flower behind my ribs. I have no claim to Cillian, he is in every right to take up this female on her offer of *comfort*.

"I asked you here on official business, priestess." He responds. I lose a breath when my magic suddenly swirls to life in delight at his apparent disinterest in the seductress. I pull back quickly when his eyes jump to the door.

Shit, did he hear me? I wait, refusing to breathe again until I know I am undetected.

"Oh, how disappointing." Halyca responds, and I can hear the faux pout of innocence in her voice without even looking at her.

When Cillian doesn't respond immediately, I start to move back towards Nova's study to avoid getting caught outside of his door.

"Nova's death obviously upset the Goddess." Cillian's words flow down the hallway clearly and I pause my steps.

I move back to my previous spot but resist looking into the room.

"The Daughter of Gaia, being killed before becoming queen... does it surprise you that she would be upset?" She's deflecting.

I saw her face when the final rite didn't go as planned. Even she was shocked.

"I need to speak with her." I hear him walking around the room now, his voice closer to the door.

Halcya releases an unflattering snort. "Nova is dead, returned to the elements. I'm not sure what you think I can do about that."

"Not Nova, Gaia." He states, his words filled with annoyance.

"You have to go through me to communicate with the Goddess, Prince." Her words are sharp but still drip with sex. "I'm happy to ask her anything you want and report back. Maybe in your private quarters next time?"

My blood, *or maybe it's my magic,* simmers at her implication. Hasn't he made it clear that he isn't interested in her? You would think a High Priestess would have a little more decorum. She is no better than the parasite princesses. And the overly sexy act is overplayed.

I hate to admit that I still know Cillian, understand him on some level. But at this moment, I *know* he is done with her antics. His words come out firm, "We agree the Goddess was upset. Ask if the storms are connected. See if the humans were involved."

"And why are you inquiring about this instead of your parents? Or better yet, the future king? You are *the spare.*" It sounds like she finally got the message because her words come back sharp. *Belittling.*

He doesn't take her bait, "They're all busy with the coronation. I don't want to burden them with anything more."

"And you only wish to help?" Her voice is skeptical. "How generous."

Why is he looking into this and not his father or brother?

I don't know what the Vaylors have done in the past to stop the storms. But one thing is clear, the storms are still destroying the magic and the synthetic options the Vaylors have brought in are not working as they promised. Are they benefiting from the synthetic options in some way? Why else would it not be a higher priority- *the only priority*- to stop the storms? Restore the full fae powers.

"To be honest, Halcya, I don't care what you believe as long as you get me answers. Soon, priestess," he snaps. I hear her clear her throat but doesn't respond to him.

The magic that I've been holding back builds stronger as I wait for her response. It reaches out, pushing me towards the door. I am about to acquiesce and try to get a glimpse into the room when the door swings open in one fluid movement.

In a blink of an eye, a hand lands on the wall next to my head, the other holding the open door open at my side, effectively boxing me in.

My eyes go wide and I press myself tight against the wall, as the scent of fresh spring water fills my lungs.

"Can I help you?" he asks through his teeth.

Still clinging to Nova's journal at my chest, I drop my shoulder and lift my face to him in defiance, "Nope, I'm good. You are free to return to your mistress- sorry I mean *priestess*." I give him a cunning smile, even as I internally condemn myself for letting my envy show.

He cocks his head to the side, eyes roaming across my face and taking in my words.

"She's gone." is the only answer I get.

"Why are you looking into the storms instead of Caspien? I don't buy that you don't want to bother them," I whisper, having a hard time catching my breath with him so close. My magic charged with us this close, making it hard to breathe.

His body goes rigid at my question, his eyes dropping to my painted lips. I swallow with his intense eyes on me, my blood rushing to my ears.

"Caspien doesn't always do what he should, or take care of those under his protection."

My brows knit together at his words, helping me ignore my mind and magic pushing me towards him. "Like Nova? Are you saying Caspien should have protected her?" I hesitate, trying to decide how much to share, before adding, "I know he was cheating on her."

I expect him to be shocked but instead a sarcastic smirk appears on his lips. I suppose Caspien's dalliances aren't much of a secret. Maybe their *agreement* was common knowledge.

My eyes drop to his lips. He dips his head towards me slightly and for a moment I forget what we're talking about.

Until he clears his throat. "Nova's death does nothing to benefit Caspien. In fact, it makes his life a lot more difficult. He doesn't like to be inconvenienced." His mouth is close enough to feel his words on my lips.

The wind catches in my chest, until his words register. *Am I the inconvenience?* I blink a few times clearing my mind, shaking away the hurt, "So, what were all the questions about? Why are you looking into Nova's death?"

"You mean when you were listening in on my private conversation?" When I just smirks back at him, his smile grows wider.

He chuckles. "I've missed you." he says teasingly. My heart beat flutters and the smirk drops from my face.

"You don't even know me anymore," I challenge.

"We may not be close, but I do know you. *You* haven't changed. Always snarky but with the best intentions. You care about others, and while you want to fade into the background, away from all this insanity, you still stand out in the middle of it."

I shift under his assessment, my cheeks turning pink beneath the ridiculous makeup they cake on me each morning.

"And I know..." His words are slow, cautious, as his hand reaches towards my face. "I know that all this makeup isn't you." His thumb presses into my lower lip, nudging it open. "You don't like it, and you *don't* need it."

My heart and my magic flare to life at his touch, an earthquake to my very being. I swallow before I begrudgingly push his hand away. "You're right about one thing. I think they overdid the makeup. But thanks for the compliment."

I move to push his hand off the wall, done with this bizarre conversation.

"And I know you didn't want this life, so I'm sorry you're here." My eyes flash with surprise and I slowly look back into his eyes, a regretful expression staring back at me.

I blink a few times, and ask, "Why are you looking into Nova's death, Cillian?"

He doesn't hesitate with his answer, "I'm trying to figure out why Gaia is attacking the elemental lands, and now the kingdom. Our magic is being destroyed, and no one seems to care enough to ask why. The pathetic attempt at a synthetic option is failing. Castara won't be strong enough if we're attacked. And since that's apparently now a possibility, someone has to do something to fix this. Nova's death could be related."

I tilt my head, taking in his words, "And you're going to be the one to figure it out?"

His jaw ticks. "I may not be the future king, but I'm still a Vaylor. We're the chosen family to protect the Fae. Even if Nova's death isn't connected to the storms, we owe it to her to find out what happened."

"You want this life, don't you?" I say. "Nova was like you. I wasn't made for this. Not like her." I pause. "Or you."

"Except I wasn't." he reminds me, lifting a single eyebrow. "You'll make a great queen, Nissa. If that's what you want."

I look at the floor, unsure what to say. I don't want this but I won't tell him my plans. I can't trust him. But anger grows in my gut at the Goddess who is just playing games with our lives. No one is in the position they want to be, except maybe

Caspien. *How could this all be so messed up? How could there truly be a plan?*

Nova shouldn't be dead, Cillian should be able to help the kingdom as he sees fit, without being questioned as the spare. Hell he should have been considered for King.

And I... I should not be thinking about how much I want to lean forward and press my overdone lips to this male in front of me. The one that abandoned me years ago. The one that even if I wanted, I couldn't have.

I look back up at him, "It doesn't matter what I want. Gaia doesn't care, as long as we follow this ridiculous cycle of royalty. It doesn't matter that you would have been a perfect king and that I would rather disappear than have to take this role. We have no say."

Pain fills his face. And if I didn't know better, I would believe that I could physically feel his despair.

"And for the record, I missed you too."

Shock washes across his features. He takes a step back from me and I instantly regret the words.

TEN

NISSA

My attention drifts out the window, over the forges and town smiths that stand between the city and Ignaria. Squinting, I try to make out the remains of the elemental lands ringing the outskirts of Solevara. As a child I used to stare out these same windows in awe of the fae fires that appeared to be burning at the edge of the world. One of the four elements necessary to feed into our people for a thriving kingdom.

Allegedly the fires still burn in the fire lands, but I can't see them between the lack of wind from Aeronia and the rain storms that keep the fire stifled. I can make out little more than gray smoke on the horizon that rolls into the sky like the dying breath of Ignaria itself.

What a vindictive bitch, I think as I watch what Gaia has done to her own land.

Cillian is right about the power being drastically diminished. It's broken my heart to watch the crops of the Homestead produce less and less as our energy from the earth has been destroyed. It used to be a vibrant sight to behold, but now even with the synthetic fertilizers and machines, the healthy green fields are not the same.

The previously fertile soil now crumbles in your hands, missing all of its natural nutrients, causing the roots to rot and the plants to wither. Those that do survive aren't what they used to be. The flavor is tainted with chemicals and, as a result of the reduced energy, they don't hold the power and healing nature they once did.

Selfishly, I never considered the full degree of the storm's impact on the safety of the Fae as a whole. The synthetic options were celebrated when Kiel and Isolde introduced them —fertilizers, wind machines, water purifiers, and chemical fuels. But we soon learned they did nothing for us. While the elements appeared to grow with them, they created dead produce, fake flames, wind that doesn't breathe, and water that doesn't replenish.

I may not be the Chosen Prince, but I'm still a Vaylor.

Cillian's selflessness digs at me like a pest burrowing beneath the bark of a tree—persistent and apparently inescapable. I'd built this image of him during my visits: the prince living a pampered, idle life with no responsibilities. Yet here he is proving me wrong. Proving that he's the male I always believed he would become.

Guilt washes over me. I've used my magic to secretly replenish some of the land on our Homestead but it hasn't been enough to make an impact. And here I am, ready to run from this world the moment I figure out what happened to Nova, while he's doing everything he can to save it.

What would it be like to be the queen? Digging into what has upset the Goddess. Helping Cillian to help solve the problems the Fae face. My eyes slide over the clay roofs of the houses that stretch out through the city limits. Homes filled with ordinary Fae that don't deserve this depleted life. We could work side by side to stop the storms, regrow our elemental lands, and protect the Fae. *Side by side...*

"Are you even listening?" Isolde snaps her boney fingers in front of my face, pulling me from the startling thought.

We're three hours into this lesson, and I have as little interest in learning about the proper etiquette for dinner parties with different social levels of the Fae as I did when I was a child. I've never understood why we should act differently with a servant than with the highest Elite. Ophe has always been a better friend than any of the Elite City's Fae.

With the exception of Cillian before he cut me out of his life.

"Umm..." I clear my throat. "Yes," I say as I straighten the utensils in front of me, twisting the plate a fraction of a leaf. I may have been raised on a farm, but I do know how to use a fork.

Isolde leans down to move a spoon back to where it was before I adjusted it. I roll my eyes. *Okay, maybe not to this obsessive level, but I can eat a meal without embarrassment.*

"No, you weren't," she bites out, that fire in her eyes thinning to slits as she straightens.

She's not wrong. I can't seem to get her son out of my mind, the one who *sees me.* And wants to help all the Fae of this world, not just those who can dress nice and attend royal events. Unlike this female in front of me.

Nova was just killed, and she's more worried about who will continue to arrange social events for the Elite than the death of the Daughter of Gaia. The princess, who Isolde raised as much as our own mother. Yet the queen seems unfazed a week after her death.

Isolde's indifference buries the guilt at rejecting a life that I don't want. Nova was easily replaced. Cillian is stepping up to solve problems that Caspien and the Kiel haven't been able to, or maybe haven't even tried to, figure out. Someone else can step into my role of event coordinator as well.

As soon as I figure out what happened to my sister, I'm getting the hell out of here.

"My apologies, your Majesty," I say, fighting sarcasm. "You're right, I was thinking about my sister." The words come out sickly sweet.

So far, she has refused to answer any of my questions about Nova. I decide to try a different approach. If I've learned anything about the queen over the years, it's her disdain for humans. I've heard she was pivotal in the decision to cut off access for any more humans to move into our world. The first humans came here unwillingly—as changelings. Later, families moved here voluntarily. I'm not sure why anyone would want to be a servant to this woman or the Elite, but humans outside Solevara have a good, quiet life.

"The thought of the human's being responsible for what happened to Nova ..." I shake my head in disgust.

She freezes, and I hold the wind in my chest, waiting to see if she's going to take the bait.

"Yes, well, they are an untrustworthy species. You should be cautious of that little friend of yours."

My mouth almost falls open. I didn't realize the Vaylors kept up with my life away from the castle. Ophe was born here. She may be biologically human, but other than one short visit to the human world, she knows nothing beyond the Fae. And she's more trustworthy than any Elite.

Isolde reaches for another utensil, but I cut her off before she can dive into the riveting history of a miniature spoon. "Have there been any developments in finding the humans who attacked her?"

She huffs out a sigh. "I am not privy to that kind of information." And again she returns her attention to the spoon in her hand.

The budding hope that I could use the role of queen to help the Fae withers away. I would just be a smiling face, planning events.

"Of course you aren't," I mumble as I look down at the array of cutlery, adjusting pieces of the silver again.

Isolde pops the top of my hand, and I look up in shock.

"Stop fiddling with the utensils! It is unbecoming and makes you look nervous. And what does that mean? '*Of course you aren't*'," she mimics.

I'm unable to hold my tongue after having my hand popped like a petulant youngling. "I just don't see much importance in this role. One of the many royal servants could help coordinate the events. Where my forks are placed has no relevance on those of this world. This spoon being marginally smaller than the last won't change that those at the royal galas are going to eat extravagantly while the rest of the Fae worry about the diminishing crops. Why am I even here?"

She gives two slow blinks at my outburst before responding. "You are here because you are the Daughter of Gaia, the Princess of Castara, which is a huge honor and responsibility."

I swallow thickly at her alarming calm. "Oh yes, royal event planner. How rewarding and important."

Her eyes blaze.

"This is pointless." I gesture towards the place setting, but I think she realizes I'm talking about more than silverware. "I'm not the chosen one. Nova was! And if the Goddess didn't deem it all that important to protect her, then she must not believe it's all that important for there to be a queen. So again, why am I here?"

"The Goddess does not give us a choice in this. We all have

to accept our role," she bites out, her calm slipping. She takes a slow breath. "Whether we want it or not."

I search her face at the potential confession.

In an instant the fire relights in her eyes. "There is importance in our role, Princess." Her voice resumes its unnerving calm. "We are here to support the king. While you may only see frivolous events, you and I are in a unique position that other queens have not been in. With the energy levels depleting, we have to keep the spirits of the Fae up. Events are a way to keep life moving as normal, despite the fear that is building. It distracts everyone and shows them that we believe there is no reason to fear. If the events and normal functions of the kingdom stopped, they would panic. We instill normalcy to the world. Stability."

She talks like these events are for all of the Fae. Most are for only the Elite. But she's right—they would panic if their fancy parties were stopped. *Maybe a little panic would be good.*

I fight my building frustration. "And what is being done to stop the storms?"

She huffs out an even deeper sigh, like this is the most asinine question I could have asked. "I'm not part of those discussions. Now, back to the lesson."

She begins listing off all the different occasions where I'll have to get dressed up and lie to the Fae that all is okay.

Royal event planner. Yeah, I'll pass.

CHAPTER
ELEVEN
NISSA

Two days later, I'm walking back to my room from the kitchens, where I've been trying to casually ask questions—*I hope it seemed casual.*

It is one of the rare days I have off from Isolde's lessons and I had planned to use the time to find some answers. In a castle filled with fae who love to spread everyone else's stories, I'm shocked at how little is known about Nova's death. Or at least, how little is being shared with me.

In the past, no one would have thought twice about spilling all the castle secrets to me. But going from the forgotten sister to the new Princess is exhausting. The Fae fawn over me and the staff act like I'm a Vaylor now, too scared to talk to me. My spirit feels like the broken trees in Terrania, leaving a dull ache settling in my chest.

The time is ticking down. *What will I do if I don't figure out what happened before the Coronation?*

The hallway opens up and I'm surrounded by voices as I make my way across the Grand Entryway. With my head down, I sigh when I hear my name rise above the steady murmur of the room. Letting my hair fall around my face, my feet quicken to make it across the large space. I'm too defeated to put on a fake smile right now.

"Nissa," a voice breaks through over the others and my magic responds, urging me to slow down. I search the room but I already know who I'm looking for. My magic only reacts this way to one fae, *to one male.*

Cillian is striding towards me, Niko following close behind. Each step closer sends a thrill through me. I'm still not used to his bright eyes being back on me. A high that I had come to love and then missed every year after it was pulled from me.

Niko still wears his Guardian attire but Cillian is dressed more casually. His seafoam green shirt grips his biceps and the tapered dark navy pants that are tucked into a pair of worn grey leather boots. A smile threatens the corners of my mouth, as I watch them approach.

"You look..." I trail off letting my eyes wander up and down his toned body. I've had a hard time getting him out of my head over the last few days. Feeling the heat of his body so close to mine in the hall outside of his office, his thumb on my lip... My cheeks warm as it all rushes back again. The memories have left an imprint on my magic. Memories that *may* have transitioned into fantasies that have taken root in my dreams over the last few nights.

He clears his throat and my cheeks tint pink as he observes me with a heated stare as I blatantly admire his body. My eyes jump to Niko, who is watching us with guarded curiosity.

"Not spending the day with my Mother?" Cillian asks, bringing my attention back to him.

"No, I have the day off. Thankfully," I respond, the latter under my breath, causing the smirk he wore to transform to a full on entertained smile.

"You should join us then," a hint of excitement creeping

into his voice. He looks over his shoulder to Niko whose eyebrows have raised in response.

"Is there an issue with her coming along?" He asks the Lord Commander.

"Current protocol in place states the Princess should remain in the castle at all times unless..." Niko's eyes jump between the two of us, unsure.

"Join you where?" I interject looking between the two of them, a crease between my brows. The thought of being outside of these walls is very appealing.

"We are visiting the elemental lands," Cillian says, still facing Niko. "As the future Queen it would be beneficial for her to see the damages," there is an edge to Cillian's voice. Niko seems unconvinced, his jaw clenching but he doesn't question the prince. Giving a slight nod.

Cillian's eyes return to me, a light to them that is nothing short of nourishing. My withering energy blooms back to life, a bud of interest growing. The only time I have seen the damage first hand was in Terrania after the Memorial. It would get me out of this castle for a little while. And maybe Niko would slip up and tell me more than he shared when I moved in.

And it couldn't hurt to see the portal again. Maybe do a little planning.

"I would love to see them," I state a little too enthusiastically.

While Niko goes to file the record of my departure, I change into something less formal. The dress I slip into is hemmed to mid calf with a slit to make it easier to move around. The shortened length showing off my brown leather boots. I feel more natural in this than I have in the two weeks since I've been here. Heels and dainty flats aren't functional on the Homestead.

We meet back in Cillian's study to leave, "Where to first?

Shall we save the lingering scent of smoke for the journey home?" Niko asks.

Before I can respond, I feel Cillian step up behind me. My breath hitches as he slowly runs his hand down the front of my arm, intertwining his fingers between mine, his palm covering the top of my hand. Instinctually I close my fingers around his, lacing us together. Stepping flush against my back, he lifts our hands, placing our stacked hands to my stomach, his arm wrapping protectively across me.

The air stills in my chest. "What do *you* want?" His voice rumbles next to my ear sending bumps across my skin.

"What?" I whisper out, breathy, lifting my chin to look up at him over my shoulder. His blue eyes shine down at me. A smile pulling at his lips as he tugs me tighter to him.

"Where would you like to start, Lila?" He says, a heat filling his eyes that never existed before. We were just younglings learning what love was but this-

My magic becomes hard to contain, the rest of the world falling away. This is the second time we have found ourselves in this position and my magic seems to be building when I'm around him. A storm of its own raging to be let out. Heat fills my stomach where our hands meet, a tightness coiling deep in me. I've had years to practice hiding my powers. I never wanted to show Nova up.

Or have the Vaylor's attention on me. But it is becoming harder and harder around Cillian.

It must be the heightened emotions, wreaking havoc on my elemental system. Grief because of Nova, anger at Gaia, frustration at all the dead ends, annoyance with Isolde and her lessons. *And Cillian's hands on me...*

"Cillian-" Niko's voice snaps both of us out of the haze we were lost in. We followed his line of sight to the desk. The fish

in his desk are frantic, trapped in the churning waters that now fill their glass enclosure.

My attention returns to him, watching the confusion wash over his face. Is he doing that? How long has his magic been manifesting? I'm guessing not long based on the shocked energy buzzing through the room.

Dazed and distracted Cillian says, "Let's save it to the end."

We both just stare at him for a moment, still in shock. "The sooner we can wash the smell of smoke out upon our return, the less likely it is to cling to the clothes." He says looking back at us with clearer eyes.

Niko nods hesitantly. "See you in Ignaria." he says, taking his cue from Cillian, ignoring what just happened. .

"Wait, I thought you said-" but before I can finish asking my question we all disappear from the room. Heat blooms across my face the moment we materialize but a cool steady rain drips from the clouds. I expected the area to be unbreathable but instead only one area in the distance has smoke billowing straight up into the grey skies.

While the air is sweltering there is little fire to note surrounding us. The veins of molten lava that used to pulse through the land are nothing more than obsidian scars now.

I drop to my haunches and reach out to run my fingers over the black glass but am jerked back to my feet before I can make contact.

"Lava still runs deep below. The rain is cooling the top too quickly to remain molten but the heat is real. As an earth fae, I would avoid touching it." Niko chides as Cillian releases me.

If possible, my cheeks warm even further as I look back at the shining rock- steam rising with each droplet that hits it. *Of course it is hot.* I scold myself.

We follow one of the fissures towards the crater at the

center of the fire land, ash coating the soles of our boots with each step.

When the ground opens up in front of us, I gap at the boiling fire below. Even with the water keeping the intensity subdued, it is nearly unbearably hot. I never came here before the storms so I can only imagine how consuming the heat would be at full flame.

It is a sober moment for me. Opening my eyes to what is happening in our world.

We don't speak as we stare out over the pit. The energy that lives here- that should fill this space- doesn't feed any of us. But it should be fueling a fourth of Castara's Fae.

I have been using my magic to secretly help the crops on our Homestead and my own herbal garden as well. But that is insignificant. It isn't enough to make an impact beyond my little plot of land.

And who is going to help the Fire Fae? Will Caspien? I don't see him here touring the lands, meeting with the High Priestess to fix the storms. Can Cillian figure this out on his own?

I look over at the Prince by my side, soot streaks down his sharp cheekbones from the steady drizzle. Sweat causing his shirt to cling to him.

As I study the male, I can sense the weight of Castara on his shoulders. A weight that wasn't forced there by a Goddess but a self inflicted wound from his own desire. His love for the Fae of this world. A weight that he is carrying on his own.

When he turns his attention to meet mine the darkness that fills his eyes shifts with a spark of light. Like the moon reflecting in the dark swirling waters of night. A real smile tips up the corners of his mouth and my heart responds. Doing that flutter thing that it did when he looked at me as younglings.

Could I take on some of that weight for him? Could I help him save these lands while giving myself more time to figure out what happened to Nova? My shoulders drop a little as I study his face.

"What?" He asks, his smile turning to a question of concern. I shake my head a little, swallowing the lump forming in my throat- swallowing a future that I can't allow myself to envision. Because even if I stayed in Castara it wouldn't be him I was standing next to, but *Caspien*. My time is ticking down. This isn't my elemental land. There is nothing I can do here with earth magic.

I shake my head a little, the soot bringing water to my eyes. "I thought you said we wouldn't start with the smoke." I say playfully as I reach up and ruffle his hair to distract both of us. He chuckles, brushing a piece of ash that falls from his soft brown hair to his nose.

"Should we go ahead and show her?" Cillian asks Niko.

A light breeze cools the beads of sweat on my brow and I glance up following the billowing smoke.

Niko notes my attention, "The smoke has been blowing towards the neighboring Aeronia for- ." He hesitates, "well since the storms started." The wind lands that are his elemental land and I note the sadness in his voice.

"A strategic offering from a gracious Goddess." I state sarcastically. No one says anything, no one argues. Cillian just wraps an arm around me and reaches out to clasp Niko on the shoulder. And we all disappear.

The moment we materialize in Aeronia, I break into a coughing fit. Where the air element should be at its purest, it is thick and stifling. Just like they warned, filled with smoke blown from Ignaria.

"Keep your feet grounded. The cliffs are steep." Niko right-fully warns us. I can't see anything through the motionless haze that surrounds us. The wind notably absent. One wrong step and I would be at the bottom of the gorge.

Nova and I came here when we were children. The stone edges connected by cloudlike pathways that swayed in the wind over the deep expansion. It scared me to death at first but Nova's laughter as we swung freely in the wind was infectious.

"Have the bridges survived?" I ask no one in particular as we skirt the edge of a cliff.

"No, the winds are unpredictable," Niko explains. "Some days they are notably absent like today. Others are chaotic and volatile. Most of the skywalks have been ripped from their anchors by the spinning gales that Gaia sends to frequent Aeronia and Terrania."

Sadness fills my chest. For Niko, for other wind Fae. Those like Nova who loved this sacred place.

We don't stay long. It isn't necessary even if we could see the rest of the terrain. The winds have betrayed the elemental Faes that depend on it by ushering in the smoke that now suffocates the land.

We all drink in the fresh air of Aquaria as our bodies fight to expel the smoke that filled our chests. After a few coughing fits, I'm able to right myself and take in the devastated beauty that surrounds me.

Cliffs that obviously spilled over with water in a past life, now stand barren. Rocks and large trees have dammed the waterways so even if the Goddess would send rain to the region, it would have nowhere to flow. The few areas that do retain water are murky, filled with debris.

The ground at our feet is cracked and dry, not too different from what we are seeing in the fields at the Homestead. At a distance I can hear the roars from the deep waters that used to act as a trade route to Varthiel. I've heard rumors of the crashing waves and sea life that fight to pull anyone that dare attempt the trek into the depths of the waters.

The iridescent tattoo shimmers up Niko's neck. His eyes

lose focus momentarily, as he takes in the message that is telepathically transmitted to him. Touching his collarbone, the tattoo alights again for a brief moment before his attention returns to us.

"I'm needed back at the castle," he states, his eyes cutting to me and then back to Cillian.

"You can return. I will keep her safe." Cillian states confidently, a little huff leaving my nose. Bristling at the implication that, *yet again*, he thinks I need protecting. But I suppose with my new title and what happened to Nova it is smart to be more cautious.

Niko looks between the two of us, clearly unsure about leaving us. The tattoo alights again and his lips go thin in frustration. "Ok, but head back after this. And don't go into Terrania without me or more Guardians."

Cillian starts to protest but Niko holds his hand up, "Please, I can't risk it."

The friends stare at one another for a moment before Cillian nods. "Ok, no Terrania."

Niko thanks him before quickly disappearing into the wind. Leaving us completely alone.

TWELVE

NISSA

Cillian grabs my hand and we begin walking towards a muddy river bed as soon as Niko blows away. His energy is different here and it settles the roots that had begun twisting in my belly. A feeling that I always get when left alone with him.

"Where are we going?" I ask with a smile on my face. The excitement that is flowing from him is contagious and I barely even note the tingling in my fingers that are intertwined with his.

He looks over his shoulder with a broad grin but doesn't say anything. I giggle at the mischief that lights his eyes as he drags me further into Aquaria.

When we stopped at the edge of the river, his excitement shifted to something of uncertainty. As I take in the murky waters he kneels down, his boots sinking into the mud. A sour, rotted smell fills the air around us.

A white crust coats the base of the plants at the edge of the waterways. They hang wilted and defeated by whatever it is that is killing them from the roots up. Bending down I rub the blight between my fingers. Standing I lift it to my nose, trying to identify the substance.

"Is it..." I begin.

"Salt." He answers without looking up at me. He is still crouched at the edge of the water, unmoving. "With the fading current in the fresh waterways, the waves from the ocean have forced their way up the rivers. Bringing the salt with it. When the balance is broken like this..." his voice changes, low, reverent like he is grieving. "The fresh water is drowning, it isn't strong enough to fight the tide and the poison it brings."

He reaches his hand out slowly, hovering above the silt filled water. I drop down next to him when I notice a slight tremble in his fingers. The hem of my skirt drinking up the element and the silt that surrounds us.

He looks over at me, the corner of his mouth lifting. Returning his attention back to the stagnate water, he lowers his hand. Ripples stretch out in response to his touch and he shuts his eyes.

I sit quietly giving him the moment he needs. But then something happens. I feel it before I see, or understand, what is happening. The river lets out a breath, the current shifting in response. As if the water recognized Cillian as an old friend that had come to visit his dying companion in their last moments.

Cillian doesn't open his eyes but he starts to move his hand, skimming his fingertips through the surface of the water.

Suddenly the silt begins to settle and the tide begins pushing the salt back towards its rightful home. It is slow. So slow, I think it might be a trick of light that is shining down from the sun. But it isn't. The water is changing. Transitioning from a brown, rudish color to pale before finally clarity blooms through the water.

Not all the way across the river, but right around Cillian's hand. I can feel the land around us reacting. Dryrds calling out in the distance and I swear even the reeds perk up like they are looking for the source of potential relief to their pain.

It is too much to contain. "Cillian," I laughed out his name in a huff of disbelief. I have not seen anyone else develop powers before their majority.

"How long have you had your magic?" I asked, still staring into the now clear window of water.

"I- um," I look over at him after he releases a shocked laugh himself. "today, it seems." His eyes are wide when they stare back at me and a bark of laughter erupts from him.

A smile cuts across my face at the thrill that I can sense from him. Reminding me of my first show of magic and the exhilaration it brought with it.

Nova and I had been playing in the garden when we realized it. It was small for both of us but it was clear what was happening.

We ran to tell mother and found her with Isolde. Nova burst through the doors ahead of me, "Mother look!" She squealed, tugging on the flowing silver skirt of her dress when we weren't immediately provided with the attention we requested.

"Our magic mama!" She squealed again, forgetting the proper titles we were instructed to use in a moment of childhood excitement. This time sending the smallest breeze across the papers they studied. Isolde froze and mother's attention shot to us.

Mother crouched down in front of us, cupping Nova's face. "Show me again!" she whispered. I watched on as the tendrils that fell around our mother's face blew backwards like they stood outside in the breeze, not in a stuffy office.

But I also watched Isolde's face. Her jaw clenched so tight I thought it may shatter. When she turned her wide eyes on me, the fire simmered there.

"And what about you? Have you found your powers as well?"

She said it kindly, but something lay beneath it, like the lava that now flows under the obsidian in the fire lands.

Nova turned her bright eyes to me, ready to share the news with them.

"No," I quickly said before she could answer for me, like we so often did back then. "Only Nova." The smile that lit my twin's face drops, her eyebrows dipping low. But she knew not to say anything. We could read each other.

"How is this possible?" Cillian questions as he stares into the water. He pulls his hand out of the water and we both look on as the silt slowly begins to swirl again as soon as it senses his absence.

I press my hand to his shoulder, giving it a small squeeze as I stand. "I have done a lot of research over the years. There wasn't much- *well anything*- in the Solevarian libraries since no twins have existed through the histories. But in the human world they are common." He stands to face me, wiping his wet hands down the side of his pants.

"Ophe did some digging when she visited the human world. It seems there are a lot of legends there about twins who had heightened powers before and after the worlds separated." I pop my shoulder. "Based on that I believe it has to do with the fact that we are twins. And well-" I gesture towards him, "this supports that."

"But Nova didn't have her powers. Caspien doesn't." A soft smile spreads across my face. Even through all the ash, smoke, and mud he is still so handsome.

"Nova did." I say, sadness edging my voice. I look down at the water, staring at the previously clear spot.

"No, she didn't." He is so sure.

"No?" I ask with a smirk. He runs his hand back through his hair. "Nova and I got our powers the same day. Your mother knows but didn't seem too happy about it. I left not long after

96

that so I didn't know for sure until recently but she was told not to use them. Or at least to not share that she had them." I found notes in Nova's journal about how hard it had become to contain her powers as she got closer to our birthdate.

We walk around Aquaria a little longer discussing what this could mean for the elemental lands but it is clear that right now the magic won't maintain against the Goddess' destruction. Whether it is because we aren't strong enough yet or because Gaia's power *is* so strong, we don't know.

When we rematerialize in the castle I immediately head back to my rooms to wash away the day that coats my skin. But as I come to the end of the hall voices float towards me.

Despite my desire to be clean, the magic in my veins alights, urging me in that direction. Tiptoeing, I approach Isolde's study. Pressing myself to the wall. I refuse to look through the crack having learned that lesson last time when I got caught.

"Let me get to know her better." Caspien's words slip through the door jamb.

"Absolutely not." Isolde snaps back.

Are they talking about me? My brows furrow. Why would she not want me to get to know the male I'm supposed to be bound to for the rest of our lives? Her own son at that.

"As I said, we need her," Isolde adds.

Caspien snorts a laugh, confusing me even further.

"Keep yourself distracted with whomever you need to. And for Goddess sake stay away from her. She is already too skittish."

Is Isolde encouraging him to cheat? On me? What messed-up dynamics are going on here? Was Nova running away from this?

"*Do* we need her?" Kiel's deep timber pulls me from the swirling thoughts.

The air is suddenly thick around me, my limbs heavier. I've asked the same question over and over: *Am I important?*

But the little girl inside of me—the one who has always felt disposable—recoils.

"Do not be foolish," Isolde answers. "If it were up to me, I would send her away again myself. But we can't risk her not being on that altar. I shudder to think of the risks."

The ringing in my ears drowns out the conversation.

I should be relieved. They just confirmed that they want me for nothing more than my birthdate. *And* they don't think they actually need me either. I'm just a safety net. I already suspected all of this. It should eliminate any guilt around me leaving.

I should be furious. So why does my heart feel like it was just ripped from my chest?

THIRTEEN

NISSA

T hree days after overhearing the Vaylor's assessment of my worth to them, I am still livid. I've endured lessons with Isolde for two days and it has done nothing but fuel my rage. She is over my barely contained attitude and being in the same room with her just makes me more angry. And more motivated to get out of here.

I feel like a caged animal with the wolves trapped in here with me, circling. I only have a few weeks left to figure this out. If Nova was running from the Vaylors when she got herself killed, then I owe this to her. And the sooner I figure it out the better.

If anyone would have insight into Nova's life it would be Caspien. While I can't trust anything he says, Isolde seems determined to keep us apart and I think it is time I try to figure out why.

I work my way through the castle seeking out the heir apparent. I head for the studies first and find the hallway eerily quiet. Taking a few turns, I find myself standing outside of the thick wooden door to his room. I fill my lungs with courage and lightly knock, unconsciously hoping he isn't there. Surely the next king would need to wake up early and be working already.

Unfortunately, the door swings open and a half naked Caspien greets me. My eyes drop down his bare chest to the rows of abs. He does nothing to hide the smirk creeping across his face as he takes me in.

"Nissa," he drawls as he leans against the doorframe, his arms flexing as he crosses them over his broad chest.

Ophe would be stripping right here at the threshold. An unladylike snort bubbles out of me. He is undeniably handsome. Hell those muscles are impressive but it only makes me wonder what Cillian looks like without a shirt.

My mouth goes dry. Internally cursing, I shove aside the thought. Caspien eyes me curiously as the humor evaporates. I run my hand through my hair and look up into his intense gaze. "I was hoping we could talk."

"Come on in." He gestures as he pushes the door further open, exposing the deep red interior.

I freeze. I'm not really sure why. Guilt? My twin sister always did her best to keep me away from her mate. But more than that, I'm shocked at how the magic hiding in my veins flares to life. Could this be some sign that there would be a bond between us if I went through with this? If so, I'm not sure I want a mate bond.

Turn around, Nissa. Leave.

I taste bile as my stomach pitches and twists. It doesn't matter what the magic is trying to tell me. I'm leaving Castara as soon as I get answers about Nova being at the portal. Hopefully soon if he can give me some information.

I will my magic to calm and take a determined step forward. Multiple sources of fae fire light the large room. Intense heat and the smell of spices hit me the moment I cross the threshold. The rumpled black satin sheets look as if the fire is dancing across them as Caspien sits down on the edge of his bed. He leans back, making the muscles of his chest flex.

Magic is warring inside of me. *Leave.*

I settle across the room on a scorched leather chair and lace my hands together in my lap, my back straight. I understand what other females see in him, but it just doesn't do anything for me.

He watches me and waits while I glance around the room, gathering my thoughts. Metal shelves cover one wall, filled with an assortment of fire-forged items, including the simple gold crown he wore when we were children. It looks so tiny now, with one tip bent inward.

"How are the lessons going?" he asks. "I know how difficult they could be for Nova. I can't imagine trying to absorb all that information so fast." He looks at me like he genuinely cares about my answer. Like he sincerely cared about her.

How could that be possible with what I've learned?

"It's been exhausting, but they're going well," I respond cautiously. I look at anything in the room other than him. I played out this conversation over and over in my head last night, but I can't seem to dive into it.

"I'm sure it will all be worth it once you're on the throne as queen."

My magic won't settle. The bile threatens to make a reappearance. I don't want the throne. I've never wanted the throne.

"I don't know how Nova did it for so long. I would think the lessons would wear on someone after so many years of it." And based on the emotionless Princess I saw last Beltane, they did. I just didn't understand what was happening with her at the time. It makes me sad to understand her more now than I ever did when she was alive. I could have been there for her if she had let me in.

Leave. Go now.

I ignore the nagging voice in my head. I owe it to Nova to see this through.

He makes a non-committal hum. "She understood the sacrifice that came along with this life—and the benefits."

I bristle, my eyes snapping to him. Sacrifice? Like watching your betrothed cheat on you repeatedly? I shove down the accusation I want to fling at him, and pull the wind deep in my chest. "So she wasn't struggling with this life? Maybe wanting something different?" I refuse to look away now, trying to gauge his reaction.

I'm here for answers, for some indication as to why Nova would be at the furthest edge of the Elite City with no Guardians. But a small part also wants to feel a little closer to my sister. The last two weeks have offered me more insight into her life than I've ever had before, made me feel more connected to my twin than since they sent me away.

"If you came to ask me something, Nissa, just come out and say it." There's an edge to his voice, but nothing shows on his face.

I may not understand my magic yet, but I can tell it's sending me warning signals to back off. I can't find it in myself to heed that warning. If anyone should be asking questions about Nova's death, shouldn't it be Caspien? His betrothed was attacked and killed in cold blood.

So, why does it seem like I'm the only one who wants answers?

Well, other than Cillian. Unless he's been lying to me.

I set my jaw. "I'm just wondering what would send my rule-following sister to Terrania and the portal to the human world. It isn't in her elemental lands. Why was she out there, especially with no Guardians? I'm curious if you think your cheating played any part." I cut my eyes to his bedsheets, eyebrows raised in question. I didn't plan on being so direct, but I can't hold my tongue any longer.

"Cheating?" An expression that oddly resembles amusement crosses Caspien's features. "I'd think you of all of us would relate to wanting some freedom. None of us has had any say in our own lives from the moment we were born. Nova and I both understood the pressures. She wanted me to be able to blow off steam, wanted me to have a little freedom. And it was *her* idea, not mine."

Nova's idea...? She'd always seemed so jealous.

"So no, Nissa," he says, "I don't believe it was *my* fault that she was there that day. I was devoted to Nova in my own way. If I could change what happened at the human portal, I would."

My gaze drops to my hands. "So why was she there? Why did the humans attack?" I almost plead, feeling the hope of any lead slipping away.

"Honestly..." His voice is slow, considering. "There's no evidence that humans are hostile towards us at all."

I search his eyes. "But the report said—"

He cuts me off. "I know what the report says—it looked like the humans attacked. But there was no indication they had reason to." He says it even more slowly, like I should know what that means.

It looked like they attacked... Possibilities swirl in my head. "You think it was a set-up? That the humans were made to look guilty? Who would do that?"

He leans forward, resting his elbows on his knees. His black eyes are aglow with... *anger? Suspicion?* "I think it was *Varethiel.*"

Suddenly it's hard to breathe. "Why would the other Castara kingdom want to kill their own princess?"

"Because they can't be content with the power we've already granted their king and his council." His jaw ticks. "There are mummers of rebellion in Varethiel. That they want out from under Vaylorian rule. *Ingrates.*" If possible, his eyes are even darker. "I believe they staged the whole thing to make us look weak."

My heart is pounding. I had no idea Varethiel was unhappy. And Caspien is, in fact, looking into Nova's death. And from what little I've learned from the servants, internal politics makes a lot more sense than the humans.

Caspien's eyes move towards the door and back to me. "I need to get ready for a meeting. Just know I'm looking into this. Don't worry, I'll keep you safe. You're going to be my queen." He smiles. Then he's on his feet, moving us to the door.

When I go past him at the threshold, he halts me with a hand on my upper arm. An icy chill pricks my skin. His other hand lifts, and he tucks a piece of hair behind my ear. "Thanks for coming by," he says, leaning close.

I swivel my head to the side, for some reason afraid he's about to kiss me. I don't know if his lips ever even meet my skin. But when my eyes land on the doorway across the hall, I'm fighting a sudden wave of dread.

Cillian is standing there, watching us.

FOURTEEN

NISSA

Cillian's ocean blue eyes flare as they bounce between the two of us. Tension wraps tight around my heart. I watch as his flat expression takes in the state of his brother and the intimate hold he has on me. Every muscle in his body is taut, his jaw tight as he grips the doorframe with a single hand that I'm worried may splinter the wood.

"Brother," Caspien greets, unaware of the fact that my world has just come to a screeching halt.

My heart stutters at the word, or maybe it's the look on Cillian's face. It shouldn't matter to me that he thinks I spent the night with his brother, but my brain cannot function knowing that he does.

Cillian ignores his twin, eyes slowly moving from my head to my toes and back again, like he's searching for some evidence to confirm or deny what he suspects.

He clears his throat. "Princess, I was just coming to find you." I flinch at his even tone and the use of my official title.

"You have a dance lesson today. My mother asked me to assist."

Unable to form words, I nod and slide fully into the hallway, making sure not to touch Caspien on my way out.

I start off towards the ballroom, and Caspien calls, "Have fun," after us before I hear the echo of his door closing behind me.

My entire being is at war with itself, my heart heavy in my chest. I don't owe Cillian any explanation. He ended any type of relationship we had years ago. And I'm betrothed to his brother.

But he is also completely selfless when it comes to the Fae, doing a job that isn't his. And despite the anger and hurt I am experiencing from what I overheard his family say yesterday, every fiber and cell of my being is urging me to explain that what he just saw is not what he thinks.

When he steps around me to pull the solid wood door to the ballroom back, my gaze stutters on the muscles that tighten his arm. He stands there unmoving and silent until I realize he is waiting on me to enter first.

"Cillian—" I start, deciding my conscience won't let this go until he knows the truth.

"The dance master is waiting." He briskly cuts me off and holds his hand out towards the waiting room.

I stand there with that unsettling heaviness still weighing on my heart before squaring my shoulders and walking inside. If he doesn't want to give me the benefit of the doubt, then maybe he deserves to think what he wants.

An unenthusiastic Isolde is standing in the center of the room with a male Wind Fae who is speaking to her animatedly. He is probably close to the queen's age, but the smile and excitement in what he is telling her, gives him a childlike quality. The stark difference between the two almost makes me giggle. I unconsciously turn to share the humor with Cillian. He doesn't even glance down at me as he quickly passes by, moving to meet them at the center of the room.

Well, this is going to be fun.

Isolde gets straight to the point unaware of how just seeing her makes my blood boil, "Princess, after the midnight ceremony, you will attend a reception to celebrate the coronation and your bond."

Cilian's jaw ticks.

"The Elite and your family and friends will attend. You, as the new queen, will do a first dance with King Caspien, the first of many you will do together as a mated couple. Obviously, the divine bond will be in place. Everyone will know you are blissfully happy." An edge of sarcasm tinges the words. "The dance is more proof of this."

A crease forms between my eyebrows. I may not believe the bond will be there, and from what she said last night I'm not surprised that she agrees. But I am shocked that she is being so obvious about it.

"Caspien is unfortunately unable to attend today, but Cillian generously offered to step in." *Couldn't attend or she told him not to attend?*

Cillian says nothing. Isolde cuts him a tight-lipped look of irritation before leaving, handing the floor over to the dance instructor.

The instructor quickly goes over a handful of steps for my benefit and then steps to the side. A steady rhythm fills the room, and Cillian and I step up to one another. The air crackles between us with tension, and the wind catches in my throat. The stubborn part of my personality wants to punish him for thinking the worst of me. But looking up into those stone-cold blue eyes that refuse to meet mine, I know I won't be able to.

We are frozen, just leafs apart, but neither of us makes a

move to touch. The music dies in my ears, and the instructor is suddenly next to us.

"Oh Goddess! I didn't realize you didn't know the starting position." He tries to sound encouraging, but it comes out with a tinge of annoyance. He thinks I'm a clueless idiot.

I may not be great at dancing, but I do know the starting stance.

The instructor reaches down between us to take my hand. With unnatural speed, his wrist is in Cillian's grasp.

"Don't touch her." His deadly tone, a low and hard warning, fills the little space between us. I swear I hear the instructor's bones crunch in Cillian's white-knuckled grip.

Shock and pain apparent, the instructor tries to pull away. "I-I... yes, of course. I wasn't thinking," he stutters as he's finally released from Cillian's death grip.

I feel bad for him, but the shock has me remaining quiet.

"My apologies, Princess. If I could just explain-"

"She knows. And if she doesn't..." Cillian says cooly as his blue eyes finally set on me. "I'll show her." My magic shivering in response to his intensity.

The instructor nearly sprints away as Cillian holds his hand out to me.

I slowly lift my hand to his. He wraps his other arm around my waist but his body remains stiff. He keeps distance between our bodies as we move into the steps. Every point of contact tingles with the magic running through my blood trying to break through. It's different from earlier in Caspien's room. With Caspien, I just felt... nervous. And there was that niggling voice of warning in my head. This feels natural—safe —despite me being in the arms of a male who is clearly livid.

"I don't think the instructor was a threat," I say, tone light, hoping humor will break the tension.

Cillian's eyes remain trained over my head. He easily

moves through the dance steps as we go a few more beats. Whereas I continue to stumble multiple times.

The feeling of Cillian's simmering anger wraps around us with each step and turn, despite his look of indifference. The intensity, not helping with my nerves.

"I went to talk to Caspien," I say as we continue through the disaster of a dance.

"His idea?" He grunts, his jaw still locked into place.

"Mine."

He offers me no response. His hand on my back fists the fabric of my dress, and we move into a turn. When I stumble, I hiss out his name, and he finally looks down at me.

"All we did was talk, then I left," I blurt out, "For some insane reason, I thought he was going to kiss me so I turned my head. That's all you saw. I didn't spend the night with him."

He releases the wind in his chest in a slow frustrated breath, and glances down at me for only a second. "I believe you."

I begin running my thumb up and down a tensed tendon at the back of his neck. I feel his muscles begin to relax under my touch. A blush creeps up my cheeks as thoughts run through my head that are anything but appropriate.

He uses his grip on my dress to pull me a fraction of a step closer. His breathing picks up too. "What could you have possibly been talking about so early?" His words come out strained.

If I wasn't planning on leaving this Goddess-forsaken world, I would remind him that Caspien is my soon-to-be mate and there are a million things we need to talk about. But there's no need to mention that since it won't ever be happening.

"Nova," I say quietly so the instructor doesn't hear.

He nods slightly but doesn't respond, trying to reconcile my answer and what he's conjured in his mind.

"He has a theory about what happened," I say.

This gets his attention, lines forming at the corners of his eyes when he looks down at me. "Does he?" he asks skeptically, searching my eyes.

The song is coming to an end, and I step back.

The instructor's cautious steps approach us, but he stays more than a branch away. "Let's run through it one more time. You had it towards the end, but the beginning—" He breaks off his criticism of me with a nervous glance towards the prince when Cillian narrows his eyes at him.

"Such an improvement." The instructor is suddenly beaming at me. "Let's just run it one more time."

"Turn the music on and then you are dismissed. I can teach her the dance." The cold look is back in Cillian's eyes waiting to see if the instructor questions his command.

"Yes, of course, Your Highness." He nods, music fills the room followed quickly by the door slamming shut.

Cillian is more relaxed this time as he pulls me close as a slow melody flows through the room. "Now, we can actually talk. What does my brother think happened?" he says, tone sarcastic, his eyes now lit with amused curiosity.

"He thinks Varethiel may have staged the whole thing to weaken your family."

Cillian's brings us to an abrupt halt. His eyes go distant for a brief moment. "That... could make sense," he says, words slow. He quickly picks the pace back up, continuing the conversation. "With Aiden, anything is possible."

"Who's Aiden?"

"The King of Varethiel's son," he mutters, as if there's a bigger story to go with the name.

Whatever the story, he's not sharing it now. It makes me even more curious. "Caspien mentioned a king and ruling council. He never mentioned this Aiden. Maybe he doesn't think he was involved?"

"Varethiel's king has passed most power to his son. Aiden makes the decisions for their kingdom even though he hasn't formally reached his majority yet. If a move like that was executed, Aiden's hands would have been in the fire."

"So you agree that it's possible?" I'm doing my best to ignore how we seem to be moving closer than necessary and how charged my skin feels anywhere he is pressed against me. Does he feel it too?

"It's possible. Varethiel has been on the edge of rebellion for a long time. They want the Two Kingdoms to actually be two kingdoms. My father gave their king his throne. He's more of a figurehead than a ruler. Aiden has been pushing for more. He feels our laws are outdated and restrictive, but..." His words trail off as we continue to sway and step to the song, his thumb at my back, rubbing up and down.

"But...?" I question.

"He's arrogant and abrasive, but to kill Nova..." He shakes his head. "That would be extreme."

"But he has more motivation than the humans?" I'm already getting an idea.

"I'll look into it, Nissa," he says, eyes narrowing as if he can see the wheels churning in my head. "Stay out of this." He holds my gaze. "Aiden could be dangerous."

We sway to the mounting symphony in silence, each step in each other's arms as natural as walking. It's a silent battle. I lift my chin in challenge, me staring at him, him staring back at me.

As the music slows, his ocean-blue gaze slips to my parted

lips, and his eyes darken. Clearing his throat as the last note finishes echoing through the room, he steps back.

My body cools the instant his heat is pulled from me. My magic searching for the missing contact.

CHAPTER

FIFTEEN

NISSA

When I see an opportunity to bring up Varethiel in my lessons, I take it.

Isolde leans back in her chair, assessing me. "On rare occasions, the king and queen visit the other kingdom to keep up appearances. Because of safety concerns, we do not spend much time there."

"What safety concerns?" My mind immediately jumps to Caspien's theory about Nova. I ignore Cillian's insistence that he will "handle it." We've been arguing about it for the last two days.

As always, my question annoys Isolde. "The ruling council of Varethiel has a different set of morals and values than Solevara. They have a much more *free-spirited* mindset and much less structure to their society."

"No Elite?" I know this already from my research, but I play along.

"Worse." Isolde gives a delicate shudder. "They welcome other species there. King Kiel and I did not agree with this decision, but until we restore the elemental lands, we have decided to keep the peace with their council."

I know humans, of course. But I've never seen the witches and vampires of the other worlds. It makes me even more eager to finagle a visit to Varethiel. Regardless, of how bossy Cillian feels about that.

The rest of the morning creeps on with a recitation from Isolde on Gaia's divine will and the Goddess's superiority over her counterparts in the gods pantheon, Asteria, Apollyon, and Elohim. All I can think about is continuing my research on Varethiel and their prince, Aiden.

The moment the lessons conclude, I rush to the study I've been assigned since my first week in the castle. Like my bedroom, it's decorated in an Earth Fae palette of browns and greens. But with added floral touches, which I love. The botanical smell surrounds me, bringing a small smile. Ignoring the beautifully carved wooden desk, I drop down onto the moss pillows at the base of the bookshelf. I pull out Nova's journal and place my hand flat on the front, sending a breeze through the room.

An hour later, I sink into the swing in the corner of the room with a huff. I tilt my head to the ceiling, absently brushing my fingers across the flowers that have bloomed among the entwined vines and leaves. I've combed through every page of Nova's journal, looking for anything on Varethiel. I found some mentions of other species, but little insight into the politics between the Two Kingdoms.

The sparse notes on Aiden grabbed my attention though. Every mention about the prince was about how rude and disrespectful he was. Very little rattled my sister, always the diplomat, but this male grated on her nerves.

I sit up when the door flies open, no knock, and Cillian

strides into the room. My heart rate increases even more at his expression.

"I got a response from Gaia!" His blue eyes brim with excitement.

He reminds me so much of the young boy I once played with in the gardens. I smile. "And what did Halcya say?"

"Nothing. So I consulted another priestess."

My eyes widen. "I thought only the High Priestess could commune with Gaia."

Cillian gives a snort. "Halcya couldn't even get Gaia to respond at Nova's memorial. This priestess is young, and she warned me it might not work. And it didn't at first. Gaia refused to answer any questions. She just said the future king should know. After pushing a little though, this priestess was able to glean a vague response. It seems the Goddess is upset that the kingdoms are not being ruled as she made them to be."

"Definitely vague." I chew on my lip, looking back up at the ceiling, considering. "What do you think it means?"

When I lower my gaze, he's staring intently at my mouth. I feel a hot lick of liquid heat at my core. Unconsciously, I lick my lips at the attention and he chokes off a groan. It's like this whenever we're together. Sometimes I feel his pull all the way from across the castle. My magic hums, growing like roots, reaching out for him more strongly each day. He has to be feeling it too. But neither of us is acknowledging it.

What's the point? Cillian thinks I'm going to marry Caspien and be the queen, while I know I'm going to run before that happens.

He clears his throat and walks to the shelves, looking at the flowers that bloom there. He continues, "I've been thinking about it. Gaia made this world for the Fae. For us to be as strong as possible against the other species. But humans live here. And there are vampires and witches in Varethiel. Maybe Gaia is unhappy about that."

He sinks into the swing beside me and sighs heavily. "That is all I have come up with. If the Goddess is causing the storms because we let some threat into our world, it would make sense that the storms were so bad when humans attacked Nova. Or if not them, then mutinous witches or vampires sent by Aiden."

"Well, at least Gaia gave us a clue. Something to investigate." I pull him to his feet. "This is progress. There's no reason to brood. Even if this doesn't help with what happened to Nova, the storms are hurting the world and the remaining magic. We won't be able to survive much longer with the synthetic options. I want to help you figure out how to fix things."

"Do you know how magnificent you are?" He strokes a slow finger down my cheek.

Without thought, I lift up on my toes and wrap my arms around his neck. His arms slowly snake around my waist, holding me firmly to him. The moment our bodies are locked together, I can feel his magic humming. Mine springs to the surface in response, buzzing through my body. The euphoria of our energies fighting to reach out towards one another is overwhelming. Much stronger than it's ever been and a whimper involuntarily leaves my body.

His whole body goes impossibly still before he grips my hips and places me firmly on the ground just in front of him. Embarrassment burns my cheeks as I glance up at him to apologize for essentially attacking him. Our eyes lock. With my magic ready to tear me in half, urging me to step back into him, the words never form.

We stand there, held together with an invisible tether. My hand moves up his heaving chest, the two of us locked in each other's gaze for what feels like an eternity but may be only a few heartbeats. My mind, my body, my magic, all war inside of me.

I want to lean into him, urge him to give into the moment. *Why shouldn't we?* It would ease this ever-increasing tension, cool this fire, and we could move on. But I know I wouldn't move on. I know it would make it harder for me. I already plan to run from this life, and Cillian only complicates things further. I don't want to make things harder for him too.

"We can't... *I* can't," he barely whispers. He drops his forehead against mine, and I feel it everywhere. Our chests rise and fall at the same time with heavy, deep breaths. His lips dip closer.

All thoughts of why this is a bad idea vacate my mind. My resolve to be strong is ready to surrender to whatever is about to happen between us.

I feel his heated breath on my ear, his voice scratchy, as if he hasn't spoken in weeks. "*I* can't kiss my way down your neck..."

A tickling sensation slides down the column of my neck. I swallow as an answering shiver runs down my spine.

"And *I* can't run my hands up the inside of your thigh..."

My lungs push the wind from my chest. My heart is pounding in my chest. Liquid heat pools at my center. *Oh Goddess.* His eyes are locked on me, and his hands are fisted tightly, knuckles white at his sides. He isn't even touching me. But my magic is mimicking the dirty fantasy he's laying out in my mind, running up and down the inside of my thigh. Like fingers gently caressing.

"And, *Lila*"—his pet name for me is low and sensual—"*I know* that I can't lay you across this desk and explore your body until I learn every place to touch, suck and caress... until you make that noise you just made..."

My magic finally reaches the spot where I want *him*. But it isn't enough, and another whimper leaves my throat as I rub my thighs together, searching for more friction. Based on how strongly my magic responds purely to his words, this is nothing but a dull tease of what he could offer.

A strained chuckle tickles my ears. "Yes, noises just like that." The tip of his nose gently grazes mine.

My whole body is trembling, off balance. Does he know what his words are doing to me? To my magic.

He takes a ragged breath as his eyes roam over me one last time. "No, *I* can't do any of that. But it doesn't mean I don't want to." He sounds as resigned as the look that fills his eyes.

He turns and strides out of the room, without looking back.

SIXTEEN

CILLIAN

I woke up before daybreak to finalize my plan. I'm rarely included in the council meetings with Varethiel. I was surprised last night when Caspien agreed I should join today's visit there. This is my chance to learn more about how their elemental lands are faring and to view firsthand the politics of their kingdom with the other species cohabitating. And then there is the issue of Aiden's possible involvement with Nova's death.

Nissa won't be happy that I'm looking into things without her. That can't be helped. I need to make sure she isn't putting herself at risk. If Varethiel killed Nova, then Nissa could be a target as well.

I don't believe Aiden would go after Nissa with the royal family and the Guardians there, but if it was him, he somehow convinced Nova to leave security. And she knew better.

Nissa. I run my hand over my face and through my hair, groaning. I've ignored her for a week but images from that day still haunt my dreams.

What was I thinking?

I have never put anything over the wellbeing of the Fae, and I cannot start now. Especially with something so important. I'm not a youngling daydreaming about being mated to my best friend anymore. She is the princess now, and we haven't been friends in a long time. I don't know why I can't stay away.

The last thing this world needs is a whole different set of issues from me getting too close to her again. I don't know how I even stopped yesterday. Her floral scent in my nose, her soft whimper against my skin.

And my magic... it has never felt as powerful as it did in that moment, barely a breath from her lips. Even in Aquaria, when I was able to use my magic for the first time it wasn't like that. Not like it was with Nissa...

My cock hardens at the thought of the look on her face when I realized she would surrender herself to me if I pushed. How I almost lost full control of my body with the surge of power pulsing between us.

The sensation shocked me to my core, my magic completely erratic. Was it a glimpse into how it will be once our magic comes of age? If so, it's going to take a lot of willpower to learn to control it.

I breath the wind in deeply and refocus. Caspien was uncharacteristically quick to agree to my request to join today's visit, so I need to use that to my benefit.

I wait until the last minute to join the group. My shocked eyes find Nissa, surrounded by Guardians. She shifts her feet, uneasy. Caspien is off to the side with our mother in tense conversation.

I hang back, taking everything in. The security force is going over plans. Earth and wind travel is unpredictable. It's safest if everyone stays together. Each Earth and Wind Fae is paired with another Water or Fire Fae.

As if she feels my eyes on her, Nissa turns to look in my direction. Her shoulders drop slightly, and she offers a quick smile. I keep my expression neutral as I continue to kick myself for everything I whispered in her ear. She shouldn't be here. Or relieved to see me—*no matter how much my magic and my cock like it.*

My eyes jump to my twin to see if he is watching her too, but Caspien seems too amused by whatever our mother is lecturing him about to notice.

Niko walks up and slaps me on the back. I note the dark circles under his eyes have improved in the past few weeks. After all the whispering about him after Nova was killed, he's taking it in stride. There is no question in my mind that she would still be here if she'd notified the Lord Commander of the Guardians, or the Guardians stationed outside of her home that she was going somewhere. But my family doesn't seem to care that Nova appeared to have a literal death wish that day by sneaking out.

"I heard you and the princess were joining us today." Niko pulls me aside, giving me a conspiratorial look along with a quick grin.

"What's that look for?" I question before glancing back towards Nissa.

A low chuckle. "She'll be mistwalking with you to Varethiel."

"What the hell?" I hiss, not bothering to feign ignorance. "She needs to be with your strongest Guardian. Hell, take her yourself." I fight to keep my voice low. I want to strangle him.

"You know I can't be paired with anyone, especially the Princess. Breezewalking is too unpredictable to have her with me. Plus, I have no interest in dealing with a prince of Castara wanting to murder me when I touch her." His tone is amused, a side of him only those closest to Niko get to see.

But he's right—every muscle in my body tenses at the thought of her in anyone else's arms. "Forget me. You need to help keep her safe from Aiden."

Niko is the only Fae who knows I care about Nissa. At Beltane a few years ago, being around her for two days had me going out of my skin. One too many elemental experiences, and I tried to talk to her, but she kept avoiding me. Afterward, I ranted about her and the weekend to Niko. Now that she's supposed to marry Caspien, he keeps reminding me of that.

"Nothing will happen to her on a short trip to the Varethiel," he says. "And I won't leave her side once we're there. Especially with your concerns." He isn't laughing any more, and the haunted look has returned to his eyes.

I roll my shoulders and let some of the tension fall off, knowing I can trust him.

"I haven't been able to find any evidence to support Caspien's theory about Aiden," he continues, "but I'll be on the lookout today. If it wasn't the humans, whoever did it had immense power to make it look that way."

I nod, clapping him on the back. I follow Niko to the group at the center of the entry way. My mother and brother have also joined the team and both of their eyes snap to me when the assignments are read aloud. I do my best to seem unaffected as Nissa also looks between Niko and me.

Taking the last deep breath, I do my best to prepare myself for her touch.

CHAPTER
SEVENTEEN
NISSA

My feet hit the ground in Varethiel, and Cillian's strong arms let me go as fast as possible. Despite his tension when he wrapped an arm around me, my response to him was the same. My body melted into him the instant we touched, and I'm over pretending it didn't. Something about our magic wants us together and it has not liked that he has been avoiding me for a week.

The instant the thought enters my mind, Cillian is striding away, and my magic withers back to that dormant place that it hides.

You're betrothed to Caspien, I remind myself. Which doesn't really matter since I'm *leaving*. And Cillian loves this kingdom —he loves all of Castara. I knew it as a child, and he's proved it over and over since I've been back. He would never abandon the Fae, especially not when they're in such a state of turmoil. So why am I even thinking about this?

I raise my eyes to help blink away the pressure building behind them. I'm sure it's from the cold air of this kingdom or the mistwalking, not that my chest suddenly has an overwhelming weight of loneliness. Loneliness that will only increase once I run.

I'll have to get used to this feeling. It would be too risky to stay in touch with Ophe. I would never put her at risk, and I can't involve Cillian. That would be a selfish burden to put on him. Especially since nothing has actually happened between us.

Pivoting towards the door, I focus on Varethiel's breathtaking castle. The dark stone edifice towering above me is carved to mirror the castle I grew up visiting in Solevara, but this rock is almost black instead of pale limestone. The dark hue stands out in stark contrast to the snow that covers the ground. The burning lamps lighting the castle in the gloom, shine blue, instead of the red-orange of our kingdom.

A chill creeps up my arms, and I pull my fur-lined cape tighter around me. Varethiel is located in the northern region and has cool weather year-round, but this feeling is more than that.

My eyes roam the intricately carved frames of the diamond-paned windows. White galanthus flowers fill window boxes in a hauntingly beautiful contrast to the dark stone. Despite the beauty, this shadow castle fills me with an eerie unease. Looking high above the entrance, my eyes are drawn to a small open window, where a silhouette of a female peers out. I tilt my head, squinting, a line forming between my brows as she quickly disappears, leaving swaying curtains in her wake.

"Are you ready, Princess?" Niko says at my side. He follows my line of sight and then looks back to my face, motioning a hand towards the steps.

A frozen breeze that sweeps against my cheeks has me following his lead to the front doors. Entering the large foyer, the heat licks around me but does little to send warmth through my bones. The similarities and differences of the two palaces are jarring. The entryway is structurally identical, but instead of artwork full of images of war, royal events, and past rulers, the art gracing these walls are of Fae living within the kingdom and the elemental lands. Peaceful images.

As we make our way down the hallway, four meticulously woven tapestries loom above us. Each piece of art represents an individual elemental land of their kingdom. I pause in front of Terrania as the others begin to file into what I assume is the council room. The weaving of the masterpiece is so intricate that it appears like a window opening up to the elemental land itself. The image is clearly from before the devastating destruction of our Goddess.

If Gaia's wrath is a result of letting the "enemy'" into her world, weakening us against those enemies seems a funny way to express it.

I study the forest depicted in front of me. Pops of color show through the snow from the winter aconite, hellebores, pasque flowers, forget-me-nots. All plants that I've studied but haven't actually encountered since I've never been outside the warm weather of Solevara until today. A thin, worn path cuts through the flowers and snow, evidence of a time that Fae frequented their elemental lands.

The path leads to a dense forest of black spruce, subalpine firs, and paper birch. I tilt my chin up to take in the snow-topped trees in their original majesty, standing tall and covering the forest floor with their thick foliage of moss and ferns. I can see in my peripheral vision that, aside from Niko, I'm now alone in the vast hallway, but I can't seem to pull my attention away from the tapestry.

I stare at the pinpoint of the walkway in its center. I step forwards, my hand reaching out unconsciously, drawn to the image.

"Stunning, wasn't it?" A deep baritone voice right behind me echoes in the space, breaking my trance.

I jerk my hand back from the priceless piece. With a pounding heart, I do my best to save the image to memory.

Niko stares calmly past my shoulder, but his hand is firmly placed on the blade at his hip.

In anticipation of who I'm about to face, I am reminded of how close I am to my majority birthdate. Reminds me that I'm essentially defenseless until my magic is fully at my disposal.

Don't be afraid, Nissa. You're safe.

Turning, I find an undeniably handsome male about my age. He has a squared jaw, with dark brown hair cut short up the sides, the longer top styled back. Fragments of tattoos peek out of the collar and cuffs of a plain, long-sleeved black shirt. His smoky gray eyes could freeze anyone in their tracks, and they are firmly locked in on me.

His gaze holds no warmth. The stranger takes me in from head to toe with a slow perusal that has Niko taking a step towards him. But my magic doesn't seem to sense the overwhelming threat that Niko does. It's there, humming again, but I feel no sense of warning tied to him. In fact, something about this male—and the way he is assessing me—intrigues me.

His eyes return to my face, his expression inscrutable as a heavy arm falls across my shoulder.

Caspien smirks at the male in front of me. "Aiden, I see you've met my betrothed."

A chill moves down my spine. My muscles lock into place as the name is assigned to my new acquaintance. Aiden still hasn't taken his eyes off of me.

Niko takes a step away, apparently satisfied with Caspien as my guard. Then my fingertips tingle with stronger magic, and I sense Cillian filling the space Niko vacated.

"Is that who this is?" Aiden quirks a brow at me, letting on nothing, but his gaze still feels like it's searching for... *what exactly?* He blatantly ignores all three of the heavily muscled males flanking all sides of me.

I do my best to remove the uncertainty from my voice and attempt to stand taller under Caspien's heavy arm. "I'm Nissa."

He gives a non-committal grunt before an older male steps out of the room we're standing outside. "Aiden, why don't we let the Daughter of Gaia come meet everyone at once so we can get this over with?"

There is a tense moment where no one moves. Aiden holds eye contact with me before he finally smirks and turns towards the room.

Shuffling inside, the older male makes his way to the head of the table, identifying himself as King Orin. I cut my eyes to Caspien when he quietly snorts at the title, but no one reacts.

Aiden makes his way to the chair to the right of the king, and I note the two individuals sitting across the aged wooden council table.

"Nissa, this is Enzo." Aiden motions, and the other male stands.

I try not to stare as Enzo gives a slight bow in my direction, taking in a slow, deep breath through his nose. He is as tall as a Fae, but his skin is pale and his ears are rounded, not elongated and pointed.

When he gives me a slightly predatory smile, two sharp canines slip out. "I'm a vampire," Enzo announces. "In case you haven't met one of us before. And this is Hazel. She's a witch." He gestures to the delicate female seated in the chair next to him.

She is short with flawless dark skin. She exchanges a knowing look with Aiden that I can't decipher, and then she turns a welcoming smile at me. If I hadn't seen the look she gave the prince of this kingdom, I'd feel as if we were long lost friends, like she knows all my secrets and fears.

Instead, an unsettled feeling washes over me, like they have their own secrets.

We make our way to the empty seats at the council table. Caspien takes up a position at the other end from King Orin, his father's position as ruler since Kiel isn't here. I'm instructed to sit to Caspien's right. I expect Cillian to take the empty chair across from me, but he moves to the open chair at my side. Unlike Caspien who seems as calm as ever, Cillian's posture is rigid, his eyes narrowed on Aiden.

Aiden who hasn't taken his eyes off of me except to share that look with the witch Hazel. She was more subtle about it, but they both look as if they're trying to gaze into my soul and find the answer to some unasked question.

Enzo seems amused and keeps grinning at Aiden between glances at me and the others, waiting on someone to speak.

The king finally clears his throat, but before he can begin, Caspien addresses the room. "Orin."

Aiden stiffens when Caspien doesn't use his father's title.

"It is important to me," Caspien says slowly, "that you all meet and acknowledge Nissa, not only as my future bride but as the Goddess's choice as queen." He holds out a hand to me, the corner of his eyes crinkling as he looks at me with a benevolent smile.

The room goes deathly quiet.

I want to tell them that I will never be their queen. But I can't do that yet. I need answers. Tension fills the space—and me—as I place my hand in Caspien's and he takes his seat, leaving our hands intertwined on top of the table.

"Yes, Nissa, it is about time we meet you," Aiden drawls as he leans back in his chair in calculated calm, his eyes sliding between my face and my hand as Caspien rubs his thumb up and down the top. He says nothing about Gaia's will or me being queen.

Goosebumps break out across my skin, and heat rises to my cheeks. I'm not sure what game Caspien is playing with Aiden, but it feels juvenile. I would consider calling them both out if I weren't distracted by Cillian's cold-eyed stares at them both.

There shouldn't be anything wrong with Caspien holding hands with his betrothed, but I feel like we've been caught cheating. Cillian sits straight as an oak tree next to me. I'm not sure he's even breathing. When I steal a glance in his direction, he's flexing and fisting his hands in his lap.

"What could you possibly be implying, Aiden?" Caspien muses from next to me.

I must have missed something while distracted.

The prince of Varethiel has finally moved his attention to Caspien, his eyes showing little emotion. "I'm simply asking the new princess if she feels safe at your castle. Nova was under your protection when she was attacked, no? We wouldn't want Nissa *hurt* as well..." He cocks his head to the side, a brow raised.

The jab may have been sent towards the Vaylor family, but I feel like it struck me. Throwing my sister's death in their faces is one thing, but this seems like there's an underlying message.

Is Aiden gloating? Could he really be so bold as to kill my sister and then imply they can't keep me safe? Does he think he covered it up so well that he isn't suspected? Or does he know they suspect him but feels untouchable?

An unusually quiet Isolde stands from across the table, blatantly ignoring the tension that has settled across the room. "Princess, the council has much to discuss and work out. Let us leave them to it. I will escort you on a tour to see the rest of your new kingdom." She gestures a hand towards the door.

Caspien unlaces our fingers, pulling back, but it's Cillian whom I glance towards. His lips are thinned into a tight line. He's clearly not pleased with this plan.

As I stand, Aiden rises with me. "I think that's an excellent idea," he says. "But first I wanted a moment alone with the princess to get better *acquainted.*" He purrs the last word. "In case we don't get time after our meetings. Allow me to escort you to the door."

He's stepping away from the scarred table before I can form an answer.

Cillian shoots up from his chair. "I'm not sure that's a good idea," he says, his voice hard as he looks across at Niko. "The princess is safer here."

The pressure in my chest is still heavy, but it eases a little knowing Cillian isn't intimidated by Aiden. Isolde is frozen across the table, the color drained from her face. For the first time, the queen looks unsure of what to do.

Caspien laughs, eyeing his brother and mother. "I have no doubt Nissa is safe within our kingdoms, right, Aiden?" Amusement envelopes each word.

A challenge? Is he baiting Varethiel's prince—with me?

But Aiden isn't listening to Caspien, he's watching Cillian. "I have nothing but her best interest in mind," Aiden says, the edge missing from his tone.

Before Cillian can object, I'm on my feet and making my way to the door. Aiden joins me in the corridor and offers me his arm. I don't dare look back at Cillian. This may be my best chance for answers.

When Isolde steps behind us with Niko, Aiden turns on her. "As I've clearly stated, I would like a private moment with the princess. Do not make me repeat myself."

Niko takes a step towards us, his hand again poised over his weapon. Despite the marks on his collarbone and up his neck, evidence of his extensive Guardian training, I'm unsure who would win if this came to blows. I'm glad I've left Cillian safely behind in the council room. Aiden towers over us all and has a lethal air about him that I don't think I'm imagining.

To my surprise, Isolde places a hand on Niko's arm and tells him to let us speak. She accompanies this with a warning look at Aiden that I can't decipher. Is Isolde protecting me? With a slight bow, the head of our security backs away with her, but Niko makes it clear he won't be far behind.

I look up at Aiden through my eyelashes and offer a shy smile, my voice as charming as I can manage. "Did you know my sister well?"

"Don't do that," he says with an annoyed glance behind him.

"Don't do what?" I blurt, my demure facade already slipping.

"You can be yourself with me. None of that docile bullshit they are inevitably pushing on you."

I blink at his words, "I—um, okay... Did you know my sister?" I say in my own voice.

"Yes, I met that shell of a princess a few times before—"

I rear back at the rudeness. Obviously, there is no love lost there, supporting what I read in Nova's notebook.

"There's no time for this." He shakes his head slightly. "I will always do what's best for *my* kingdom, and I have no doubt this offer will cause all sorts of trouble for me, but..." He closes his eyes for a heartbeat and opens them with a deep breath, the silver color shining brighter than before. "If you ever feel like you're in danger, you're welcome to come here. There are instructions in the pocket of your cape on how to get back here without the Vaylor family being able to detect your movements."

I swallow thickly and look back at a closely watching Niko, who should be jumping into action any moment.

Aiden follows my gaze. "They can't hear us. Hazel's shielding spell made sure of it."

I stare at him in confusion. "She is a witch," he hitches his eyebrows like I'm slow. "All they hear right now is me offering you congratulations on being the Daughter of Gaia and expressing sympathy about your sister."

Shocked, I return my focus to him for the few private moments we have left. "And why should I trust you? Why would I come here?"

Is this how he tricked Nova? Offers of safety from... *what exactly?* Was he the wolf in sheep's clothing all along?

"Honestly I don't give a shit if you trust me," he says. "But the offer is there if you ever need it."

We approach the front door, and he turns to me, bowing low. "I've notified our Guardians of your tour of our kingdom. Some of our best will join you, for extra protection. Though you shouldn't need it here." He gives a pointed look towards Niko, and without another word he walks back towards the council room.

I'm left with more questions than answers, but he definitely didn't sell me on his innocence.

EIGHTEEN

Isolde and I exit the castle surrounded by a mix of Guardians and guards from Varethiel. Unlike Solevara, no walls separate the royal residence from the city. We walk down the stairs and straight onto the streets.

"What in the worlds was that about?" Isolde hisses at me, close enough for our dresses to brush with each step.

"He just wanted to express his condolences about Nova's loss." The lie spills out as I slip my hand into my cape pocket and finger a rolled slip of parchment.

"And he couldn't do that with us there..." she mumbles, as if thinking.

I don't respond. Although I have no reason to protect Prince Aiden, the information on the parchment may benefit me when I run.

"The prince has deep feelings for you," she says, abruptly changing the subject.

I give her a quick side glance before continuing to take in the other kingdom laid out ahead of me. "I haven't had much time together with Caspien since my sister—"

She cuts me off. "I am referring to Cillian. He has always been infatuated with you, and he seems to be having a hard time concealing it now."

"We were close as younglings," I say after a slight falter in my step. I recover quickly and keep moving. "It's easy to fall back into that old friendship." My whole body is heating inside my thick cape, but it would be too telling to remove it on the snow-covered streets.

"You and I both know it is more than that. I saw the way he looked at you when Aiden insisted on talking to you privately." She clicks her tongue. "It isn't a good idea, Nissa."

My name from her lips makes my head jerk towards her. I don't recall her ever using my given name before.

Her face is taut. "This is a hard life to be born into. None of us asked for it. Don't repeat the mistakes I made and believe you can have what you want. You are called to marry Caspien. Gaia won't let anyone come out unscathed if you try to go down another path. Don't drag Cillian into your selfishness."

The wind stings my eyes as her vague confession settles deep in my stomach like a rock. I want to push and ask what mistakes she made, but with the lump in my throat, all I can do is nod and keep my pace beside her.

After a moment of silence, she begins telling me about Varethiel. How cold-weather crops and herbs are transported from here to Solevara.

I try to focus on the unfolding city, but it does little to distract me from the growing nausea. She's right about my selfishness. What she doesn't realize is that my relationship with her son isn't the only thing she should be worried about.

As we make our way down the cobblestone alleys, guards surrounding us, we gain the attention of only a few passersby. Most ignore us. A stark difference from Solevara, where the Fae fall all over any royal they come across.

Among the usual restaurants and shops, a few places unexpectedly stand out. Glassblowing galleries and stores filled with fabrics that I have never seen. An armory that has every shape and size of blade you could imagine. The Guardians all carry weapons but this is the first time I've ever seen a place to buy them.

"Varethiel creates the strongest weapons available to the Fae," Niko explains as we get closer, noting my interest. "The Fire Fae here have a specialized process that combines the cold of the snow and the extreme heat of their blue flame." When we reach a market, he explains this is where the witches are able to find spell and potion supplies—crystals, herbs, and other rare ingredients.

"A waste of space." Isolde's voice drips with condescension, making her opinion clear. She doesn't approve of the kingdom catering to foreign species.

Next to the market, there's an alcove with a door painted with symbols. Grimoires are stacked in front of the window. I strain to see inside but the dusty window obscured my view.

Outside the threshold, an elderly woman is sitting in a peeling chair that was once red, carving something. A sign is propped beside her, advertising card readings and communications with those who have returned to Gaia. The words faded from years out in the sun.

She doesn't look up, but I still send a small smile in her direction as we approach. Her wrinkled skin and hunched back give away her age. Like Fae, witches live for centuries, but they age differently. At least that's what I've been told. I've never seen anyone like her until today.

"Well, well, one of the mirrored princesses in the flesh. As I live and breathe..." Her raspy voice is weathered but strong despite her advanced age.

The Guardians with us crowd closer to the queen and me, as if urging us to move along. Isolde's fingers brush my elbow.

I step away from her grasp and push towards the elderly witch. "Madam, are you speaking to me?"

The witch's eyes swivel up from the trinket she is working on, straight up at me, shocking me with the crystal-clear white around her irises. Her body may be failing and aged, but her ethereal blue eyes look as clear as a child's. I take a step back at the intensity of her gaze. It feels almost as if she's touching my skin.

"Of course, darling, you are one of the mirrored princesses, are you not? I never thought I would live to see the day." She's taking me in now, a soft smile on her face, looking me up and down. Like she's trying to memorize every detail about me.

"This is to be the Queen of Castara, crone. Do not speak so carelessly!" a young Guardian snaps.

"Princess, let us continue. Now," Isolde commands from behind me. It sounds as if some of the Guardians have already pulled her farther away.

I don't turn to confirm it. My eyes are frozen on the witch. She pushes from the chair to stand up. Her clothing hanging loosely from her frail body. The young Guardian reaches for my arm, and she pops his wrist with the stick she was carving. He drops his hand.

"I know who she is, you fool! *Do you?*" she hisses at him.

Suddenly, Niko is there and takes a position directly behind me. I ignore him. "Madam, what do you mean when you call me a '*mirrored*' princess?"

"Oh, darling"—her voice is softer as she turns back to me —"they have hidden so much." She makes a tsking noise, shaking her head, but there is sadness in her eyes.

"Enough," Isolde calls out with a hint of urgency. "Bring the princess to me."

The old woman strikes out with another burst of speed. With surprising strength, she grips my wrist. Her sharp nails dig in but not enough to break skin. When I instinctively pull back, she jerks me a step towards her.

"She needs to know!" Her words are focused over my shoulder in the direction of Isolde. "She needs to know why the star burnt out!" Her eyes are wilder with each word.

Niko does interfere now, inserting himself between the witch and me. Shouting at everyone else to remain calm, he puts me at his back. My arm is stretched around his body, still in the witch's grip. As he carefully but firmly attempts to free me, the intensity in her gaze has me frozen.

"Trust no one but the future king," she whispers over his shoulder, just as Niko separates us.

Her words to Isolde begin to sink in. Someone shoves me towards the other Guardians, and I crane my head back towards her. "Star? Star... you mean..." My mind is reeling. "Are you talking about Nova?" I'm nearly shouting now, my voice rushed.

A Guardian lifts my feet from the cobblestones, dragging me away.

"The prophecy, child." Her eyes look frantic, and she is barely whispering, but the words carry to me on the icy wind. "The prophecy will tell you all."

It's the last thing I can hear her say. A small bell above her door chimes. A Guardian shoves her into the shop while I'm carried down the street.

"Stop!" I'm pushing against a Guardian's chest. "I want to hear what she has to say!" They can't possibly see this tiny, elderly female as a threat. "Stop!" I yell again. We're now well down the cobblestones.

When they finally release me, rage is humming through my blood. I shove the guard that had me in his hold. Turning towards Niko, I say, "What is wrong with you and your men?! She was a little old lady! I wanted to hear her out."

His head dips towards the ground immediately, "Princess, I apologize, but with the current situation, it's my duty—"

"She was a witch," Isolde snaps as she steps between the Lord Commander and me. Any concern in her voice is gone, replaced with rage. "A witch who assaulted you. I'm aware that you aren't accustomed to them, but we could not risk it. They prey on those who have lost loved ones. It's common knowledge that your sister passed. Don't let her antics manipulate you. You'll have to be smarter than that as the queen." She practically spits the last part.

"Assaulted me? Are you serious?" The witch definitely did not assault me. I look to Niko and the other Guardians for some agreement, but they don't seem to be interested in contradicting Isolde.

"We should return to the castle," she says through gritted teeth. "I'm sure the council will be wrapping up soon."

My mind spins. Was the witch trying to manipulate me? Or is everyone else manipulating me?

I look from Isolde to Niko to the castle where the three princes are waiting. I'm not sure who, but someone is lying to me about Nova.

And I will figure it out.

CHAPTER
NINETEEN

NISSA

The guards must have sent word ahead. The doors are thrown open, Aiden on the castle steps. When Cillian sees me, he rushes down the stairs two at a time, taking long strides towards me. Caspien follows, his steps slower and his hands in his pocket.

The witch's words echo in my mind. As if she were still whispering them into the wind from wherever she is now.

They have hidden so much.

Trust no one but the future king.

Then I hear another voice. *You're safe.*

I stumble backwards a step. When Cillian reaches to steady me, I straighten on my own and move away from him.

"Nissa?" he says gently. His hand drops, but he continues to check me over for any outward injuries, face filled with concern

Everything happening around me slows, and all the voices drop to a white noise. Time seems to be moving in slow motion as I scan from person to person. Caspien is watching us closely, his eyes thinned to slits, taking in his brother's focus on me. Isolde closes her eyes briefly, shaking her head, mouth tight. Her suspicions are undoubtedly confirmed.

Aiden is nonchalantly leaning against the castle wall, a small flame dancing between his fingers. He watches us with all-knowing eyes, raising a single brow at me, a smirk pulling at the corner of his mouth.

My heart is a drum in my ears. Panic continues to fill my chest. Cillian says something else to me, but I don't register his words.

Guardians from Solevara and Varethriel are watching both of us, some faces confused, some sympathetic. I lose the wind in my chest as I watch each person form an opinion on whatever is happening between Cillian and me.

But there is nothing happening. I've merely been caught up by the memories of our childhood and by what seems to be his selfless devotion to helping the Fae world. Nothing has happened. *Nothing will happen.* I won't drag him through the mud just to turn around and leave.

I close my eyes for the briefest moment, blocking everyone out, before straightening my back and transforming into the princess I need to be in this moment. The sister, Nova needs me to be so I can get to the bottom of all of this.

Sound floods back to me like lightning striking, and Isolde's shrill voice hits me, complaining about the dangers of Varethiel. With my mask firmly in place, I walk around Cillian towards my betrothed. Towards the future King of Castara, of the Two Kingdoms, of the Fae.

The one the witch said I could trust.

Sliding my hand into his, every nerve in my body fighting the idea, I look up from under my lashes. "Can we go home now?"

THE ACRID SMELL from smokewalking still in my nose, I throw the door to my room open. My body is shaking, as if it wants to rid me of everything happening. Of the pressure of the day, of spending time with the male who potentially killed my sister, of the whole lot of them who are lying to me.

I'm just not sure who that is yet, or about what.

As much as I feel like the witch was telling the truth, I can't shake the feeling of wrongness I have after traveling with Caspien's hands on me. Will his connection to Nova ever leave my mind?

He's not your mate.

Another tremor racks my body, and I let out a small cry into the empty room. I try to calm myself, taking multiple deep breaths and still unable to get my thoughts straight. My little green wisp appears at my request, and I release a breath when Ophe's voice fills the room transmitting through him.

"Tell me you are finally getting some and are calling with all the juicy details," she whispers, deliberately keeping her voice quiet.

I should know better than to reach out to her this late. Her father will be furious if he hears her. I don't want to cause her any issues. But at the same time, I need her. She's all I have, for now.

"Let's not use the word 'juicy' when discussing *getting some*," I say, releasing a broken laugh.

Silence stretches in the distance between us.

"Who are we returning to their element?" she finally asks. "I'm sure any number of these farm tools could be used as a weapon."

There are rummaging sounds, like she is actually searching for some form of a weapon. Her blind support fills my lungs with a calming wind for the first time since I was dragged away from the crone in Varethiel.

"I can come." Her voice softens when I don't respond. "I can leave right now if you need me."

I want to scream yes. I could even send someone to get her here faster. But who could I even trust to send? And her father is just now off her back about coming to see me after the announcement... It would be too selfish.

Selfish. A term I am becoming accustomed to. Selfish to run. Selfish for pulling Cillian into this. Selfish for wanting my best friend...

I sit down on the edge of the bed and rub and hand down my face. "No." I try to add some strength to the word. I almost add, *I'm fine,* but she is the one person who would see through it.

Cillian would see through it too.

I swallow, shoving away the invasive thought. I clear my throat, and repeat, "No," more for myself than her. "I just needed to talk."

"I'm here."

I sigh out a small amount of the pressure in my chest. She *is* here and always has been. Through the good and the bad. We have had each other's back and supported each other even when the other couldn't find the words.

"I went to Varethiel today to meet their prince and royal council."

"Oooo, is he——" She breaks off abruptly. "Nope, nope, nope," she chants. "Not asking that. Go on."

I can't help releasing a small chuckle. The familiarity of it provides comfort, and I relax a little more into the bed.

"Yes, he is quite attractive," I answer her unasked question. "And very" ——I search for the word to describe my encounter with Aiden—"attentive."

She lets out a slow sigh. "You're making this very difficult to not take this conversation down the wrong path. What does that mean? Attentive?"

"I don't know. He was almost protective in an 'I don't care about you' kind of way," I say slowly, trying to work it out in my head.

"You suck at this. Just tell me what happened."

I give her a quick recap.

"He sounds broody and dangerous—I love it! Little Nissa who avoids all attention now has three sexy males trying to catch her eye. How very slutty of you! Tell me you're putting at least one of them to good use."

My mind flashes to Cillian, my magic's reaction to him and how it took everything in my body to not take him up on his words right then and there in my study. I shake the thought away with the reminder of Isolde's warning.

"That's the thing... Aiden didn't actually seem interested in me. Just very curious and oddly... protective. But that isn't why I wisped you."

"That isn't an answer," she grumbles under her breath.

I dive into every detail of my run in with the old witch and everything she said. Waiting on a response, I fidget with my dress. I stick my hand into my pocket and feel the sliver of paper still there.

The instructions that Aiden left me. The instructions that could give me the way out that I need. It could be a trap, but if I can just use it to get to Varethiel without anyone knowing, then I could use their portals to leave. It's a risk, but the best solution so far.

You could leave now.

The voice is back in my head. I thumb the small piece of paper, and my magic goes still in my veins at the thought. While part of me feels like I need to protect Cillian from myself, there are still too many unanswered questions for me to run. I can't leave—*yet*. But now I know how to get out when I can.

"I don't even know where to start asking questions." Ophe finally says once I'm done.

"I probably won't know the answers anyway. Each time I find more information, it feels like the Goddess throws something else at me."

"Could Aiden's protectiveness have something to do with whatever the witch is talking about? Do you think he's worried about the Vaylors hurting you if you find out something?"

It is one of the many things that has taken root in my mind since being pulled through the streets of Varethiel. Could Aiden be the good guy in all this?

"I don't think the Vaylors plan to hurt me. They need me for Caspien's coronation with Nova gone... But they're hiding something. We can't trust them." I nod to myself. "Except Caspien, if we're to believe the witch."

"Do we believe the witch?" Ophe muses. "I'm not brushed up on knowledge of the witches and their level of trustworthiness."

"Isolde insists they're notorious for manipulating and twisting words. I'm going to check on that. But something is obviously going on, and I do feel like I'm being lied to. I've felt that way since the day Nova died." I just didn't feel like *Cillian* was lying to me.

I press my temple, trying to ease the pressure that has been building there. Is the witch, right? Can I only trust Caspien? I realize that doesn't entirely fit. Obviously, I trust Ophe. And could Cillian really be deceiving me? Have I been completely blinded by our past and his pretty face? Okay, it's more than pretty, but that just makes it worse.

I heave a sigh.

And the helper in Ophe kicks in. "Okay, so if we believe the witch—which at the moment let's say we do—then your first step is to figure out what this prophecy is. And you can't trust anyone. I wouldn't even trust Caspien. There are just too many variables."

For the next hour, Ophe and I make a plan.

TWENTY

NISSA

I wake up before daybreak with a new resolve. I'll jump through whatever hoops Isolde demands, but my main goal is to find a prophecy that talks about a "mirrored princess."

I slip out of my room before the servants even arrive to wake me. Inside the Royal Archives, I'm greeted with the warmth of the fires that burn through the long, narrow room. It's been over a decade since I've been in here, and I stop in the doorway to appreciate the room's beauty.

The ceiling's domed windows send streams of light shafting throughout the space as the sun rises to start the day. The bookshelves stretch two stories, and the wall on one side of the room has been built around an ancient tree. Its trunk has grown into a staircase to the second floor, its massive limbs creating walkways around the high shelves where most of the books are stored.

On the first floor, four seating areas are spread out down the center of the long room. Each of the four sections has chairs surrounding a large copper bowl. Each bowl showcases an individual element—a roaring fire, a stunning water feature, an artistic display of leaves, feathers, and petals caught in an ever changing wind. The final bowl is filled with moving flowers and vines, their colors and shape changing and shifting, like dancing foliage.

I remember the display of elements being grander. Maybe it's that I'm not a youngling anymore. Maybe it's the failing energy.

I step inside, and the great doors whoosh closed behind me. I jump, even more startled when I realize two golden eyes are staring straight at me through the flames rising from the fire element vessel.

I watch for a few breaths. I can't make out a body through the flames, but whatever it is it seems small. But that doesn't mean it isn't dangerous. I swallow and take another slow step forward. "Hello?" I say tentatively.

Unmoving, the creature blinks as it regards me. Then the tiny white and gold head of a dryrd pops out from the side of the flames. The tousled feathers on the top of the little head bob.

"Well, hi there, handsome." I giggle, and his eyes light up. "What are you doing here?"

The little guy makes his way around the lip of the flaming display. Sitting back on his golden, scaled haunches, he wraps his tail around himself and looks up at me.

Getting down on my knees, I smile at his sweet little features that are analyzing me. "Can I touch you?" I ask, lifting my hand up to him and waiting.

Dryrds are notoriously skittish creatures, but so far nothing about this one seems shy. They are a hybrid species of the long-extinct dragons and the wild birds of the human world. I've never been so close to one.

The creature regards me for just a moment before blowing

warm air from his white leathery snout and lowering his head towards me. The corners of my mouth lift as I use the back of my knuckle to stroke the soft feathers that start at the top of his head right before his golden spikes fall down his back. On the second stroke down his back, he lifts onto all fours and stretches his golden-lined, webbed wings away from his body. I pull my hand back slightly, but he pushes his head into me, nuzzling me to continue.

"Do you like that?" I gently scratch right between his wings and am answered with a contented rumble. I give him one more little pat. "Unfortunately, I need to look for a book," I say, pulling my hand back.

The archive is well maintained, not a speck of dust to be found, the smell of old paper surprisingly absent.

I glance above at the rows of shelves, then search around me for any type of index or recordkeeping system that could help me find the information I need. Not finding anything obvious, I climb the tree staircase, wandering aimlessly until I see the tiny dryrd's reptilian eyes staring at me from the shelf right in front of my face.

"Back for more?" I chuckle, reaching up and scratching the side of his neck. His eyes shut. "Any chance you know where the books on Fae prophecies are?" I joke.

His eyes open and regard me for a moment before he takes a few steps and jumps to the wide branch. He scuttles along the bottom of a few shelves before pausing and looking back at me as if waiting for me to follow.

My eyebrows come together as he huffs. "Really?" I mumble.

He leads me up around the second floor, climbing and hopping between the shelves until he lands on one and stares at me.

I study the titles: *The Gemini Sisters: An Account of the New Worlds and the Goddesses that Created Them... Pantheon of the Past ... The Song of the Elements: Prophecies of Fire, Water, Wind and Earth...*

On and on they go. Book after book about Fae history. Recounts of our time in the human world, creation of the new worlds, and *prophecies* from Gaia.

"You may be the best thing that's happened to me since I moved in here," I say, lifting my hand up to the little dryrd.

I had no idea these creatures could understand us. Or maybe it's just this one. Either way, thank the Goddess he can, because it would have taken me ten lifetimes to find these books without assistance.

He jumps on my hand and runs up my arm to my shoulder. Laughing, I rub him while I scan the titles etched into the leather bindings. "Any chance you know which one talks about the mirrored princesses?"

He's looking at me, just leafs from my face, but this time he doesn't lead me to any more books.

Gathering up five volumes with titles that refer to prophecies, I make my way down to the chairs around the earth vessel. The little library dryrd crawls down my dress and curls up in a little ball next to my seat, warming the side of my leg as I flip through the books.

"I am going to need to figure out a name for you, little one," I tell him.

He blinks up at me a couple times before he closes his eyes.

Several hours later, disappointment washes over me. I stand and look around the archives one last time before I need to leave. The fact that I've found nothing yet makes me hesitate. There has to be something in all these shelves of history.

"I'll be back to see you later, I promise," I tell my new

friend. I can't wait another minute without risking a scolding from Isolde.

~

AFTER THREE DAYS of fruitless searching during every free minute I have, I am losing hope. I give the dryrd a little parting rub and slide out the door. When I see Cillian and Caspien stopped up the hallway, anxiety replaces frustration as I take them in. I've managed to avoid them both since we returned from Varethiel.

No longer. Since they both are looking straight at me.

"Good afternoon, Nissa." Caspien greets me first, embers burning in his eyes. "What *have* you been up to?" He glances at the room at my back.

A creak from the door I just closed saves me from a reply. A little white tufted head and two familiar eyes peek out of the square-cut opening centered in the wood. The dryrd pops through the smaller door, bright eyes lock on me.

"Cyndr." Cillian's deep timber says in a firm but playful tone. "Where do you think you're off to? Coming to find me?" He regards the little dragon with affection and reaches around me to rub his neck.

"Cyndr?" I look between the two as my new friend nuzzles into Cillian's hand.

"The stray vermin he took in a few years ago." Caspien wrinkles his nose. "He found it almost dead in his elemental lands. My brother insisted on bringing it back to the castle."

I note his use of "it" when this dryrd clearly has a name.

"Cyndr adopted the archives," Cillian explains. "Once he was feeling better, he made the space his home. I put in the door so he could come and go as he pleases."

Just when I'm trying to distance myself, I find out that he's out there saving abandoned animals.

"I hope he didn't give you too hard a time," he continues. "He's very protective of his space." Still rubbing the little dragon.

"Actually, I think he may have been following me out," I confess. "He seems rather attached."

Cillian's hand pauses on Cyndr's head. "You bonded with Cyndr?"

"Is that unusual?" I question.

A snort leaves Caspien's throat. I look between the two of them.

"He doesn't typically let anyone near him," Cillian answers.

"That's an understatement." Caspien laughs tightly. "The little monster hates everyone other than my brother. There are scars on many to prove it."

I turn back to Cyndr. "You aren't a monster, are you?" I reach up, and he immediately jumps on my hand, scurrying up my arm to the crook of my neck and snuggling in.

Cillian's mouth falls open.

Could this male that saves helpless animals really be lying to me about my sister's death? I try to read the emotion on his face as I rub the back of the apparent terrorizer.

Caspien clears his throat. I flinch, pulling my eyes away from the sharp planes of Cillian's face. I've been staring too long.

"I was hoping we could find some time to get together." Caspien quirks a brow at me. "With the coronation approaching, it would be good to get to know one another better."

"That sounds perfect." *It doesn't* but I have to remember my mission and I need to keep Cillian at a distance. Isolde was right, we are both getting too involved. I aim for an airy, flirty voice, even though the words feel wrong coming out, reminding me of Aiden calling me out on the fake persona.

Caspien doesn't seem to mind. "Dinner tonight?"

Nodding, I fight the sense of unease filling my chest, and remind myself this fits with Ophe's and my plan. If the witch believes I can trust Caspien, then maybe he has some insight into the prophecy.

I quickly hand off Cyndr to Cillian before I can change my mind.

CHAPTER
TWENTY-ONE
NISSA

Isolde makes me stay late, reviewing information she says I should already have committed to memory. I know the answer to most of her questions, but she still looks disappointed in me when she calls it a day. It seems to be a constant emotion for her when I'm around.

On the way to my room, a servant approaches with a message from Caspien, requesting that the dinner be pushed to tomorrow. Without much time left before our birthdate, I decide to put the unexpectedly free evening to use. After telling Ophe about my mother's ominous warning after Nova died, we both agreed that she could know something. Visiting her is also a good excuse to get me out of the castle. Away from Cillian.

I make my way to her house, leaving two Guardians with persistent scowls outside the front door once I arrive. I find her sitting at the wooden table alone, picking at her dinner. Candle light dancing across her face accentuating her sharp features. The scene pulls at my heart as I make my way into the dim room.

"Nissa, the staff is making you a plate. You should have sent a wisp yourself to let me know you were dropping in." She doesn't even look up from her food.

"So, how did you know I was coming?" I look around the lifeless house, only muted sounds coming from the kitchens.

"You put in a request to visit, I believe. That Guardian, Niko, wisped me to confirm no one else was at the house. 'Securing the location'. 'Extra precautions' and all that." She swirls a hand in the air.

I take a lap around the dining room, looking for any signs of my childhood and the happiness that once existed here. I don't find any.

My mother looks drained of life, her facade of normalcy gone. She seems to have even lost the frustration she harbors for me. A shot of guilt shoots through my chest. The distance she put between us after my father left always hurt, but I don't like to see her so dejected, so alone. Her whole life was Nova. Who does she have left?

"How have your lessons been going?" she asks, over the rim of her goblet. I almost laugh at how often I get asked this question. Either the Fae are very concerned about my ability to be queen or they don't know what else to say to me.

I make a noncommittal noise in response and pop a shoulder. I'm not sure how to bring up what the old witch said in Varethriel, but I don't want to talk about the exhausting lessons either. Lessons that she always felt like I shouldn't be included in as a youngling.

I lean my hip against the table, facing her. The blue of her eyes —the blue that matched Nova's —weigh down on me, reminding me of my purpose here. The silence stretches between us, and she continues to eat her meal. Only the faint singing of a wind chime fills the space between us.

Silence is nothing new for us, but the longer it goes on, the more tired she looks and the more frustrated I grow.

I'm about to ask her about the prophecy when the door swings open and a young male human brings in a plate, then scuttles out. The vines on the legs of the chair scrapes against the floor as I sit down.

"Did you ever find the necklace?" she asks. Her face is impassive, but she shifts in her seat.

It takes me a moment to remember the lie I told her when I was searching through Nova's room weeks ago. The lie I told right before my mother warned me to be careful about digging into the past.

I cock my head and study her face. *Maybe she does want to talk about it.* "Have you ever heard the term 'mirrored princess'?"

Her face loses the little bit of color that was left. Her lips press together so tight they begin to turn white. She balls her napkin up and abruptly stands, picking up her plate, and moves to the door. "No. No, I haven't."

"Convincing..." I mutter as she hands off her plate to someone on the other side and dismisses them for the night.

I turn, watching her aimlessly walk around the room as I just did, wringing her hands. She doesn't keep a full-time staff, but dismissing the servants this early is unusual. At least it was when I lived here. I don't really know what is normal for her anymore.

What has she even been doing since Nova's death? She used to be so involved in the lessons. Did that stop long ago or did it stop when I was the one getting the lesson instead of Nova?

"Lovely to see you, darling." She gives me a fake toothy smile as she sidles from the room, dismissing me too.

I sit there, staring at nothing, trying to decide how to get her to talk to me even after she has apparently decided the conversation is over.

About the time the noises from clean up in the kitchen stop, she reappears, dressed up like she is about to go out.

"Nissa, you're still here," she says, breezing into the doorway. "Haven't you finished your dinner?"

"Just tell me what you know about the prophecy, and I'll leave."

Her back straightens slightly while she digs through her bag, looking for something. "As I said before, I don't know what you're talking about." Her voice is quieter but still holds firm.

"You aren't a very good liar," I mumble.

With a shake of her head, she huffs out a laugh. "There are a lot of prophecies out there, darling. Don't waste your time digging into things that don't matter anymore. You have more important things happening in your life."

Anymore. That confirms it—she knows what I'm asking about.

"Would it matter if I told you it's connected to whatever happened to Nova?" Nova is the only thing that has ever mattered to her. It's my last card to get her to talk.

Instead of the anger I expect, her eyes go soft. She lifts them to the ceiling and blinks away the sudden shine.

When she refocuses on me, her gaze is hard. "All I know about Nova's death is what I was told, and it had nothing to do with a prophecy. However, *if* it did"—she emphasizes the *if*, "then I would think it wise to stay as far as possible away from whatever this prophecy is." The familiar venom coats her words.

I don't know why I ever thought she would help me. I stride past her for the door, surprised when she grips my elbow.

"Nissa, leave this alone," she says in a low whisper, like she's worried someone might hear. "It isn't worth *both* of your lives."

"So, you don't believe that report either." I let out a dry laugh. She didn't outright say it, but she's implying enough. "With how much you loved Nova, the fact that you don't care about finding out what really happened to her is..." I look for the word, coming up short. "Goddess, I can only imagine how quickly you would have moved on if it were me."

I jerk my arm out of her grip and throw the door open. There's a muffled cry as I leave my mother in the room behind me.

My chest feels just like it did when I was sent away all those years ago. When she showed me that she would never fight for me. *That she didn't love me.*

I'm going to have to figure this out myself. I'm alone, like always.

So, why is my heart pulling me towards Cillian?

TWENTY-TWO

The dress I selected for tonight is beautiful and perfectly suited for me. Sage green, with a romantic, flowing silhouette, it sweeps to the floor in a way that's formal enough for the occasion but still comfortable. The floral embroidery around the neckline and lace bodice is whimsical and adds just enough detail to make it stand out.

I've pinned my curled hair to the side and let it fall over the front of one shoulder, exposing the delicate leaf-shaped earring, dangling from the tip of one pointed ear.

I summon a smile at my reflection, feeling confident, but it doesn't reach my eyes. I've been eyeing this dress since they put it in my closet, and I love how I look in it. That doesn't mean I want to go through with tonight's dinner. I can't shake the feeling that Caspien is just using me. A stepping stone he's dusted off to get what he wants. I know the witch said to trust him, but it still feels wrong.

Nova and he had time to form a relationship, no matter how distorted it may have been. They knew each other, maybe even loved each other on some level. It's conceivable that they would want to bond their lives together. But Caspien just needs me—the other twin born on the same day as him—so he can be crowned and replace his father as king. Otherwise, I suspect I would already be back at the Homestead with Ophe.

Taking a deep breath, I steel myself to meet him in the private dining room. But when I get to the break in the hallway, I hesitate and turn towards the studies instead. It's one hundred percent because I'm a few minutes early and have decided to kill time, I assure myself. It's not because I'm hoping to run into Cillian.

What reason would I have to want that?

I flex my hands and rub them over the skirt of my dress. Cillian's study door is cracked open with light streaming into the hallway. The click of my heels slows as I remember Isolde's warning.

If Cillian really does have feelings for me, they're pointless. I shouldn't encourage him. I take a step backwards. I need to turn back the way I came.

Just as I do, he slowly pushes the door open, expression on alert. His features soften when he sees me. "You look beautiful." His blue eyes darken as his gaze rakes over me. He takes a slow step in my direction.

"Thank you," I almost whisper. I try to sound a little more confident. "I'm on my way to dinner with—" I choke back Caspien's name.

Cillian's jaw tick as he realizes why I'm dressed up. I didn't bring up the dinner to hurt him, but we both need to be realistic. No, I don't plan to go through with the coronation, but he doesn't know that. And I'll be gone either way. There is no *us* in the end.

"Right. Well, enjoy." His face is an emotionless mask as he turns back towards his office.

My feet are rooted to the spot.

When he realizes I haven't moved, he leans against the doorframe. "I assume you were in the archives because of the prophecy? Niko told me what the witch said to you. If you need help figuring it out, I'm here."

My eyebrows rise so high they may very well be in my hairline. Would someone trying to hide something offer to help? Maybe if they were trying to keep me from finding something.

"Could you help me get in touch with that young priestess? She may know about any prophecies."

He immediately nods. "I'll wisp her. It may take some convincing. Gaia wasn't happy about the last time. I was thinking there may be something in the ancient archives," he adds.

"I've been looking in the archives for days." I tilt my head at him.

"The ancient archives are different. They have some of the more sacred accounts, more in-depth histories of Castara. I've been intending to go there myself to look into any history about the storms and the elemental lands. I could take you."

Every fiber of my being wants to accept. "Thanks for the offer. I'll let you know."

"I know you think everyone is lying to you right now. I have no doubt that some are. But I'm not. *I promise you*, you can trust me, Nissa."

It feels like his words wrap directly around my heart and squeeze, making it hard to breathe, much less respond. I give a tight nod before reluctantly turning away to hurry back down the hall.

Caspien is there when I round the corner, and he doesn't seem happy to have been kept waiting. Arms folded across his chest, he's scowling.

"Hi." I try to smile through the pit forming in my stomach.

After a moment, he gives an answering smile. Dropping his

intimidating stance, he leans forward and briefly brushes his lips across mine.

Ice fills every crevice of my being. The pit in my stomach turns into full blown nausea.

"Hi," he says, still smiling down at me. Like he didn't just kiss me for the first time, no matter how fleeting it was.

Still in shock, I let him grab my hand and pull me into a private dining room. He pulls out a chair for me, and I sink into it, regretting everything about this night already. But I know I have to pull it together and remember my goal. First, I need to feel him out, see if I get the sense that I can trust him. And second, I want to ask about the prophecy. See if he knows anything.

He takes the seat next to me, and I feel his hand on my thigh under the table. His touch feels wrong. The soft fabric of my dress is the only thing between him and my skin. Even with the thin barrier I feel naked, and all I want to do is cover up.

"You look beautiful in this dress," he says, giving my leg a light squeeze.

Goosebumps cover me, and I shift away. Trying not to shudder, I take his hand and place it on top of the table. I summon a faint smile, hold it for a moment to avoid being completely obvious, give his fingers a gentle squeeze.

His mouth tightens, but he doesn't call me out. I'm relieved when a servant interrupts, placing two elemental experiences in front of us.

"I hope it's okay. I ordered you verdant dewdrops," he says as he inhales the black smoke of his experience.

I lift the cupful of tiny glowing droplets to my lips. The rich taste of moss and honey fills my mouth, instantly calming me as it hits my tongue.

We spend the first course of the meal, a golden nectar bisque, discussing my lessons with his mother. The conversation moves smoothly, his charm and charisma clear as he focuses on me and my life since moving into the castle.

After we both finish the perfectly seared moonfish and spring root vegetables, I take advantage of the slight lull in the conversation. I sit up a little straighter. "How did your meeting with the council in Varethiel go?" I ask, steering the topic in the direction I want.

He takes a slow sip of his second elemental experience, a small flame-filled cup that smells of cinnamon and ginger. "It was uneventful until your return."

I'm unsure if he's referring to Cillian's reaction to me or what happened on my tour of the city. But the one thing I do know is that the last thing I want to discuss is my relationship with his brother.

Summoning an encouraging smile, I muse, "I don't suppose Aiden gave you a full confession the moment I left the room?"

"Considering the fact that he left with you, no." His voice is flat

I shift in my seat.

He takes mercy on me and continues, "But no, he didn't confess anything upon his return."

"Is he always like that? Or did the way he was speaking confirm for you that he was"—the staff enters the room to drop off a blossom-flame tart—"involved?" I choose the last word carefully. I don't want to give away what we are talking about to any humans.

I dip my fork into the vanilla orchid cream that fills the pastry.

"Aiden has always been an arrogant bastard. I can't be sure if he was just trying to mess with me or if he was gloating. I'm continuing to look into it though." His dark eyes track my fork as I lick the cream off.

My cheeks warm. I blurt, "Do you know anything about a prophecy that refers to me as a 'mirrored princess'?"

He leans back in his chair. "I've never heard of any prophecy that includes that term." He thinks for a second longer. "The High Priestess reviewed the history and prophecies after our births. I'd think she would have mentioned something like that. Why do you ask?" His burning gaze sweeps back to me.

His question throws me off. I'd assumed Niko filled him in about the witch. "Just something I thought someone called me." I return my attention to my plate, moving the dessert around.

He places his hand over mine. "You seem nervous, Nis."

The name sounds wrong coming from him—*forced*. I swallow the instinct to tell him not to call me that. We're supposed to be bound together in a matter of days. I can't afford to make him wonder. The touching, the nickname... he's using this dinner to build intimacy between us.

It's exactly what I implied we needed not so long ago at the memorial.

So why does the realization make me want to run and not stop until I'm—*where*? Back at the Homestead with Ophe? Out of this world all together? Heat fills my stomach when I realize where I want to run. Or rather to whom.

Caspien leans forward and tucks a stray strand of hair behind my ear. "What am I doing wrong, Princess?"

I fight back a guilty wince at his use of my title. I look up to the ceiling, shaking my head. "You're not... I just..." I take a breath. "It's just all happening really quickly. In my head you're still Nova's betrothed, not mine. This life was never mine."

The words may not be the whole truth, but they are true.

"I understand." He nods to himself. "The mate bond will

take away all these thoughts." He runs a knuckle down my cheek to my jaw, giving me a knockout smile certain to work on any other female.

But it's doing nothing for me. In fact, it's having the exact opposite effect.

I'm supposed to be bound to this man in a week, and my body wants nothing to do with his touch. My chest tightens, and it's hard to breathe. My mind flashes to the one person who does make my body react. If I weren't already planning on leaving Castara, this would lock the decision in stone.

"We'll get there," he soothes, his features soft as he reassures me.

After that he shifts the subject to something lighter. We spend the next hour trying to get to know each other better. Which only solidifies for me that I have nothing in common with this male.

Once the plates are cleared, he insists on walking me back to my room. With each step, he subtly brushes against me. With each touch, another chill slides over my body. I'm glad when we reach my door, eager to make a quick escape. Instead, he grabs my waist and pulls me towards him.

I freeze as he snakes his hand around me to the exposed back of my dress. The heat of his hand feels like ice on my chilled skin. Before I can react, he leans down and presses his lips to mine. It's forceful this time, not the soft brush of the earlier kiss. His tongue pushes against my tight lips.

Shocked, I gasp, wriggling to free myself from his touch. Ice is spreading through every nerve of my body. He steps us backwards into my door, his wet tongue sliding across the seam of my lips, demanding entrance.

The cold is seeping into my bones now and snaps me out of the shock. I shove his chest. He doesn't budge. Instead, his hips press into me, leaving no doubt how aroused he is.

I push again, this time wrenching my head to the side. "Please." The word comes out shakier than I want.

He moves his lips to my neck.

My body begins to shiver uncontrollably, but I can't form words. I push harder, and he finally pulls his head away. When I look up at him, there is no denying the frustration in his eyes.

He must feel the tremors because after a few blinks, he asks, "Are you okay?" Tilting his head, he runs his hands up and down my arms.

"I th-think I'm s-sick," I manage, shivering harder.

His eyes narrow, as if he's trying to decide if I'm lying, but he must believe me when the shaking gets worse.

"M-maybe it was th-the food."

"I'll call a servant for you." Interest gone, he takes a large step back.

I just want him to leave. I shake my head and mumble, "I-I just need sl-sleep." I flee into my room, shutting the door in his face.

CHAPTER

TWENTY-THREE

NISSA

I'm buried under my fur-lined cape and every blanket in the room when I hear a muffled knock. While I didn't want Caspien to call a servant, I'm thankful someone is here to light a fire. I don't have the strength through the cold to do it myself. Even my powers seem frozen in my veins.

The teeth chattering has barely subsided enough for me to call out a weak, "Come in."

The door creaks open behind me.

"Can you pl-please light the fire?" I manage.

"What the hell, Lila?" a deep voice growls.

The relief of hearing Cillian is overwhelming. I want to cry, but truly believe the tears would freeze on my cheeks.

He is kneeling in front of me seconds later. "What did he do?" he grinds out as he cradles my hand. He instantly jerks away, his face shifting from anger to utter shock as he stares at my icy fingers.

"I'm s-sick," I'm able to get out between more tremors.

His eyes grow wider as he grabs my hand again, this time

holding it tight and covering it with his other. I let out a broken whimper when the heat from his skin seeps into my fingertips.

"Am I hurting you?" he asks.

I close my eyes and shake my head. "Helps," is all my tired body can get out.

"I'm going to light the fire for you." He begins to stand.

I clutch his fingers with the little strength I have. "No, please. Don't leave me."

He looks across the room at the fireplace, but I can't let go of the little heat he is giving me.

"What can I do?" He crouches back down in front of me.

"In the drawer, get me..." I squeeze my eyes shut, trying to clear the fog in my brain. "The echinacea and... goldenseal tinctures." I shiver through the words.

Keeping one hand on me, he digs through the herbal remedies I have in the table next to the bed. When he finds the right ones, a broken cry escapes me when I attempt to sit up.

"I have you." He twists the amber bottles open, gently places a hand under my head, and lifts it. "Open," he quietly instructs.

I obey, and he uses the dropper to give me the needed amount of the tinctures. After lowering me gently back to the pillow, he closes the bottles and sets them on the table next to me. My eyes fall shut, but I can feel him watching me as he pulls the blankets up to my chin.

I open my eyes and see what looks like a new resolve wash through him. He quickly crawls over my body and climbs under the covers with me. Taking one of my hands, he wraps himself around me and covers us both back up. If I didn't actually believe I could be dying, I would appreciate how well we fit together when he settles against my back.

Then my back bows, and I cry out as cold and heat clash

through our clothes. He pulls me tighter into him, and I try to suck in a ragged breath through the pain.

"You need the heat. You're okay, you're going to be okay," he murmurs into my hair.

I can't tell if he's trying to reassure me or himself, but it helps me pull the wind deeper into my lungs. It only takes moments before our combined body heat begins to release my tensed muscles. I relax into his embrace. My eyelids are heavy, cold and sleep pulling me under.

The last thing I remember is his gentle whisper. "Lila."

THE SUN IS BARELY COMING through the windows when something wakes me. I lie there for a moment, trying to get my bearings. The rattle of glass drags my attention to the corner of my room.

Cillian's wrinkled shirt stretches tight across his back as he digs through a cabinet.

"Snooping?" I ask in a sleep-filled voice. I clear my throat as I sit up a little.

He gives me a mischievous smirk over his shoulder. "If I was going to snoop, I'd do it when you weren't in the same room." He resumes his search.

The moment feels so normal, so natural. For a moment I pretend that we could have a life like this. That there's no worry about whether his family is lying to me. No divine requirement to become Caspien's queen, a duty that makes every fiber of me want to run.

"What are you looking for?" I ask.

"I thought I'd make you some tea. You feel warmer to the touch, but it could help make sure that chill doesn't return."

The melancholy retreats, and a smile breaks out across my face as I watch him try to tend to me, digging through the glass jars I brought from my flat.

"And what do you have to make that tea?" I eye the medicinal herbs he has set out. I giggle as he names off a few things that are for completely different ailments.

"Okay, okay." He gives me a feigned look of affront. "What should I be using?"

After I list off what my body needs, he steeps the tea and settles into the bed next to me. "How are you feeling?" he asks, as I blow on the steaming liquid.

"Much better." I eye him over the mug as I take a sip. One corner of his lips tips up into a sexy smirk. My eyes jump back to his. I shake my head a little to clear the thoughts. "Will you tell me about the ancient archives?"

"Why don't I just show you instead."

CILLIAN PULLS BACK a single large mahogany door. The hinges groan, like the entry hasn't been used in a long time. Peering around him, I stare down a dark staircase barely illuminated by fae fire.

As we wind down the dark stone stairs, the deeper we go, the mustier the smell. The stairs are slick with algae, and my legs are still weak and unsteady from the night before. I run my hand along the edge of the wall to help my balance, determined not to fall and make a fool of myself.

Without a word, Cillian places a hand on my lower back to steady me as we descend deeper under the castle.

The stone steps end and open into a narrow corridor lined with a handful of doors. He leads me to the second door on the left. The moment his free hand makes contact with the door knob, a vibration radiates through the corridor.

Cillian grabs one of the fae fire torches from the wall and leads us into a dark room. As he places the torch in a metal pit in the center of the space, the room comes to life, fae fire winking in glass-paned bookcases. I can barely make out the ancient scrolls and leather-bound books inside through the layers of dust obscuring the glass.

I make a lap around the small room, taking in the date markers on a few of the panel doors. Running my fingers across the two drafting tables on the right, I leave dust tracks behind.

"Doesn't look like this room is visited often," I muse. "No Cyndr?"

"No." Cillian is taking in the bookcases as intently as I am. "I was shown these archives as a child during a history lesson. I've never actually been down here to research anything myself. And obviously they aren't maintained by the staff."

I walk back around to the shelf that appears to have the oldest of the parchments and peer in through the grime. "May I?" I ask.

He gives me a quick nod, and I grip the golden handle and pull. The musty smell of old parchment and leather assaults me when I peer inside. I sigh when I don't see any sense of organization to the piles of aged literature in front of me. Again, I'm wishing for the helpful little dryrd.

Gingerly lifting a stack of scrolls, hoping the whole lot won't tumble from the shelves, I move to the tables to unroll one. Cillian takes up the table next to me, opening a leather-bound book that is clearly from a more recent time.

As he flips through the book, I study the first page of my scroll—a map of Castara. I scan the diagram of our lands, taking in the Kingdom of Varethiel longer than the rest. When I shuffle to the next page, there is a map of Pollara.

"I've never seen the other worlds." I run my hand over the depiction. "Have you ever been?" I ask Cillian without looking up.

"Not often. A few times with my family for royal events." He comes over and looks over my shoulder at the table. "Pollara is beautiful. Their crystal and salt mines are like nothing else I've ever seen." He points to an area on the map. "The stars at night look as if they're so close you could reach up and touch them." He pauses and then peels the page back to a third map.

Alhena—the Vampire world. Even the image appears to be drawn darker than the others.

"Royal visits to Alhena are even rarer." I don't have to be able to see his face to sense the change in him. The tension is rolling off of him. "It is not somewhere I'd like to visit again."

"Why?" I instinctively whisper, like the vampires will be able to hear me through the parchment.

"It's a vicious, brutal world. Humans are still the vampire world's main source of food."

I jerk my head up to him in shock. We have humans here as workers, but they are treated well. Most prefer life here.

"It's different there," Cillian adds. "Humans are used for whatever the vampires want, and humans have no say."

"How do humans end up there?" Why would anyone willingly go to a world like that?

"Apollyon has never forgiven Elohim. He turned his people against the humans. They aren't just a food source, they're the enemy. Many of the humans there were manipulated or stolen by vampires that have snuck back to Elohim's world, but some humans go there in death."

"But Enzo, the Varethiel guards—" I cut myself off, shaking my head. I don't know any of them, but they didn't seem to fit what he's describing.

"Yes, the original demons are irredeemable in their anger

and vengeance. But some of the made-vampires remember being human and disagree with the treatment of their former kind. It's actually why Aiden opened Varethiel to a few who have proven themselves." He pauses, thinking. "It was a risky decision. But helping those that wanted out of Alhena—I admire it."

His eyes turn towards me for the first time. "Just be careful if"—he hesitates—"when you have to go there." We stand there, staring at each other for what feels like minutes but could have been only a few heartbeats.

I'm not sure where he means. Alhena or Varethiel. The words are on the tip of my tongue that he doesn't have to worry about either. I have no intention of becoming Castara's queen, requiring me to go on any type of royal visits. It is on the tip of my tongue to tell him. To share with him my biggest secret.

Trust no one but the future king. The witch's words ring through my mind, and my lips stay sealed.

He blinks after a minute and returns his attention back to the tome on his table.

I watch him read for a moment before I move on to the next page. A detailed account of each world. I scan the words, knowing they won't give me any insight into what I'm seeking but still fascinated by the accounts. I roll the scroll back in on itself and return it to the bookshelf for another.

"So Cyndr..." The little dryrd has been on my mind.

"He seems taken with you." A small chuckle leaves Cillian's throat as he shuffles through another cabinet and bringing another set of tomes to the table.

"What's his story?" I question as I return the parchment I just looked over with no success.

"A particularly brutal storm hit the lands. It was one of the worst to date. Many of the animals had to flee for safety to other parts of the kingdom. I traveled with my father to Aquaria to check on how bad the damage was. Just like the other areas it was devastated. Rocks had fallen, stopping the water ways, preventing the rivers from flowing. The droughts in this particular area came later, so there were large areas that were nothing but flooded waterways." He takes a deep breath, flipping through a few pages, lost in thought.

"I found Cyndr half drowned in one of the flooded ravines. I almost missed him, but the sun came out just long enough to reflect the gold on his wings. I was able to swim out to him. He didn't even fight. He'd given up by that point." He shakes his head. "I don't know if it was from being in the water so long or from something else, but he's never gotten his fire back. He wouldn't have survived alone in the lands. He was too weak, and the others had left him. I couldn't do the same."

"So he lives in the library now?" I asked, having abandoned my search, listening to the story.

"He stayed in my room at first but never settled. One day I visited the library, and he immediately went to the fire vessel. It was the first time he had left my side since I pulled him from the water." Cillian's face lights at the memory.

"I woke up the next morning and he wasn't in my room. I panicked at first. Until I found him curled up at the archive's door. I went that day and had part of the door removed and replaced with the smaller door so he could come and go as he wished. He rarely leaves now. Never leaves actually."

"So he sticks to the library to *harass* people?" I joke, amused at Caspien's warning that the little creature could cause much harm.

His smile drops for a moment before he recovers it. "He doesn't like many Fae. But he liked you."

"Who wouldn't. I'm wonderful," I joke, calling on a little bit of the confidence Ophe has pushed on me.

"True..." he murmurs. Our gazes lock.

Then he returns to the book in front of him.

Cillian and I go back and forth between the shelves and the drafting tables for at least an hour in silence. The space is small and each time he returns a book to the shelf, he touches me in some small way. At first I think it's just an accident, a subtle brush of our arms or shoulders as he turns to go around me, but the longer we're down here, the bolder his touch, a hand to my lower back as he walks by, a gentle squeeze on my hip.

Each time my body warms, and my magic rushes to the spot he's found. I turn back towards the bookshelf to return another useless scroll and take a slow, deep breath, trying to calm my body down.

My arm is still tingling from his fingers running down the bare skin when I start to skim through the next scroll. It is an account of the birth of the first Vaylor Prince and the first Daughter of Gaia. Parchment after parchment of scribe documentation of the births of each heir to take the throne.

I flip to the last page, the ink fresh compared to the centuries old chronicles of the earlier pages. I read through the dramatic birth of the first Fae Twins and the chaos they brought with them. And then I'm brought to the last entry of the scroll.

I gasp as I read the title to the start of our birthing story.

"Did you find something?" Cillian asks, stepping into my back, hands casually resting on my upper arms as he peers over my shoulders.

"Look," I point down to the parchment.

'The Birth of the Mirrored Princesses.' The title is followed by a detailed recollection of my mother's labor and the birth of Nova and me.

"It's the last page. There isn't anything about the prophecy but whoever wrote this had to have known about it." I tap my finger on the two signatures at the bottom of the passage, indicating the scribes who documented the events.

"Do you recognize the names?" I ask.

"Only the bottom one. He is the Royal Scriptor but I don't know the second." We both stare down at the second name. *'Celyste,'* scribbled messily in tiny script.

"Could you ask him about her? Find out who she is?" I ask, studying the words before us.

I look up at a nodding Cillian. For the first time, I realize how close he is. He looks down at me over my shoulder and gives my mouth a quick glance.

Our gazes collide. My tongue slips out of my mouth to wet my lips.

"Yes," he says, his voice deeper than before sending my magic into a frenzy. He leans in slightly, and I tilt my head back further. He runs the pad of his thumb over my jaw, and I shudder.

"I don't have much time." My voice comes out breathy, and his eyes snap back to mine. "To find her. It's only a week from the coronation," I try to clarify. It just sounds more incriminating.

I curse internally. There's no reason why I would need these answers before the coronation. In fact, it would probably be easier to get answers as the queen.

"Then we need to be quick. Lila..." His name for me sounds like a prayer. Concern and resignation fill his face. He closes his mouth, like saying more will make me disappear right then, or maybe make the Goddess appear.

Does he know?

Releasing his hold on my arms, he moves back to his table. He runs his hands through his hair. I try to ignore the flexing muscles in his arm. When I look up at him, he doesn't look suspicious. For some reason, he looks relieved.

"I'll reach out to the Scriptor today."

I study his face. He would stop me if he suspected my plan to leave.

Wouldn't he?

CHAPTER
TWENTY-FOUR
NISSA

After our discovery in the ancient archives, the next two days are filled with preparations for the coronation and mating ceremony. Isolde insists on including me in all the event plans for the reception, forcing me to look over different types of food and experiences and decor that will emphasize the fire and earth elements coming together. I spend hours at dress fittings and hair and makeup trials, waking up every morning in full dread that I won't have answers before our birthdate.

Caspien has been noticeably absent during the planning. Which is a relief.

Cillian and I haven't given up on answers though. We've split up, dividing the research while we wait to hear from the Scriptor. He's continuing in the ancient archives, while I'm with Cyndr, sneaking away whenever I can to look through the ordinary histories.

Each hour that passes increases the pressure in my chest until I can barely breathe. I drag myself out of my bed and stare into the mirror at the dark circles under my eyes.

I've failed Nova. Even if we find Celyste before the coronation, that doesn't tell me who killed Nova. There are just too many questions unanswered.

And on top of that, I'm about to abandon the Fae and this world. I can only hope that I'm right, and they don't need me. Either way, by running, I'm ignoring an all-powerful goddess's will. The storms and destruction are proof of Gaia's power. And soon, that destructive power might be directed at punishing me.

A servant throws the bedroom door open and scurries inside with a tray. It's the human girl from Nova's study. "Happy day, your Highness. I have some fruit and tea to start off the morning."

"I don't believe I'll be able to eat anything today, Dahlia."

"At least have some tea." She sits the tray on a table and begins pouring a cup despite my protest.

"I really don't—"

She shoves a napkin into one of my hands and then stands there holding out the filled cup expectantly. Her eyes are wide with unspoken words.

I take the cup from her slowly. The napkin is, in fact, not a napkin but a folded note.

"I will leave you to get dressed, Princess. Unless you need assistance today?"

"Um, no. I'm okay. Thank you." The instant she's out the door, I discard the unwanted tea and unfold the note.

LILA,

I know you'll be happy to learn I've located your long, lost friend. I'm unsure whom you would want to share the joyous news with, so I felt it would be best to communicate it to you privately. I've made arrangements for a brief meeting for the two of you tomorrow. I believe you'll need one final fitting with the seam-stress. Dahlia will come to get you in the morning and bring you to me.

Cillian has found Celyste.

Each time I reread the note, the smallest amount of pressure eases and I feel the tiniest spark of hope. Hope for what, I'm not entirely sure, but hope nonetheless.

The next morning, I'm up and dressed at sunrise after barely sleeping. I sit, bouncing my legs at the end of my bed unsure what else to do with myself. A light knock fills my room, and my heart jumps into my throat.

I hurry to the door and crack it open. It takes everything in me not to rush out the door the moment I see Dahlia.

"Princess Nissa," Dahlia says, "I apologize for bothering you on your day of rest, but it's time for your final fitting. The *seamstress* is waiting for you."

"Yes, of course," I say with a regal nod, playing my role.

I silently follow her down the halls until we're in an older part of the castle. The servants' area isn't kept up as well. There is no art on the walls, and smaller doors line the narrow halls. We make another turn, and she takes us down a thin, empty passageway that ends in a heavy door. When she shoves it open, sunlight floods in from outside.

As my eyes adjust to the bright sun, Cillian is pushing off a castle wall. Dahlia gives him, then me, a quick nod and shuffles back inside with a wave and smile. The door slams shut behind her, and I flinch.

Cillian smirks at me with a silent laugh. "A little jumpy?"

"You found her?" I roll my eyes. I'm not in the mood for jokes.

"Yes, she isn't a Scriptor. She was an upcoming priestess assisting Halcya at the time of our births. When the Royal Scriptor couldn't leave my mother's birthing room she volunteered to go record the Daughter of Gaia's birth in his absence."

"So she is a priestess?" I consider the new information, "Makes sense that she would have knowledge of the prophecies."

Cillian nods. "She was, but she left years ago. We should hurry," he says, expression turning more serious. "We have a long trip ahead."

I blink at him slowly a couple times. "Can't you mistwalk us there?"

"To start, but we may have to do some searching for her. I don't want to waste any time."

I don't want to waste any time.

A shiver runs through me. The coronation is in three days.

I must not hide my reaction very well. His eyes soften, and he takes a step towards me, lifts a hand to my cheek. I lean into his warmth, into his comfort.

"I'll do my best to get you answers before you leave" His words are barely a breath on the wind.

My eyes shoot to his in a panic. I move to take a step away, but he grabs my wrist. His grip is gentle but firm. When I pull, he drops his hold and enfolds me in his arms. Just like every time we touch, my magic is there, but it's only a faint echo of the usual rush.

Even my magic showing caution at the potential risk.

"You don't need to lie anymore. I've known since I saw you in Terrania after the memorial."

I stare at the hard chest. When I don't answer, he tips up

my chin. I swallow and roll my shoulders back slightly. "I can't marry Caspien."

I tense in anticipation of his response. Did he even find Celyste? Is he going to tell them and lock me away until the coronation? His eyes search mine as I stare up at him in defiance, waiting on whatever he's going to do.

He leans forward, his lips brushing mine as he speaks. "I know. And I'll come with you. Wherever you go."

My face goes slack. A breath later his lips firmly press into mine and the world around us explodes.

My magic responds faster than my mind. Every cell and fiber of my being feels like it's been thrown into the deepest level of pleasure. A whimper works its way out of my chest. I can feel him everywhere, his hand presses into my lower back... another under my chin... moving into my hair.

When he angles my head, tugging my hair for more access, my mind finally catches up. I clutch his neck, going up on my toes to deepen the kiss. The ground shakes around us, and I open my mouth for him. A deafening rumble of thunder surrounds us, but all I hear is his moan as my tongue finds his.

He turns us, pushing me back into the warm stone of the castle. His hips find mine, and I feel how hard he is, pressing against me. Pulling back, breaking our kiss, he places his forehead to mine.

"Together," he says through deep, heaving breaths. "We will leave here *together*..."

We both look up to the heavens as lightning strikes somewhere nearby. Thunder claps again, shaking the entire castle, and he curls around me. When the immediate threat quiets, we both peer up into a sky as dark as the day Nova died.

I swallow and look at him with wide eyes. The dark sky brings some semblance of rational thought back to my brain. "You can't leave with me," I argue, determined. "I may be running from the Goddess the rest of my life. Hiding in another world, away from friends and family. She'll be angry if her princess doesn't marry the new king. I don't want that for you. You love this kingdom, this world. You were born for it. You can't go with me."

"I can go, Lila," he grinds out through a clenched jaw. "Goddess be damned if she is mating you to *him*. You are *mine*. I'll give up anything in this world to be with you." He's almost shouting into the storm, which is now pelting us with thick rainfall.

"Be quiet!" I swing my gaze around desperately, as if Gaia herself is about to show up and damn us on the spot. When no one appears out of thin air, the wind fills my lungs again. "You love the Fae. I would never ask you to abandon them. That isn't who you are."

"You didn't ask, and the only Fae who matters is you. If you run, I'm coming—"

Thunder and lightning explode around us. A wooden wagon the servants use splinters only twenty twigs away from us.

"We can argue later." He grabs me around the waist. "If we're going to talk to Celyste, we need to go *now*."

I shut my eyes, braced against the instantaneous heat and nausea that threaten from a mistwalk.

Just like before the air in the Aeronia is thick and suffocating. But with the storm is raging even some of the smoke has dissipated. The ground shakes with the rumble of thunder and it echoes through the cliffs nearby.

"What are we doing here?" I yell through the rain.

"Celyste isn't in Castara," he yells back over the noise of the world being ripped apart around us. "Niko found her seeking refuge in Pollara."

My heart skips a beat as he tugs me towards a portal to the

witch world. I realize that I'm in almost the exact same situation that Nova found herself in before she died—away from all Guardians, in an elemental land that isn't my own. At one of the portals.

I freeze.

Cillian swings around. His hair is sticking to his face and rain drips from his chin. His blue eyes shine back at me. "Do you trust me, Nissa? Because you're the only Fae in this world that I trust completely. Maybe that's stupid since we've been separated for so long, but I know, I know *in my soul, in my mind, in my magic, in my heart,* that I can trust you. So even if you have only the tiniest feeling that you can trust me, I ask that you do it, right now. Trust me. I'm taking you to Celyste. Let's just pray she has the answers you need."

I swallow the last of my fears, because he's right. I still need answers. And the one thing I know for certain is that I can trust Cillian. I've always known that we were connected somehow. That he would protect me at all costs.

So, I give him the smallest nod. I'm not even sure he sees it through the rain, because we are already racing for the witch portal together. Hand in hand, we step through. The immediate feeling of weightlessness carries us as we fall through space. Red gas wraps around us, hiding anything that exists outside of our connected bodies.

My pulse picks up as the fall goes on longer than I expect, but when I look into his eyes, a sense of peace fills me.

At least it does until we find ourselves in a world that I don't recognize, with a storm still raging around us.

We look at each other. What are the odds that the Goddess has sent her storm across worlds? The gods are supposed to have an agreement—to leave the other worlds to the god who created them. For the storm to follow us across portals could mean that Gaia is defying that to chase me.

No matter where I run, that *we* run, we may never get away from her.

I try to push the thought away as Cillian grabs me around the waist. Kissing the side of my head, he mistwalks us again.

This time we land near a cream-colored stone cottage set in a dark green forest. The vine-covered roof is thick with twining leaves dotted with budding pink flowers. The windows look dark, but we proceed hand in hand up a rock path inset into the mossy ground.

An invisible barrier halts our progress. Cillian reaches out, probing, running his fingers along the blocking magic. I place my free hand against what feels like a solid, cool breeze. It tickles my palm, and then my hand easily pushes through. It's as if someone suddenly unlocked a door.

We look around to see if there's anyone around but it is hard to see through the pouring rain. On alert, we approach the front door. Cillian shields me behind him, then knocks. There's movement inside, and the door pulls open. A stunning silver-haired female Fae in a white robe dress stands just inside. Her eyes widen, and she tries to shove the door closed.

TWENTY-FIVE

NISSA

Cillian swings his arm out to stop her. The perfect milky skin on her cheeks goes red as she stumbles backwards, only avoiding falling when she catches herself on a table inside.

"We aren't here to hurt you," I call out as she continues her retreat. I step out from behind Cillian, my hands held up in a non-threatening gesture.

The fear on her face contorts to a moment of confusion. Then horror returns to her delicate features. "Nissa," she breathes out, her eyes frantically darting between Cillian and me.

Both of us go unnaturally still. "You know who I am," I say as I take a step into the doorway.

"Of course. I would recognize those eyes anywhere." She grips her forearms and looks to the floor, "may stone and soil steady your steps," before straightening again, looking between us. *The earth fae respect.*

"I was hoping to ask you some questions, Celyste," I speak

slowly and softly to not spook her any further. "May we come in?"

"And him?" She tilts her head towards the prince behind me. Cillian has a hand on my lower back in support.

"And him." The storm is raging at our backs. What sounds like a tree crashes in the distance.

This gets Celyste's attention too. She finally gestures for us to come inside. Walking carefully backwards, her distrust obvious, she leads us to a room off the hallway and offers us seats.

The inside of the cottage all feels very *mortal*, or at least what I have learned of it. Very little evidence of the elements are present: a single plant, one wind chime by the window, a candle glowing on a shelf, and a tiny recirculating water feature in the corner. Other than that, there's simple seating, lamps, and a table at the center of the room.

Cillian and I settle next to one another on a couch. I welcome the heat of his skin as his body brushes mine.

Celyste looks down at our wet legs pressed to one another. After a moment she tosses me a blanket. I wrapped it around the two of us.

"What can I do for you, Princess?" She sits nervously on the edge of the cushion, hands tangled in her lap, and back straight.

It doesn't go unnoticed that she's only addressing me. I give a quick glance to Cillian and decide to take the lead. "I was hoping you could tell me about the prophecy that calls me a 'mirrored princess.'"

Her eyes dart back to Cillian and hold. "Why come all this way when you can just ask him?" Her voice is cold.

The thunder above shakes the trinkets on the shelves.

"I'm just here to help Nissa find the answers she is looking for," he says. His tone is stern, demanding. One of the royals.

186

She lets out a humorless laugh. "And bring Gaia's wrath to my doorstep?" She gestures outside to the storms.

"You think *this* storm is from Gaia too?" My heart sinks into my chest in a downward trajectory to my stomach. This confirms my worst fears. "Please," I plead, "Is my sister's death a part of prophecy? Do you know what is causing the storms?"

She studies my face while the wind continues to howl outside the windows. Pity fills her eyes. "Nova may be part of the storms now," she offers, her tone softer. "But it started with you."

"Me?" I stare at her, confused.

"I left because of you. The storms are because of you. The answers to all your questions come back to *you*."

That can't be correct. I've only been the Princess for a few weeks.

Cillian threads his fingers through mine. "We're going to need more information than that." The deep timber of his voice sounds lethal.

"*Your* family," she snaps at him, "wanted me to lie to the Fae about what the Goddess wanted. What was prophesied from the beginning! And I wasn't going to lie to you." She looks at me now, the look of a mother trying to comfort a child.

"Why would they want it hidden? What does the prophecy say?" I fight the quaver in my voice. I'm not a younging. I've come for answers.

Cillian grips my hand tighter, both of us waiting, worried this can only get worse.

"The prophecy that *you* are to rule," she states matter-of-factly.

I snap my attention back to her. "*Nova* was supposed to rule," I say, finally finding my voice. "Halcya said so at our birth!"

She nods slowly at my outburst. "Yes, but so are you.

Halcya may have been ok with disregarding an ancient prophecy but I wanted nothing to do with it. And they wanted me killed for my knowledge. So here I am." She gestures to the room around her.

I shake my head. "I don't understand."

She sighs. "The mirrored princesses." She stands, moving to a shelf across the room. She pulls out a scroll but the parchment isn't aged like those in the ancient archives.

"I knew they would try to get rid of all evidence so I copied the prophecy before I ran. If it still exists, you can find the original in the ancient archives or with the High Priestess."

She rolls out the single piece of parchment in front of us. A manicured nail points to the passage at center of the page.

**When twin daughters bloom beneath the
veiled skies,
Born of breath and root, where old power
lies,
A realm once whole shall split once more,
Two Crowns to rise from ancient lore.**

**One shall guide the winds that roam,
One shall stir the seeds of home,
Each to thrones the stars foretold,
In mirrored lands both fierce and bold.**

**Joined by flame, embraced by sea,
Fourbound fates shall come to be,
Yet secrets shield what must remain,
Until the storm reveals the flame.**

But shadow waits behind the veil,

To test their will, to see them fail.
Should mirrored daughters heed the call,
Two thrones shall rise, or kingdoms fall.

BLINKING, I read the lines over and over.

"It is clear both of you were to rule," she continues. "I interpreted it to mean Nova would rule Solevara with Caspien, and you would rule Varethiel with Aiden." My head jerks up at this.

"Aiden?" I blurt out, cutting her off.

"Yes, based on the birth order-"

"Wait- wait, Aiden has the same birthdate as us?" The words rush out of me. My head is spinning. "Did you know that?" I turn towards Cillian.

"No..." We sit there for a moment staring at each other, both of us unsure what to make of this new information.

Cillian's deep voice fills the silence. "Is there any other context? What did the rest of the text say?"

"Nothing that I felt of importance to record." He eyes her for a moment as if trying to determine if she is trust worthy. This is simply a hand written document by a former priestess. Without the original we can't verify the validity of it.

As if prompted by the uncomfortable assessment, she continues, "The Vaylors set Varethiel up with a ruling council before any of you were expected. I'm assuming they had never heard of the prophecy and didn't realize the implications. Halcya instructed me to keep the prophecy quiet after the births so the kingdoms wouldn't panic about the change that would come."

She shakes her head, looking down to the floor. "But they never had any intention of you ruling. That was confirmed for me the moment they sent you away. And clearly Gaia realized it too since the storms started soon after."

I just stare at her, speechless. I had never put together that the storms started after I left. I was so young and lost in my grief of being separated from Nova and Cillian.

"I tried to fight it. *I tried*, Nissa, I really did," she implores. "When I continued to question Halyca and tried to go directly to the Vaylors, I was removed from the Priestess ranks. She made everyone think I was crazy. Once you left, I knew the Vaylors wouldn't let someone who knew about the prophecy live. So I copied the important part and ran. I had planned to come back once you were older but... I was a coward. Then word of your sister's death came..." She looks down, tears falling onto her lap. "I knew it didn't matter."

Hands fisted at his sides, Cillian continues to study the page. "When did the prophecy surface? Who was the source?"

"I don't know when it surfaced." Celyste swipes away tears, gathering herself. "Asteria and Gaia had a hand in the prophecy. I wasn't far enough into my studies to be sure why the witch Goddess was involved in our politics."

"My parents knew the whole time." Cillian grips my hand. "This settles it. You're not safe in Solevara." He searches my face with intensity that overflows my heart.

"Halcya met with your mother often back then. It was clear she knew and orchestrated many decisions. Though I can't imagine your father wasn't part of it."

"But this doesn't explain anything about Nova or help us stop the storms," I argue. "I can't fulfill this prophecy, whoever I marry," I wave at the parchment, "since she's dead. There's only one of us to rule."

"The Vaylors"—she spits out the royal name in disgust, glaring at Cillian—"don't care about stopping the storms. All they are interested in is maintaining their power even if it is at the expense of those they rule."

"*I* care about those we rule." Ignoring the venom she's directing his way. "We can't do anything about the fact that

Nova isn't here anymore. So, how do I stop the storms?" Cillian demands.

He still wants to fix it for the Fae, even though the prophecy can't be completed.

"How can you be sure it is about the prophecy at all if the storms are still happening?" How can you be so sure?" I challenge the female in front of me. She has a lot of opinions but only one thing is confirmed in the words in front of me. That I am to rule. Everything else is just guessing.

"You're right, I can't be sure. But if I were to guess why they are still happening and why they followed you here..." She drops her eyes to our linked hands.

A loud boom echoes through the forest. I look out the window and spot a fallen tree. This forest is being as battered and beaten as Castara and the elemental lands.

Is me becoming Caspien's queen the key to making the destruction stop...? Has the prophecy shifted now that Nova is gone. Do I just need to be on the throne?

My mind whirls as I try to put the pieces together. "We need to go. We've learned all we can here."

When we make it to the hallway, Celyste's voice follows us. "I really am sorry, Nissa. For every part that I played and everything that has happened to you and your sister as a result of it."

I turn back to face her. "Do you know what truly happened to her?"

"I don't," she states simply.

And I believe her.

The wind whips my hair around me as soon as we step back into the storm. Cillian turns and pushes both hands into my hair. Holding it back, he tilts my head up and looks into my eyes. I wonder if I look as haunted as he does.

"Where to, Nis? Anywhere you want, we'll go," he offers thickly.

"We have to go back." The words are barely audible over the storm. But as soon as they leave my mouth, the wind disappears and the rain slackens. Thunder still rumbles but only in the distance, a low warning.

Cillian jerks his head around in shock.

"I think that answers one question," I say, not sure whether to laugh or cry. "Gaia agrees. She wants us back in Castara."

"I won't just hand you over to Caspien. I can't." He is shaking his head, jaw tight. "I won't."

"According to Celyste, I was never yours to hand over," I say. He looks like I've slapped him. "I'm not trying to be cruel. I just mean that we need to figure out what all of this means. What the Goddess wants from me. Maybe I'm supposed to marry Aiden? Who's to say Caspien is the right choice in this? Or that I'm now the Goddess's chosen princess for him? Nova and I may be the 'mirrored princesses' in the prophecy, but everything else is just guesses..." I finally take a breath, wind filling me.

As he digests my rush of words, I heave a sigh. "My point is that we don't even know what Gaia is truly angry about or how the prophecy changed with Nova's death."

His hands run down my arms like he can't let go. "Lila..."

"No, Cillian." I place my hand on my chest. I take a step back, breaking the connection between us. "We can't run. We have to figure it out. We have to go back. You know we do. You of all Fae know how detrimental these storms have been."

"Why does it have to be you?"

"I don't know," I say. "But how can I walk away knowing I could end the suffering of our entire world? Of the entire Fae population. I have to at least try."

TWENTY-SIX

NISSA

When we land outside of the castle, the sun is setting. The only evidence of the Goddess's wrath are the wet cobblestones and a pile of scorched wood from the destroyed wagon stacked against the castle wall. His arms are still wrapped around my body protectively, neither of us are ready to let go.

We had been so close.

The moonlight shines down on us and I lean my head against his chest. Closing my eyes, the steady beat of his heart is a comfort to my soul.

"I always wanted it to be you," I say quietly. And truthfully, *I always believed the Goddess wanted it to be us too.*

He doesn't respond. He just pulls me closer, drawing circles on my lower back with his thumb.

Goddess, what do you want me to do?

I open my eyes and stare up at the waxing moon surrounded by a star filled sky. Something about its beauty pulling at me.

His chest rises like he is preparing to say something, and I know whatever it is will break the last piece left of me. So I quickly pull away, already missing the feel of our magic dancing with one another.

"I need to go think through everything we learned. Figure it out. We have to be missing something." His face falls but there is a light of determination in his eyes as I back away from him towards the door.

My heart races as I pace my room, going over ever detail of the prophecy in my mind for what feels like the millionth time. Gaia clearly wants me in Castara to rule but with who?

I begin breaking everything I know down.

The storms started around the time that I was sent to the Homestead and continued for the years while I was gone. A storm hit the Elite City for the first time the same moment Nova was killed.

And the City was hit a second time when Cillian and I agreed to leave together, following us to Pollara. Only stopping when I said we needed to return to Castara. Otherwise, there have not been storms since I have moved into the castle or when I visited Varetheil.

I shake out my hands as frustrated energy swirls inside of me, tinkling in my fingertips. The timing of the storms does seem to support the fact that the storms are related to me ruling or at least staying in Castara. But it doesn't help tell me which Kingdom she wants me in now that Nova is gone.

Why would anyone want me to rule anyways? And could the kingdom have changed with Nova's death?

Even if we figure out which kingdom it doesn't guarantee that they will stop once I am Queen. All this could be for nothing...

What is your plan here, Gaia? What am I missing?

Celyste thinks I am betrothed to Aiden. Could that explain why he was so attentive to me during the visit? So worried about my safety?Giving me a way back to him. Does he know about the prophecy or was it just a natural instinct to take care of me? The mate bond driving him.

Something is there at the edge of my mind. But what is it? What am I missing?

Knowing about the prophecy could give Aiden motive to have killed Nova... Based on the Vaylor's thoughts: *no Daughter of Gaia, no King.* Which would mean Caspien couldn't become King without Nova and Aiden would be crowned *with me.*

Maybe that is why he is so calm about everything during the meeting. Does he think the ceremony with Caspien won't work because I am betrothed to him?

When was he born anyways? What is his birth order? And where does Cillian even fit in with all of this? He was born on our birthdate as well. *He is the one I have a connection with.*

I rub my hands over my face. My head is pounding more and more with each additional theory. And that is all they are. *Theories.*

How am I supposed to know what some Goddess intended an unknown number of years ago when She prophesied my birth?

Groaning with my lack of progress, I dig through my herbs, pulling out lemon balm, passionflower, and holy basil. With the brewed tea in hand, I walk the empty hallways towards the archives. Maybe I can find something helpful now that I know the context of the prophecy and how Varethiel is connected.

Cyndr lays curled up in a ball at the lip of the fire basin, one golden eye cracking open as I walk into the room. When he sees me his little spiked tail flips up in response. He stands stretching his wings out, and then sits at the edge patiently waiting for me to approach.

"Hey friend," I smile as I ruffle the feathers on the top of his head. "I can't tell you how good it is to see you." I hold my hand out to him and he scurries up my arm, nuzzling into my neck with a content rumble. I giggle, heading to one of the chairs surrounding the earth basin.

I drop down in the vine woven seating to drink my tea, tired down to my roots. I lift the mug to my mouth and take a sip, savoring the warmth that fills me. Leaning my head back, I close my eyes and wait for the calming and mental benefits of the concoction to take effect. Cyndr takes up a new position in my lap and I unconsciously rub his back.

What does Isolde know? According to Celyste, she knew about the prophecy and still sent me away.

She doesn't know if they need me for Caspien to become king but isn't willing to risk it. Beyond those few things, I'm only guessing and I have no intention of asking her about it.

Taking another sip, I run the prophecy over in my head again.

When twin daughters bloom beneath the veiled skies...

I open my eyes staring up through the glass ceiling, the starry night stretching out above me. Beams of moon light spill into the room through the domed windows.

With the light falling across my face, I freeze taking in the moon above me. Could that be... *Oh my Goddess.*

"Cyndr, that could be it!" The little dryrd perks up, flapping his wings in response to my excitement.

"Come on, we have to find Cillian!"

CHAPTER
TWENTY-SEVEN

NISSA

The gold-framed floor length mirror reflects the most beautiful dress back at me. The straps are made from the same lace that covers the front bodice of the dress. The delicate vine runs over my shoulders and down my back before meeting right above my lower back. I run my hands down my hips along the deep green fabric that is fitted down my legs before flaring out into a perfect mermaid cut.

The guilt that has been pressing in on me since I first decided to leave has eased. I know this is the right thing. I have to trust Gaia. I have to trust that the divine bond will be there. That I will be happy at the end of all of this. But even if I'm not, Castara will begin to heal, and I will survive.

All this tragedy-—Nova's death, the destruction of the elemental lands, me believing I could run and have a normal life—all started because of Fae believing that they knew better than the Goddess, trying to change fate.

And look where it has led us. I won't make the same mistakes. I may not be trained to be the queen like Nova, but I can do better than those before us and bring the kingdom back to what it's supposed to be. Well, as close as it is can be with Nova gone.

Staring at the princess in the mirror in front of me, I keep reminding myself that I can stop the damage, help bring back the natural energy of this world, despite the fact that I am still dreading this.

THE ANCIENT SANCTUARY is the most breathtaking place I've ever seen. Walls with soaring gothic arches match those inside the castle. The open ceiling exposes everything to the night sky. The fun moon and the stars light my way, assisted by fae fire candles that help illuminate the winding stone path to the altar.

Ivy grows up the walls, trees pregnant with buds hang down over the walkway. Streams wind in and out of the beautiful flowering bushes on either side of the path. The sound of trickling water meets my ears, and the delicate floral scent fills my nose. As I stare at the stars reflecting in the stream running through the ancient haven, I realize they are actually luminescent fish, playfully following my path. Everywhere I can possibly look is a divine representation of all four of Gaia's elements within the space.

Breathing in the energy from this space is intoxicating, my magic feeling stronger than ever.

I can see Caspien approaching from the opposite side, and a chill runs down my exposed spine. Each step towards him feels like I'm a lamb being led to slaughter.

I have to believe that I'm right.

I can bring peace to the Fae.

I will be a strong, fearless queen.

I hold my head high and refuse to show any fear that I could be wrong.

I almost miss a step when I spot Cillian at the edge of the altar, standing with Kiel and Isolde. He is the perfect image of male masculinity. My stomach muscles contract and my magic reaches out for him as I watch him run his hands through his hair. My eyes quickly snap to the stairs I'm approaching, resisting the pull.

I will be a strong, fearless queen.

But I'm not stupid. I know that I can't make eye contact with Cillian unless I want my resolve disintegrating into dust. He trusts that I know what I'm doing but fears I could be wrong. But this is my calling and the bond will be there. *The bond has to be there.*

I feel the wind beginning to pick up as I start to ascend the steps to where Caspien and I will meet.

I finally make it to the top of the cracked steps that every Queen of Solevara before me has mounted. The sobering honor constricts my heart further. The wind fills me as I move forward.

I will bring peace back to the Fae. We will bring peace back to the Fae.

Caspien is dressed in a stark black suit with a matching shirt. I have to admit he pulls off the look well, even if he isn't the prince I know should be walking towards.

His eyes glow, gleaming like his gaze could burn the whole place down. He's emitting power, even more than normal, but something feels off about it. The energy feels different from the elements around us, from the magic I feel in my own body trying to fight to get out. I want to jerk my hands free.

As the full moon slowly shifts into place directly above our heads, the wind begins blowing, the bottom of my dress flowing in the breeze. It's swirling around us, the rest of the sanctuary untouched. The moon's light is shining brighter than I've ever seen, and my whole body feels like it's beginning to vibrate.

I close my eyes and breathe in the wind. I have faith in what's to come. I trust Gaia.

I will be a strong, fearless queen. We will bring peace to the Fae.

My magic seems to settle in my fingertips, and I let out a small sigh.

I inhale deeply as Cillian's familiar scent swirls around me, caught up in the wind. Before I can relax into it, my magic surges up my arms towards my chest.

Caspien is curiously taking me in, unaffected by the energy that our Goddess is surrounding us with. The divine bond clicking into place is supposed to be the first step. I fill my lungs again and am engulfed by the scent of fresh spring water. I can instantly feel exactly where Cillian is. An invisible force is urging me towards him.

My knees go weak as the divine bond wash over every cell in my body. My magic is thrilled. My eyes fill with joyful tears as I look away from Caspien to Cillian.

Caspien follows my gaze to his twin. Heat courses through my body with each pump of my heart. Turning back to face Caspien, I brace for his anger—or shock. Instead, his mouth curls into the slightest smirk when he meets his brother's gaze.

It's all the confirmation I need. Caspien knew.

I smile straight at my divine mate—Cillian.

CHAPTER
TWENTY-EIGHT
NISSA

P anic fills my chest when I try to pull my hands back and Caspien tightens his grip.

Does he think Gaia's big plan is to curse me to a life separated from my mate? I refuse to believe that.

But none of that changes that I'm still here, becoming Caspien's queen. *I need to be right about the next part too.*

Kiel steps up to us and begins reading from a parchment. I can barely understand his words. It's as if they were in a different language with how fast my thoughts are racing.

Something has my feet rooted to this spot on the altar, while my magic—stronger than ever—is fighting to go to Cillian. The trust I put in Gaia surges as his scent surrounds me. I can sense he's fighting not to rush for me. Our bounded hearts are yearning for one another, an invisible string pulling us together. *But he is trusting me.*

My hand is crushed in Caspien's grip. King Kiel's voice is a drone as he reads from the ancient scroll. His eyes dart around the altar as his voice slows. I glance at Caspien, and the blood drains from my face. His eyes are full of rage and resentment as they turn from his father to his brother to me.

Pain explodes across my face. The back of his hand connects with my cheek, the force of the unexpected blow throwing my body sideways. I crumple to the ground, unsure whether it's from pain or shock.

"This is your fault!" Caspien roars as sparks explode at the back of my eyes.

In an instant Cillian is kneeling in front of me. He cups my cheek, his gentle hand a soothing balm against my burning skin. My mate's touch is an immediate antidote to any pain. I look into his eyes. Eyes that are dark with a mix of protectiveness and fury.

I have always felt at peace around Cillian, but this feeling is sacred, aligned in the stars. I close my fingers around his. I can feel the energy from the earth beginning to shift. Cillian runs his other hand over me, assessing me for injuries, so focused on me that he doesn't seem to notice the vibration building underneath us.

The raised voices behind us go quiet. Caspien and King Kiel break off their heated argument mid-sentence. They both look down at the rock altar below our feet.

Caspien's face turns a mottled red as he glares at his father. "Don't stop! I'm the king! Crown me!"

They feel it too.

Cillian finally registers the undeniably shaking around us. My heart freezes in my chest as Caspien lunges for us. The earth cracks open in a violent quake. Caspien lurches backwards while my mate wraps his arms around me.

On unsteady legs, we stand together through the tremors wracking the world around us. The king scrambles for the ancient text and crown that have fallen to the altar, just as a thunderstorm begins to spin above us.

I press closer into Cillian's hold. *Gaia is not fighting to keep us apart*, I assure myself.

But I bury my face in Cillian's chest, braced for being pulled back to Caspien. Kiel has retrieved the text and is hurriedly speaking the address.

"Our blessed Mother of Nature..." he shouts into the raging storm as the first crack of thunder echoes through the ancient grounds.

I have to be right. She can't be sending another storm...

I fight not to flinch at the loud rumble and peek out to see vines emerging from the cracks in the stones around us. They form a protective circle a branch out from Cillian and me. A vine breaks from the circle and makes its way up the skirt of my dress. It snakes around my waist, binding us together. Fat droplets of rain wet our skin, and lightning illuminates the altar with a second clap of thunder.

Kiel stops abruptly. As he looks up at us, his voice is deliberate and slow, like he's speaking to a youngling. "Cillian, you need to stop."

I look up at the male wrapped around me, protecting me.

"No. You need to stop," he growls back at his father, the vines tightening as he pulls me even closer. Their strength, undeniable.

"No one is taking her," Isolde's even voice states from behind us. "Look around." We both twist to see her outside the circle, holding her hands out, palms up. "The Goddess has made her choice known."

I still don't understand why Gaia has sent this storm, but Isolde seems to agree that it's not to separate us ...

Kiel is taking slow, deliberate steps towards us. As he attempts to step over the vines into the circle, they whip out and bind his ankle. Frozen mid-step, he says, voice measured,

"Princess, I need to be able to reach the prince. The ceremony cannot be complete without the crowns."

Cillian has started rubbing circles on my exposed back with his thumb. A feeling that I have come to love. The storm has gone quiet, and the rain has stopped. But the clouds still swirl in a circle directly above our heads, like they are desperate to begin again.

My eyes widen as realization hits me. *Water and earth.* Our elements — Cillian's and mine — are protecting us. Our powers are keeping us together. *We* are keeping us together. This isn't the Goddess trying to tear us apart—this is us using our full abilities to connect us.

I look into Cillian's perfect ocean-blue eyes for confirmation. He agrees that it's safe. He glances back towards his father and then nods firmly.

It takes me a moment, but I'm slowly able to unwind the vines from his feet, the magic much stronger than I have ever experienced. Kiel steps into the circle and places the jewel-studded crown on my mate's head. Where we realized last night that it always belonged. The colorless stones now radiate a brilliant blue that matches Cillian's eyes.

The King of Castara. My mate.

When Isolde looks to me for permission to enter the circle of vines, I nod. She gingerly steps over the tendrils with a tiara in hand. She places it on my head, and I can feel the magic rush through me with the weight of the metal. I'm confident that the jewels that adorn each peak of the crown now shine with the same amethyst of my eyes.

For a heartbeat, I think of my twin and her eyes. Her crown that will never find its rightful place now that she is gone. *I miss you, Nova.*

As the now former king completes the sacred rite, I release the wind I didn't realize I was holding.

But Cillian tenses, preparing for battle. "Where is he?" The question is dangerously soft. A snap of lightning flashes accompanying the lethally calm tone.

His parents exchange a look. "I don't know," his father says. "Caspien must have slipped away after he was thrown from the altar."

"I want every Guardian looking for him. And if he or anyone else ever lays a hand on my mate—my *queen*—I will hunt them down through whichever kingdom or world they try to run to." His jaw is tight.

Then with a look that makes my heart swell, he gently cups my tender cheek and leans down to kiss me. It's a light, innocent kiss. His lips barely brush mine, but each piece of my bond, body, soul and magic fall into place.

We are divinely bonded.

CHAPTER
TWENTY-NINE
NISSA

"This is an unexpected turn of events." Isolde's chuckle comes from behind me. "And your energy!" She gives a hum.

My blood turns molten at her feigned surprise. I'm not even turning to look at her or Kiel. My whole life was altered, the entire Fae world assaulted, because they kept me from my mate. They might have thought that it was Aiden, not Cillian, but the result was the same. All because of the woman standing a branch away.

Cillian stiffens when I start to twist in his arms to confront his mother. I still as a voice— a voice I have heard sporadically throughout my life— echoes through my mind.

Wait, not yet.

My head jerks back as if I've been struck again. Confused, I look up at Cillian and he squeezes me. *Not yet, Lila. Trust me.*

All I can do is stand there, staring at my mate. *My mate,* who apparently can speak into my mind. And has been doing so for years!

Unaware of the internal turmoil happening in front of his

eyes, Kiel claps his hands together. "Well... time to announce the new king and queen to the Fae."

Cillian's hands move to the tops of my arms. He slowly slides them down, taking one of my hands. His eyes search mine, questioning.

I'm unsure how I'm supposed to respond. Even if I knew what to say. How do I talk in his mind? All I can do is mentally scream, *'Why? Why are we letting them have a say in anything? Tell them we know what they did!'*

I don't *feel* my thoughts reach him, but he gives me a small shake of his head.

"We'll be introduced later," he says to his parents. A dismissal. Then he tugs me towards the stairs of the sanctuary.

We aren't even down the aged stairs before he mistwalks us away.

Moments later, we materialize in a bedroom, and I'm hit by a blast of humid air. A liquid chandelier hangs from the ceiling, aglow with sparkling water drops. The bed is suspended over a creek that winds through the space to the window. Underneath, the water disappears to join the waterfall that plummets down the side of the castle. It was always my favorite feature of Cillian's room when I was a youngling.

His room is exactly as I remember. At the same time it feels completely different. The light, pastel blues have been exchanged for deeper, richer blues. The collection of sea glass and coral has been replaced with stacks of documents and tomes.

My attention pulls back to him when he releases my hand and turns to me.

"Why wouldn't you let me—" The words die on my tongue. The feral look in his eyes has my mouth clamping shut. My heart hammers in my chest as he cups the side of my face with a gentleness that doesn't match the intensity in his eyes. I can feel the power radiating off of him.

The power of a king.

"We have a lot to talk about..." He steps further into me so we are chest to chest. All I can do is nod, at a loss for words as he studies my face, his gaze lingering on my lips. "But all that matters right now is that you *are* mine. Lila... my Lila."

Time stands still in that moment, and the wind catches in my throat. Looking down at me is the male that I've hated and resented for years. The male that I've also admired, desired, and loved for even longer—and he is also *mine.*

We *do* have a lot to talk about. We have so much to work out. It feels like the whole world is bearing down on us and depending on us. But for just a moment, we both realize that we need this. That this moment is allowed, and not only allowed but is blessed by the Goddess herself. That because we trusted Gaia and each other, we're standing here together, not on the run but as one.

And together we'll do everything we can to fix the damage that's been done to our world.

In the next breath, his arms are wrapped around me, lifting me against him as our lips collide. I reach up, one hand at the nape of his neck and the other in his hair, pulling him harder into me. We're frenzied, our chests rising and falling in unison as our magic ignites within us, urging us on.

Magic that feels more intense than I could have ever imagined. Stronger than I've ever experienced. My back bows as he kisses my neck, bringing me back to the floor.

He drops to his knees in front of me and looks up through dark lashes. His jaw flexes as his hands stroke my sides, finding a stopping spot at the sides of my breasts. "My queen," he purrs, kissing my stomach.

Even through the fabric of my dress, his mouth sends a

bewitching shiver through my entire being, the feeling settling at my core. He grazes his nose up and down me, adding to the intensity, and my stomach contracts. I am about to come apart from his touch and our magic alone.

A gasp escapes me when I feel the cool touch of water on my back. A stream of water has lifted out of the creek. Like delicate fingers, it strokes up my spine and slips the laced vines off my shoulders. Wide-eyed, I catch the fabric at my breasts just as it begins to fall. With a devilish smile, he slowly takes it from my clutches, lowering it equally slowly.

His eyes glow brighter as he watches my body be exposed to him. "I just wanted to put these new powers to good use."

A shy smile breaks across my face—

A knock echoes through the room, and I instinctively raise my arms to cover myself. Cillian stops the fall of my dress, holding it against my hips.

"What?" he barks out. *Impatient.* His eyes still on me, he licks his lips.

I can feel the look down to my toes.

"Your Majesties, we need you," a muffled voice responds from the other side of the door.

He stands, his throat bobbing as if it's physically painful to help me pull my dress back into place over my shoulders. He gives me one more kiss, his shoulder muscles flexing beneath my palms. Then he eases the door open just enough for him to see who's outside.

I peek around his bicep to find a smirking Halcya in the hallway. Jealousy flashes through me in a violent rush. I know it's from the mating bond, but that doesn't dampen my instinct to scratch out her eyes.

Her smirk falters momentarily when neither of us says anything. "King and Queen Vaylor," she says, her smile return-ing. "I was asked to come find the two of you and bring you to the celebration. I hope I'm not—" her tone is tinged with amusement—"interrupting anything."

The mocking tone in her voice makes me sneer. She is acting like a friend, not the manipulator that she is. The priestess that came in to destroy lives and prevent prophecies from coming to fruition.

Does she even have the gift of communicating with the Goddess? I can't imagine Gaia would want to communicate with a High Priestess who is conspiring to stop what she wants.

"Halcya"—Cillian's voice has turned to ice—"we will be there momentarily." He begins to forcefully close the door.

"Wait," she says.

He slowly releases the wind in his chest, and pulls the door back open.

"The Heart Stone." She holds out a wooden box .

He takes the box and shuts the door in her face.

Cillian hands me the smooth box, beautifully carved and engraved with an *N*. I run my finger over the initial before slowly folding the top back, exposing the symbol of my birthright. An emerald stone shines brightly in a golden setting. I watch as the flower encased in the elemental jewel constantly shifts, cycling through an array of blossoms.

Cillian lifts the heart stone free. He walks to my back, pulls my hair to one side, and gently slips the pendant on my neck. "We can't tell them we know yet," he whispers into my ear as the energy of the gem settles between my breasts.

I lean into him as he nuzzles my neck. "And why is that?"

He pulls back, hearing the need for answers in my voice. He leads me to the driftwood chairs in the corner, and we face one another. "I know, it will be hard. I almost called my mother out then and there, but we can't. We have to figure out who knows what. My father is probably in on all of it, but I can't be sure yet. Aiden—if he knew, it could explain why he would want Nova dead. If they find out that we know, anyone that was part of it will try to hide their part. Do whatever they can to make us believe they weren't part of it."

He's right. I know he is, but I still don't like it. I would throw both Kiel and Isolde into the castle's prison without hesitation if it were up to me. But Aiden... I still need to know if he was the one who killed my sister. If he didn't, someone else did. It could all still be connected to the lunacy around the prophecy.

And our mate bond!

I smack my hand into the center of his chest. "And when did you plan on telling me that you could speak into my mind?" I almost screech the accusation.

The corner of his lip twitches.

The amusement makes me even angrier. "Seriously, Cillian! Didn't you think that could mean we were mates? Didn't you think that was important information?" I feel hysterical from so much information to take in, so many new emotions swirling through me with the mate bond. Plus, coming into my magic. It's too much.

He cups both sides of my face and kisses my forehead gently. Leaning back just enough to look into my eyes, he pops a shoulder up. "I never knew if you heard me," he says mildly. "How could it be possible anyway? No king and queen have ever felt the mate bond until the coronation ceremony."

"Why us? Why are we different?"

"I don't know. *Yet.* But when you wanted to confront my mother at the altar, I knew I had to try to stop you. You were my mate. Maybe I *could* speak to you in your mind."

"Well, it worked."

"There were other signs. I always just chalked them up to

my desire for you. Did you ever feel the connection we had?" He swallows hard, gaze intent on my lips.

"Yes." I try to nod, my face still held in his hands. "My magic. It *reacts* to you." I swallow too as those beautiful blue eyes darken. *Screw the reception. We can save the world later.*

He gives me a seductive smile, like he heard my thoughts. And maybe he did. I still don't know how this works.

"We need to get the reception over with. But soon, I plan on acting out every fantasy I have ever had about you. It'll take a while to get through all of them." Heat fills me as he licks his lips, eyes traveling down to my mouth. "But we will definitely start tonight."

Looking up at him through my lashes, I have to clear my throat. "Fantasies. Tonight," I manage in a rough grumble.

"Yes, Lila, fantasies." He tilts my head and leans down, running his tongue along my lower lip.

My lips open, and he eagerly accepts the invitation, slipping his tongue inside. He kisses me in a way that leaves my body reeling, waiting on the promise he's just made.

The coronation celebration can't be over soon enough.

THIRTY

NISSA

As the servants pull the doors wide open, nerves fill my belly. I never thought I would make it to this point. I imagined myself alone, on the run. Instead, I'm standing in front of the same large oak doors as I was the day after Nova's death. And while I feel like my life has just been turned upside down again, at least this time it's in the best possible way. With Cillian by my side. With hope for Castara.

The music from the room surrounds us as the servants get the large doors open, and the same Fae attendant presents us for the first time as the new king and queen. Silence ripples across the room as all eyes turn on us. No one skipped a beat when I was announced as their princess, but it seems that the wisps haven't had time to spread the news that Cillian is king.

Confusion fills the faces of the Elite as Cillian takes my hand, leading us into the ballroom. The former king and queen are a step behind us. The sea of Fae part, allowing us access to the raised platform. Perplexed whispers surround us as we take the stage, but all I feel is the confidence radiating off of the male at my side.

Dropping my hand, Cillian faces the Elite and gives them a smile that I know well. One that makes the sunflowers turn in its direction, makes you feel capable and calm just by seeing it across a room. As a youngling, I would watch him at events, just hoping he would find me in the crowd and give me one of those smiles. Once we lost touch, I missed it every day.

I step into him, unconsciously staking a claim in front of all of the females that look up at *my* mate.

The fire-and-earth decorations no longer fit, but that won't bother Cillian. He couldn't care less about something so trivial. He cares about the Fae that are looking up at us now.

He clears his throat and addresses the room, the wisps amplifying his voice and spreading his words to all of Castara. "Thank you all for coming to celebrate with my family tonight." He gently places a hand over mine wrapped around his bicep. "We're unsure if there was a misinterpretation of the texts at our birth or if the death of Princess Nova changed things, but as you can see Caspien is not the one standing before you.

"During the ceremony, Gaia made it known that I was to be the next king. My queen and I have come to learn that it is best to trust the Goddess. And now we ask you to do the same." He glances over his shoulder at me.

Thank the Goddess we didn't run.

Looking back at the crowd, he says, "You may be unsure of me, but know that since my birth, while you have expected my brother to be crowned as the next king, I was trained right next to him. I also have been researching the storms that have been destroying our power. Queen Nissa and I are already developing a plan. We will do everything in our power to bring Castara back to its original strength and splendor."

The murmurs start then. His parents, who are standing to the side of the dais, rarely ever mention the storms or the fact that the synthetic power sources are not sufficient. Some Fae have their eyebrows turned down, muttering under their breath, while others faces are lit up, speaking animatedly about Cillian's announcement.

It's clear he was born for this. And they may not realize it yet, but he's already bringing the Fae to his side.

For the first time, I'm excited at the idea of being queen and the power it will give me to help the Fae. At Cillian's side I know my position will be so much more than the picture Isolde laid out for me as queen. There are still unanswered questions about Nova. But there is also hope—for my future with my mate and about repairing the elemental lands now that the storms should stop.

I decline when Cillian asks if I'd like to add anything, and we make our way towards the crowd of curious faces. This part makes me feel like a bug-infested tree, but having him beside me makes it a little easier.

As soon as we hit the floor, we're surrounded. I plaster on a smile but stay as close to Cillian's side as possible. After a few minutes, I hear a squeal, and I'm all but tackled by a tiny redhead.

Cillian startles but doesn't react when he sees the smile bloom across my face. Ophe's arms are wrapped tightly around me. Her head tucked under my chin, we turn towards him.

"Cillian, this is my best friend, Ophe."

His eyes are bright as he grips both of his forearms and nods at her.

"Oh, we've already met." Ophe laughs.

I pull back, narrowing my eyes to look between the two of them. Ophe gives me a little squeeze before letting me go.

"You've met? When?" I ask her as Cillian turns his focus to a male asking about his plans on reviving the natural energy sources.

"Well, being queen suits you." She looks me up and down, smiling broadly, ignoring my question. "I'm glad you stayed," she adds in my ear.

More Fae press forward.

"How are you even here right now?" Annoyance is written on the faces of the Elite at me choosing to speak with a human over them. Good thing I don't care.

"Your *mate* came and got me," she says with a conspiratorial smile at the confusion written all over my face. "Yeah, he showed up at the Homestead and told me you would want me here since the reception included your family." I glance over at my mate, the love in my heart growing even more at the gesture. "You should have seen how red my father's face was when Cillian told him I would be *moving* into the castle." My jaw falls open, leaving me lost for words.

She giggles as another Elite dramatically clears his throat behind us.

I glance between my best friend and grinning mate before I turn back to see a glaring male. Like the constant support she's always been for me, Ophe tucks herself at my back as I do my duty and greet Fae after Fae.

When I feel like I can't possibly greet one more, there's a shift in the room. The loud buzz of voices lowers, and gazes begin to seek out whatever, or whoever, has caused the change. I see the tops of two male heads moving towards us, the crowd separating to let them pass. When they are finally in front of us, I understand why.

Mouths hang open. Some are stepping swiftly back, putting distance between themselves and the new arrivals—Aiden and Enzo, his second-in-command.

The vampire has an amused grin as he flashes his fangs at those scurrying away from them. Aiden's expression is bland, but there's an alertness in his eyes that says he's assessing every miniscule thing in the room.

"Aiden. Enzo," Cillian greets them coolly. "How nice of you to join us in this celebration."

In my peripheral vision, I see Ophe step forward. While the Elite are moving away in fear, my breakable human friend is moving straight towards the danger.

The same danger that could be responsible for the death of my sister.

"So where is Caspien?" Aiden eyes the crowns adorning our heads with indifference. He looks me up and down, his eyes lingering on our joined hands.

He's either very good at hiding his emotion, or he didn't have a master plan to kill my sister and claim the Fae world with me by his side.

"He isn't here." Cillian's civil tone has gone icy.

I squeeze his fingers as I feel his protectiveness coursing through our connection.

There's a moment of tense silence when Ophe pipes up with, "Hello there. I'm Ophelia." She almost purrs as she grips her forearms and dips her head, her eyes narrowed in on Enzo. "Glad to not be the only non-Fae guest here anymore."

He reaches out a hand, and when she takes it, I almost jerk my friend back. As his gaze slowly slides from the tips of her fingers up her chest to her face, I swear his eyes go completely black.

Enzo arches an eyebrow at her. "Indeed, maybe we can keep each other company, little morsel." Her hand still in his, he steps forward, towering over her. But instead of shaking her hand, like most would do with a human, he flips it over revealing her wrist.

Cillian goes stiff at my side, and my heart comes to a complete stop as Enzo leans down and takes a long, slow breath. His fangs slip out from his smile and then disappear when he places a kiss to the vulnerable skin.

Aiden rolls his eyes like this is all just theatrics.

I can barely pull the wind into my chest, though I'm doing my best to not cause a scene.

"We won't be staying long enough for that," Aiden says to his second, boredom filling his voice. His silver eyes dance across my face one more time. His usual intense gaze takes me in, like he's trying to read my mind. Turning back to Enzo, he says, "In fact, we should go now. There's no need for us here."

Enzo's eyes light in surprise. His gaze moves from my best friend to me, assessing whatever Aiden sees between Cillian and me.

THIRTY-ONE

NISSA

T he sun is at full height in the sky before we're able to leave the reception. Elemental experiences flowed all night, making the Elite more and more agreeable to having a king they didn't anticipate. Or at least they don't seem to care by the celebration's end.

We collapse onto Cillian's bed in mutual relief. The new rooms with our combined elements, not Caspien's, aren't ready yet. So for the time being, we've agreed to stay here.

"Does your body feel like it could rip apart if the magic isn't let out?" I ask as I roll onto my back, creating a blossom attached to a vine, midair. Moving my fingers, I twirl the new plant, helping it grow before pulling it back.

Cillian cups a hand around mine, and a ball of water appears, surrounding the little flower. The petals immediately brighten in color, and the vine dances in the added energy that encases it.

I giggle at the tingling that courses between us, tickling my skin. "This is amazing. I didn't expect it to feel so strong."

He nods. "Honestly, I didn't either. I've studied and monitored energy levels for years, past and current, natural and synthetic. What I felt during the ceremony, exceeded anything I've come across. Even before the storms began."

We both fall silent, considering this.

Maybe the Goddess is rewarding us. Or maybe it's an omen for the energy that's to come once we renew the elemental lands. A sign for what could be in Castara.

I gently touch the water floating above us, the tips of my fingers skimming along the smooth bubble surrounding it. Cillian follows my hand, but instead of reaching for the creation we made, he runs his fingers down my arm slowly. Goosebumps break out in his wake.

Our arms fall and we interlock our fingers, the combined elements above us slowly reducing to a single petal with a water droplet that floats to the bed between us. I turn my head to face him and find his gaze already pinned on me. In an instant, the mood shifts from playful to intimate.

His intense eyes swirl with desire. My gaze drops to his lips, and I watch his throat rise and fall as he swallows. Rolling onto his side, he props himself up, over me. My head falls back when he leans down, kissing his way up my neck. The smell of fresh rain fills the room. I let out a tiny whimper as he reaches the soft area near the elongated tip of my ear.

"Lila," he groans as if he's in physical pain as he nips my earlobe.

Our hands are memorizing every leaf of each other's bodies, sending my magic into a frenzy. He moves down to my chest, his lips caressing the skin of my exposed cleavage. I moan as he trails lower, his breath a cool stream against the heat of my skin. He groans into me, his hands gripping my hips with something between reverence and hunger.

Everywhere he touches, his magic lingers—a soft, rolling

tide meeting the steady, rooted pulse of mine. Water and earth, yielding and unyielding, colliding and entwining.

"You feel like home," he whispers, his voice raw, like the rush of a waterfall over jagged rock. "You always have." His forehead rests against my stomach for a beat, his ocean eyes wild and unguarded when he looks up at me.

I clutch at his back, feeling the way his muscles shift beneath my fingertips, slick with the dampness of our mingling energies. My vines respond instinctively to my will, twisting around his waist, pulling him up my wanting body, desperate to tether him to me, to keep him close. To irreversibly bind us together in the most physical way possible.

He claims my lips again, the kiss deep and consuming. Magic surges between us, a cool wave crashing into the warmth of my own power, sending a shudder through my entire being. He reaches between us, fisting the fabric of my dress, dragging it up my legs. When the skirt snags its limit, he groans in frustration.

"Roll over," he growls against my ear, the command sending an aching pulse to my core.

When I don't respond fast enough, my body flips, as if caught in an unseen wave. A giggle escapes me before dying in my throat as his fingers skim down my spine. Twisting my head, I watch over my shoulder as his reverent eyes trail my exposed back until he reaches the spot where the dress hits the dimples in my back.

As if snapped back into the moment, he makes quick work of the buttons holding the lace together. Multiple clasps pop and roll off the bed, splashing into the stream below. This time he doesn't even give me a chance before his magic rolls me back over to face him. He peels the dress down my body, his eyes darkening like the deepest depths of the ocean as I am bared to him.

"Your turn," I whisper as he watches me, completely vulnerable to him.

He strips away his clothing, and I realize that for the first time in my life, I don't feel like a prize to be claimed or a connection to be leveraged. With Cillian, I am just *wanted*. It isn't for my birthdate or my lineage, it is just for *me*. He would have given it all up, *for me*.

I stare at the male that the Goddess has blessed me with. My mate, *my other half*. He is perfect in every way. Emotionally, intellectually, and *physically*.

My eyes trail down his sculpted abdomen, and I reach up, placing my hand on his thick thigh that straddles me while tracing a single finger down that vee with my other hand.

My gaze snaps to his as I reach the top of his impressive length. Unable to wait any longer, Cillian lowers himself over me. With nothing separating us, he slowly glides his hand down my stomach. Pressing against my core, he slips a single finger into me, his thumb finding my clit.

The sensation has me arching into him as if drawn by an unseen current. My mouth falls open, gasping for the wind as his thumb expertly circles the sensitive nerves. He draws me to the edge before pulling out, leaving only the lingering sensation of his magic behind.

A whine escapes my throat, and he chuckles.

"You're so wet," he says, his warm breath against my neck. It sends goosebumps across my skin as his hand snakes between us again.

I anticipate the feel of his fingers. Instead, the thick end of his cock runs from my opening to my clit and back again. We find each other's lips as I lift my hips, searching for the sensation again. And he obliges, sliding up and down through my desire. We both moan, the sound muffled into the other's mouth.

With the next swipe of his thick erection, he pauses at my entrance, applying the slightest pressure. An unspoken question. I answer with a scrape of my nails down his back, arching into him. His fingers dig into my hip, his other hand on the bed next to my head as he presses into me, the head of his cock stretching me, filling me as he slides in. The wind catches in my throat as I adjust to his size.

Breathe, Nissa.

His voice echoes in my mind while his lips are busy peppering kisses across my breasts. When he finds my taut nipple and sucks it into his mouth, pleasure shoots like an arrow directly to where he's pressing deeper into me.

I cry out and he freezes. My hands are frantic, pulling at him to continue. "Don't stop!" I beg at the same time that I scream it in my head.

A male smile curves his mouth. Eyes hooded, he reaches a hand to my other nipple. He applies the precise amount of pressure I need—*yes!*—before pulling his hips back a fraction and then filling me completely.

This time he doesn't stop. He pulls back and thrusts deep into me, hitting that sensitive spot deep inside. I cry out in a mix of pain and pleasure. With the next stroke, we find a rhythm, unfathomable euphoria swamping any pain.

We continue this dance, and he does exactly what we couldn't do in my study that day. He explores my body until he finds every place to touch, suck, and caress that makes me moan. When I don't know if my body can take any more, the room pulses with our connection, the walls vibrating with the force of what we are, what we've become.

～

WITH MY HEAD on Cillian's chest, I listen to the flow of his heart. I run my fingers across the ridges in his stomach.

"I need to ask you something..." I trail off still trying to catch the wind in my chest but the need for answers is too strong to wait.

He hums, urging me on.

"Why did you push me away when we were younger? After everything, I thought we -," The words trail off. Even with the bond in place the pain of him cutting me out of his life echoes through me. I have to know what happened.

He squeezes me closer to him. "I came to visit you a few months after the gala." A line forms between my brows at his words. "I wanted to see where you lived, meet Ophe and the family that was raising you."

"I never saw you."

"No, I found the two of you in your herb garden. Ophe was begging you to go somewhere with her. I don't remember where, but you refused. You said you wanted to stay and wait for me to wisp you. The two of you had a huge fight and she accused you of wasting your life waiting on *me*."

I remember the fight. I was so hurt by her words and after she left my powers felt abnormally stronger, out of control.

"You don't get to decide what's worth waiting for. I would have chosen you." My words are choked and I can feel him nod against the top of my head.

"I know. And I should have talked to you about it. I was just scared of being the thing that held you back. I loved you too much to let you sacrifice your life just to live for the two days a year when you visited." His words are resigned.

The sadness, the abandonment, that has lived in my heart for so long, falters as his confession sinks into me like rain over parched soil. He didn't just say he loves me. He said he loved me then, too. The words I have thirsted for — words that begin to heal what I thought would always remain broken.

I lift up on my arm to look into his eyes. "I love you too. I've loved you for as long as I can remember." Leaning in, I whisper, "Even when I hated you," before pressing a quick kiss to his lips and then falling back to his chest.

He chuckles softly, kissing the top of my head. "I will always love you, Lila."

"Why do you call me that?" I muse.

I feel his chest shake with his chuckle. "The day before that gala, an instructor was brought in to teaching us about the linguistics of all the different worlds. I found it fascinating—"

I smile at how different we are. *Thank the Goddess I got to skip that lesson.*

"—Caspien was struggling with it. While our instructor reviewed it with him, I dug deeper into the books he'd brought from the library. One of them was an account of all the different flowers in the human world and the meaning of their names. One of them was called a *lila*, it is derived from the word 'liat'."

"And what does it mean?" I ask quietly, each beat of my quickening heart healing the wounds of my past.

"*Mine.*"

THIRTY-TWO

NISSA

O ur feet crunch along dried mud and debris that litters the ground as we take in the destruction wrought on Aquaria. Years of scant rain has left most of the rivers and lakes dry and cracked. The few remaining waterways are muddy and brackish like the one Cillian and I visited.

We have approached a barren channel, filled with large chunks of earth and the broken remains of trees from past earthquakes that shook these elemental lands. I can sense the faint heart beat of the few remaining plants that have prevailed through the devastation and my magic aches for it.

Following Cillian's orders, the Guardians are already moving into action, using a mix of magic and pure strength to clear the earth away. Fae murmur around us as they take in the ravaged lands firsthand since they were restricted from visiting years ago.

A few Elite have tagged along under pretense of helping. I'm guessing they've been drawn here by the novelty. Not only can they spread the stories about the damage they see, they can also pass judgement on their new king.

Cillian's parents discouraged our efforts. *Unsurprising.* They claimed all past attempts to repair the elemental lands just resulted in additional storms.

But we hope by putting the rightful king on the throne and fulfilling my side of the prophecy that the Goddess will be appeased. We *hope* we have done enough to appease the wrath of the Goddess and stop any future storms.

Of course, we haven't revealed that to anyone yet. Least of all his parents. I understand Cillian's reservations but I look forward to the moment that we can get justice for the Fae that have suffered as a result of their decisions.

He's continued to look into where Caspien went, with no success. And we've been unsuccessful in finding anything to support what Celyste told us beyond the prophecy.

But we need to do something—even if it's not about figuring out who knows what. So, here we are, putting in the manual labor to bring back the magic of each elemental land.

An echoing *boom* pulls my attention as a massive rock finds its new home at the bottom of an empty, cracked ravine.

Five of the Guardians move to another larger boulder. Even with their magic, they have to call for assistance to help navigate the chunk of earth out of the path of where we hope water will one day flow again.

I make my way up towards them as Cillian takes up post among the effort. He calls down to the group of Elite placing small stones, one by one, in a pile on the bank.

Cheeks pale and their eyes go wide when they realize the king is calling on them to help.

I choke back a laugh at the ridiculousness of the situation. From their panicked expressions and overly adorned clothing,

I'm confident none of these Fae have ever lifted anything more than an elemental experience in their lives.

"Don't worry, I can help." I roll my eyes as the males eye one another, trying to decide if they can get away with their queen stepping in, and avoiding manual labor.

The Guardians shuffle down, allowing me a space next to Cillian. But I don't need a space. Standing to the side, I call on the magic that pulses through my body like a second heart beat—coiled and ready to be released.

A low rumble vibrates at our feet as my magic frees the boulder from its resting place. An earthy musk fills my nose as dust and debris fall back to the ground.

The eyes of the Guardians widen at the ease of my magical strength. But it only takes a moment before they snap back into action, helping guide the boulder out of the waterway.

The murmurs of the Elite around us start immediately. A proud smile washes across Cillian's face.

As the sun moves across the sky, I am shocked by the lack of magic that those accompanying us possess. Cillian mentioned that our power is more than any he's tracked in recent history, but I don't think I truly realized the extent. These are some of the strongest Guardians and their energy is but a whisper of ours.

The realization rocks me and fills me with hope in the same breeze. Hopefully we can return this type of power to all the Fae once we fix the lands.

As the sun sinks low, the sky melting from amber to violet, we finally look down into the cleared gorge. The first of many to come, I hope.

"Now we wait for the rain to come," someone says in jest, swiping dirt from his brow.

I grin at the grime covering all of us, specifically the few

Elite who decided that being shown up by their queen didn't sit right with them.

A few gasps draw everyone's attention further up the ravine. All of our jaws fall open as a heavy stream of water begins washing down from upstream. We watch in stunned silence as the water reaches the dormant waterfall and splashes into fresh water waiting below.

"How?" a gruff-voiced Elite male asks in utter shock.

"Gaia is filling the pool from below," Cillian responds, his eyes fixed on the now free-flowing waterfall.

Laughter and cheers erupt around us as we take in the miracle.

Looking up into my mate's shining eyes, I smile at the immense sense of relief that is radiating from him. "You know what this means."

He nods, a smile pulling at his mouth.

"Our strength will return!" exclaims a Water Fae at his other shoulder.

Others chime in, some plummeting into the water in celebration, sharing excitement and making plans to clear the other lands. Eager to begin the process of restoring the power the Fae receive from the elemental lands.

Cillian and I share a knowing look. Their excitement is warranted, but they have no idea of the true meaning of the flowing waters.

Gaia is on our side. The storms will be stopping.

We already know that we are the rightful King and Queen of Solevara, but this feels like confirmation that Gaia's wrath for all these years has been a result of me being sent away. An attempt to thwart Her prophecy.

Of all the deception.

Something we still need to deal with.

CHAPTER

THIRTY-THREE

NISSA

"How is the restoration going in the elemental lands?" Ophe asked, lounging on the bed of her new room in the castle like she's a queen herself.

I've been helping her unpack all morning and am still shocked by how much stuff she has. When I arrived boxes were all over the room, tops ripped open, overflowing with clothing like she dug through them looking for something.

Thankfully we have made some progress. The room now resembling and bedroom instead of storage. It started as a plain room, with a basic human bed and furniture of a human home. No doubt brought to this room from the servants quarters.

There was not a single sign of an element or any life at all. But it is finally starting to look like my best friend's room with her stuff added in. I smile at the small garden of potted plants that she has placed on top of the dresser. She brought them from the homestead. I used to sneak them into her room, believing they'd keep her grounded — that their quiet roots might protect her when I couldn't.

"It's going well." Cillian and I have been going out every day for the last week, leading the Fae in clearing away anything that could inhibit the elements within each land. "We still have a long way to go, but we're seeing some incremental amounts of power returning. It's been miraculous to see the elements revival."

"And how is mated life," she asks with a mischievous grin.

I just laugh at her, continuing to put more of her clothing away. *Seriously, how many clothes does the girl need?*

"You never did tell me how you figured out that Cillian was supposed to be King."

I put down the dress I'm folding and twist to face her, cross legged on the floor.

"Everyone was so consumed with the prophecy revolving around Nova and me. They weren't considering the princes. It didn't make sense that there were three of them, and if you read the prophecy it says *'joined by flame, embraced by sea; Four-bound fates shall come to be'.*"

She takes in my words, nodding, "Right, so Caspien is flame and Cillian is sea."

I smile at her. "That is what I was thinking too. But Aiden was also born on our birthdate and he is a fire Fae. Then I remembered an account of Caspien and Cillian's births that I read in the ancient archives. It stated that Caspien entered the world *just as* the full moon crested the sky. Which could be interpreted as the start of our birthdate but if it was seconds before the moon hit peak-"

"Then he was born the day before..." She concludes with bright eyes.

"Exactly." I smile at her. "And if you consider the birth

order without Caspien, it was Nova, Aiden, Me and then Cillian. The witch told me to trust the future king. I didn't have any connection to Aiden but Cillian and I-," a whimsical smile blooms on my face. "I just knew we had to be mates. Our connection, our magic- it was just too much to be a coincidence. *He* was the future king I could trust."

My best friend smiles back at me, "And what about Nova? Do you still think it could have been Aiden?" She lifts an eyebrow at me when I hesitate.

"Okay, spill."

"There isn't anything to spill." I sit up straighter and shrug. "We haven't had much time outside of cleaning up the lands to do anything else. Today is the first day I haven't been out there. The only reason I'm not there is because I'm here helping you unpack."

"Aw, I'm honored that you would put the good of the world on hold for little ol' me." She places a hand to her chest.

"Okay, when you say it like that, I feel selfish. Want to go clean up the elemental lands together?" I bobbed my eyebrows up and down.

"Hmm, tempting as that is... no. I think we should go look for information on Nova! We can go to Varethiel, find the old witch, and hear what else she knows." She shoots me a toothy grin.

"I'm not sure that's the best idea," I answer.

"And why not? Cillian got his answer. He's restoring the energy as we speak. Let's go find your answers. And maybe a hot vampire for me while we're at it."

I huff out a laugh. "And there's the true motive." I lift a dress, returning to the mountains of clothes to unpack.

Her auburn hair falls around her shoulder as she pops it up and lets it fall back down. "You got your hot mate. The least I can get is one hot night."

"You're ridiculous." Laughing, I shake my head. "We can't. Cillian would worry. Anyway, I still don't know what Guardians we can trust. And honestly none of them wanted me speaking to the crone."

"Since when has something like that stopped you? In fact, shouldn't that make you want to find out what they're all hiding more?" I quirk an eyebrow at her. She is the one that doesn't let things like that stop her. Not me.

"Cillian—" My words are cut off.

"Will never know unless you tell him."

"Even if I agreed, the root systems still aren't strong enough. They don't go far enough for me to rootwalk us all the way to Varethiel without help. And the portal would notify the Guardians."

She pouts for a moment. I think she's going to give up until that gleam reappears in her eyes. "Didn't Prince Aiden give you some secret way to get to his kingdom?"

When I don't respond, she claps her hands together. "Great, let's go!"

"Ophe... I can't." I admonish.

"Nissa... you can. You're the *queen*. What good is that if you can't use your power to figure out who killed Nova?" Her eyes are sincere.

I hesitate. I do want to go, and she isn't wrong. But this is a bad idea.

"And..." she insists, enthusiasm growing, "don't you want to know all the information before you confront his family? All of this feels connected."

"The Vaylors didn't kill Nova. Her death caused them more problems than anyone else."

"So they want you to think!" She whispers loudly, eyes darting around the room like someone could be listening.

I shake my head at her theatrics. Manically smiling in my

direction, she lets me process, knowing that her logic is taking root in my mind. And it does make more sense the longer I think about it.

"You know you want to," she sings quietly. Nothing will discourage Ophe once her mind is set.

"Fine." I stand and straighten my shoulders. "Let's go."

CHAPTER

THIRTY-FOUR

CILLIAN

Blinking my eyes open, I reach out and find Nissa's side of the bed cold. She wasn't here after I returned from Ignaria. Or after my shower. She must still be with Ophe, catching up.

But the moon is at its height, and for some reason dread fills me. Reaching out to Nissa through our bond, my stomach churns as it remains unanswered.

I go straight to Niko's room and bang on the door. Eyes bright with alertness greet me despite the fact that I've clearly woken him up.

"Where are Nissa and Ophe?" I demand.

"In bed?" I tense when he stares at me like I'm an idiot.

"Niko..." I question the word slow and full of warning.

"What is going on?" He asks as he goes to grab clothing and his sword.

"She isn't in bed and isn't answering when I reach out with the bond." He nods slowly as he straps multiple blades to his chest and arm before pulling his shirt over them.

"Have you checked Ophe's room or the Princess' study?" He asks calmly despite strapping his sword to his back.

I'm still learning to use the magic that has flooded my veins but I reach out to every water molecule throughout the castle looking for my mate. "She isn't here, Niko." I bark when I can't feel her.

To be sure, Niko goes to Ophe's room and I check Nissa's study.

We arrive in the hallway outside my study at the same time. Niko looks at me, hopeful, but I shake my head. Nissa's study was vacant, just as I suspected.

"I'll alert a unit of Guardians to be on standby," he says.

If we need them. That part goes unsaid. But I hear the worry in his voice.

I appreciate that he's already setting things into motion, but it only adds to my growing concern. "Nissa still isn't responding when I reach out." I can hear the panic growing in my voice.

"Okay, let's find out if Ophe went anywhere tonight." He presses his fingers across the tattoo that lines his collarbone, activating the telepathic properties of the sirilis' poison used to create the Guardians mark. It shimmers like the scales of the rare fish it's harvested from as he sends his message out to his security forces.

As he awaits a response, I use all my unsettled energy to focus on connecting to the mating bond. *"Nissa, where are you?"* I pace, circling the room, sending the message again and again.

"Don't panic. I'll hear back from them soon," Niko tells me, trying to keep me calm. "I'm sure there's an innocent explanation."

I nod, but we both know that after Nova neither of us are remaining calm. I sink into the driftwood chair behind my desk. I rest my elbows on the glass and push my hands into my hair. Closing my eyes, I try my hardest to get anything from our bond. Only rippling silence. *Please let her have fallen asleep somewhere.*

The mark on Niko lights up with a response. He's silently taking in the message, glancing at me every few moments. I can see the anxiety in him building. "Ophe never left. No one has seen either of them in hours."

"It has to be him." My hands fist.

"Aiden?" Niko shakes his head, unconvinced. "From inside our own castle? Something doesn't add up. She never left."

"Yet she isn't here," I growl. There's a moment of tense silence. "You saw how obsessed he was at the council meeting. And now with the prophecy. Maybe he believes she's the key to his gaining power to rule both kingdoms."

He takes in my words, his eyebrow knitting together as he thinks it through. "The wisps announced to both kingdoms that the two of you are divinely mated. He saw you together. Maybe he felt he could use her as leverage..." He pauses. "I will look into it but we have to handle this carefully. We can't go in with gale-force accusations. We need to consider the best way to approach—"

My dark blue wisp is working to contact Aiden before Niko even finishes his sentence.

He curses. "Or not." As my wisp finds the connection, he sits down across from my desk. It's too late to talk me out of this.

"What the hell do you want at this time of the night?!" Aiden barks when the image comes into view.

In the background, a woman's sleep-filled voice asks what's going on.

"Is that Nissa?! Where the hell is she, you asshole?!" All pretense is gone.

Niko leans his head back and rubs at the mark across his

neck. I don't care about the consequences of accusing Aiden if he isn't involved. I need to know she's safe. I need to know where she is.

Aiden's eyes shoot to the side. His face goes stone cold—a clear communication to the other person in the room.

"Where is my mate?" I don't recognize the ice in my voice.

"What in the worlds are you talking about, Cillian?" Aiden's voice is low. I can hear the threat in it.

"Did you take her?" I roar back. "Tell me where the hell she is! How did you get to her?"

"I do not have Nissa, Cillian."

I hear the female voice again, but it's too quiet to make out what she's saying.

"Get Enzo," Aiden instructs whoever it is.

"And why should I believe you?" I'm trying to stop yelling. The concern in his voice seems sincere. But I'm not sure I want to start considering other possibilities if he doesn't have her.

"Tell me what you need from us," Aiden says. "I can have our guards scouring the city within minutes."

"Or we can come to you." I recognize Enzo's voice.

Is this all a ploy to distract me? Instinct is telling me that Aiden is telling the truth. I make a split-second decision to trust it. "Niko, what do you advise?"

Niko's eyes widen, but he barely skips a beat. "We don't want to cause alarm just yet." He leans over my desktop, speaking directly to Aiden. "Inform all your guards that we are searching for the queen's best friend."

"Ophe is missing as well?" Enzo asks.

Niko ignores him. "If we find her, Nissa should be with her. If we can't locate her, we'll reevaluate and notify everyone of who we're actually looking for."

"My wisp will transmit a likeness of Ophe to you," I add in.

"And where are these Guardians that were supposed to be with them tonight?" Enzo's voice is sharp.

Shockedly so. I don't think I've ever seen the vampire bothered.

Niko grinds his teeth. "The queen and her friend didn't leave the premises. Or at least didn't notify us of plans to."

"So they could still be in the castle or have just left to get away for a night?" Enzo inquires.

The implied accusation—that we're fools not to have considered it—grates on my last nerve. "In the middle of the night, without telling anyone? After her sister was killed doing the same thing?" I snap back. "Something is wrong." I growl.

Silence falls over the room.

Nissa, where are you?

THIRTY-FIVE

NISSA

The pain radiating through the back of my head pulls me awake. Groaning, I try to lift my hands to touch the source of the throbbing. My eyes fly open when I realize that my wrists and ankles are bound to a chair. My head spins as the light in the room floods my vision, and I'm sure I'm going to be sick.

I do my best to breathe through the nausea and confusion but the wind is putrid. I gag at the burnt, moldy odor that fills my nose. I close my eyes tightly, trying to remember what happened. I recall Ophe and I arriving in Varethiel and making it to the witch's empty shop...

A string of questions bloom in my mind. Where's Ophe now? Was this a trap? Did Aiden lure me away, just like he did Nova? But what's his plan? Kill me? Use me as leverage?

I don't know enough about Aiden or the politics to figure out his end game. But I don't want to stick around in Varethiel to find out. I need to find Ophe and get out of here.

I reach for my magic to snap the bindings that hold me down. When nothing answers, panic instantly takes root in my veins. I try again and again to pull vines through the moss and algae covered stones that cover the floor, but nothing grows.

My magic that is now normally a vibrant, mighty plant, is nothing but an unreachable seed below the surface. Even root-walking is unattainable in this position.

With the bindings still secure, I frantically look around to figure out where I am. Aiden obviously didn't bring me to his castle. Unless this is a long-forgotten section.

The gray stone walls are faded and covered in burn marks, paint is peeling off the door from years of aging and what looks like water damage. Parts of the ceiling are missing, exposing wooden beams that look ready to collapse on top of me at any moment.

Twisting my head, I find a mattress with a stained blanket and no sheets. My heartstone shattered on the floor next to it. Otherwise, the room is empty. I want to call out for Ophe, but Aiden, or whoever he had taken me, could be on the other side of the door.

I slump in the chair as I weigh the pros and cons of drawing attention to the fact that I've woken up. Surely, he has someone keeping watch outside the door.

Before I can make a decision, I hear Ophe's voice. "Hey, burnout! How about you tell me what the hell you want with us?"

A loud thump follows. Ophe goes quiet. Chill bumps break out across my skin, and I begin fighting harder to free myself. The shackles cut into me, not budging a leaf.

I gasp when the broken door begins to scrape across the floor but panic quickly erodes into confusion. The male's face is partially hidden with his downcast eyes, disheveled hair, and unkept beard. His clothes are dirty and torn, like he has been living on the streets. *Or somewhere like this.* There is no guard's uniform. There is no well-kept Aiden.

"Caspien?" I gape at him as he lifts his dark eyes to mine. There's no doubt it's him, but the lack of any emotion in his gaze only increases the anxiety that had been growing since I woke up here.

If the Guardians were searching for the prince, it makes sense they would have overlooked him. This male looks half out of his mind.

Caspien's eyes are wide, wildly scanning the room like someone other than the Fae he tied to a chair would be hiding here.

Is Cillian looking for me? Does he even know I'm missing yet? What were we thinking, going to Varethiel alone?

My frantic heartbeat has my body shaking, but I try to keep my voice calm. "Caspien... where are we? How long have I been here?"

His only response is a manic laugh that sends ice through my veins. Once he's closed the door and convinced himself that no one else is in this empty room, he turns his attention to me. He seems to be taking me in like I'm the intruder, not the person he just knocked out and kidnapped.

I can see how sunken in his eyes are. He's lost weight and looks so tired. Despite everything, for a moment I feel bad for him.

"Are you okay, Caspien?" I understand what it's like to be uprooted and discarded like you are worthless.

"Am I okay?" He breaks out in a laugh again. "Really?" He runs his hands through his hair and pulls it at the ends, then bends down to look me in the eye. His face is too close, his breath carrying the sour stench of ash and decay. "Hmm, let me think. I was supposed to be the king, and you and your damn sister had to go screw everything up!" Straightening, he looks around, spreads his arms. "Now I'm hiding out in this shit hole, while you and my brother are playing house in *my* fucking castle! I'll give you one guess, Nissa. How the fuck do you think I am?"

"Right, so not okay." Even as I mumble it, I know it is the wrong thing to say, but I can't seem to stop myself. Oh, how I wish I had listened to Isolde's lessons about holding my tongue.

"You stupid bitch." He is pacing the room again, and when he turns back towards me, a blade flashes in the dim light.

The wind catches in my lungs. "Caspien, please. It isn't my fault that Gaia selected us. You don't have to do this."

"Oh, this is very much *your* fault! If Nova wasn't dead, then it would be her and me ruling now! Not you and that traitor of a brother!"

"I wish Nova was alive too," I soothe, making a conscious decision to omit that he was never intended to rule. "I'm still trying to figure out what happened to her. That's why I was in Varethiel. Is that still where we are?" My voice is slow and calm, following up on what he's said, like I'm speaking to a toddler.

"Alive?!" He spits the word in my face. "Alive?! She's dead. How is it *not* your fault?! If you had shown up when I sent for you, then she wouldn't have died! You knew what would happen!"

My mind is reeling, trying to understand. The pounding from the back of my skull isn't helping. "What are you talking about?"

His manic laughter fills the room again. Maybe he's been drinking the wrong elemental's experiences. Maybe that's making him hallucinate, and he's confusing that with reality.

Back in my face, he's burning with anger. "I sent for you! You were supposed to come. Not Nova! You were supposed to die, *Nissa!*" He hisses out my name as he backs away, pulling at his hair again.

"You... *you* killed Nova?" I'm barely whispering, but he must still hear me over the horrible rattle that fills the room from something outside.

"No, you fucking idiot! I killed *you*!" His eyebrows knit together, and he is pacing the room again. "But when I went to get rid of your body, it was Nova! *I* fucking killed *you*." He says the last part like he is trying to convince himself of it, like saying it could make it true.

He sent for *me*. The castle must have sent his request to my mother's house, just like they did my gown and the letter from the queen. Nova must have received it. Nova who always preferred I stay away from Caspien. Of course she would have gone to see what he wanted. He sent for me. *To kill me.*

"But why? Why did you want to kill me?" I'm still not positive he isn't hallucinating, but I have to know if he truly killed her.

"Because Solevara *and* Varethiel are mine!" he snaps in my face. "I was supposed to be the one to rule the Two Kingdoms. *'Two crowns to rise from ancient lore,'*" He mockingly quotes the prophecy. "If you were what Aiden needed to finally separate from us, then *you* had to die." He looks at me like it's the most obvious answer. As if I should just agree that I should have died that day to put both kingdoms under Vaylorian rule.

"The prophecy." I whisper. A chill runs down my spine. He is the one that knew about it all along. He is the one that was trying to stop it from coming to fruition. Not Aiden.

He ignores me. "But now everything is ruined and Cillian is the king! With Nova gone, that conniving brother of mine is ruler of *both* kingdoms—of all of Castara. My brother, who claimed he never wanted to be king. Yet our whole lives he showed me up in lessons, in meetings and made me look bad. Acted like I was nothing but an ember for enjoying my position! But I'm the one who did all the dirty work!"

His black eyes turn back to me, full of venom. "But don't worry. With the storms starting back, he will lose Varethiel. And he's already lost *you*." A vindictive smile splits his face, and a new level of fear grows in my stomach. "My brother, who claimed that *my* betrothed was *his*. Funny how things play out. He may be king, but I have his queen." He slides his eyes up and down my body.

Oh Goddess, no. I can't hide the tremor that racks my body. His smile grows even wider at my obvious fear.

I swallow the bile rising in my throat. "Do your parents know you killed Nova?" Probably not the best question, but it will keep him talking. Give Cillian time to find me.

As soon as the words are out of my mouth I try to connect to our mental bond. Of all times for me to get a message through to him, it would be now. I don't know where we are, but I know we started in Varethiel. And Caspien couldn't have gotten two unconscious females very far.

"Caspien has me. Varethiel."

"Caspien. Varethiel."

"Caspien. Varethiel."

"Help. Please."

I don't know if he's hearing any of it. Tears fill my eyes as I continue to try and send anything through to him.

He ignores my question, continuing his ranting. "They tried to keep the truth of the prophecy hidden. Keep *you* hidden. Why do you think your family sent you away? Why no one ever trained you to be a royal? If Aiden did get his hands on you, we weren't going to be the ones who prepared you to be the perfect little queen for *them*."

His words bring my thoughts to an abrupt stop. "*My* parents were part of all of it?"

"Well, your mother was. Your father was never on board, but my mother took care of that. His *two* princesses." He rolls his eyes and scoffs. "Like it was an honor to have a daughter being the Princess of Varethiel." He spits the name of the second kingdom.

"But you know what is great about this city?" He looks through me, not waiting for me to answer. "With the witches allowed to live here, you can buy just about any type of potion or herb you can imagine. I already gave you forget-me-nots when you were out."

A wicked smile stretches across his face when he sees the horror in my eyes. "Yeah, you know what that means don't you?" He mocks.

I swallow thickly. *I do know*. Forget-me-nots are one of the few flowers that are cruel enough to strangle a Fae's element from the inside out. Once they take the root in, the magic will wither. Starve. Until the body finally purges it.

I don't have my magic...

He pulls a vial out of his pocket and dangles it in front of me with two fingers. "And then there is this potion. Why don't we do a little experiment to see what this one can do?"

I fight my restraints, trying to get any traction on the floor to push away.

He grabs me by my hair and jerks my head backwards. Gripping my jaw painfully, he forces it open. I send every ounce of strength I have to my magic. I feel only the smallest quake. I'm doing everything I can to fight his prying fingers and the liquid he's trying to pour into my mouth. But some of the liquid slips down my throat before I'm able to spit it out.

I immediately begin to feel its effects. My body is going numb, and for the briefest moment, I feel the smallest connection to Nova. I don't know if it's finally finding out what happened to her, or if it's our fates connecting us in our mirrored deaths, but she's here. I feel her fear as she realized she would die at Caspien's hand. The fear she felt knowing she would never see those she loved again. I feel her spirit with me.

And then she's gone, and I'm alone. *With him.* And my heart is uprooted from my chest and buries itself into my stomach.

As the potion takes its full hold of me, I no longer have any control of my body. I am limp in the chair, unable to even hold my head up.

"Now, when we were to be bound, I was excited about the fight in you. But tonight, I decided it would be better to have you a little more *agreeable*." I can feel him working the knife against the ties on my ankles.

"I'm confident that you'll be a good girl now. I should probably thank you for making it so easy to grab you tonight. I've been watching for an opportunity and you, showing up here with no Guardians..." He laughs.

I try my best to shake my head, but nothing happens. And my foggy mind does nothing to settle the dread as he finishes freeing each of my legs. I try to kick my legs out when he moves on to my wrists but again nothing.

I realize the only thing I can do now is focus all my energy on reaching Cillian.

"It's Caspien. Please! Help!"

Tears are streaming down my face.

"Varethiel. Please!"

This can't really be happening.

"Please hear me..."

After cutting all the restraints off of me, he lifts me from the chair and unceremoniously drops me on the stones at our feet. I squeeze my eyes shut, shutting out what is happening, trying harder to focus on summoning any magic I can reach in the stones that surround me.

I feel a sharp burn to my face as he slaps me. "Keep your

eyes open!" He roars in my face. I can smell his rancid breath. The cool metal of the blade against my neck. "You will be awake through all of this!"

Unable to respond, I do my best to keep my eyes open, trained on the cracked ceiling, barely blinking.

And all I can think is, *Goddess, help me...*

THIRTY-SIX

CILLIAN

Our feet touched down in Varethiel faster than ever before. Not long after disconnecting with Aiden, Nissa got a message through to me. It was weak and broken, but I was able to hear it. And now I can't get it out of my head.

Caspien has me. Varethiel.

Caspien. Varethiel.

Caspien. Varethiel.

Help.

Her pleas for help, knowing she is with my brother... it's a riptide tearing me in two. But what's almost worse is when those words stop coming.

I've sent a wisp to update Aiden to get every Fae, vampire, and witch on the watch, while Niko has alerted every Guardian. *I will kill my brother when I find them.*

Ever since her messages stopped, I've been doing my best to get a message back to Nissa that I'm coming. To give her any comfort I can.

Even though we have no idea where to go now that we're here.

Enzo and Aiden are at the front steps, waiting on us with a few of their Guardians. The rest are out with the Night Watch, the vampire guardians who work the dark streets of Varthiel.

Niko extends his hand to Enzo, and Aiden turns to me. "I can't promise anything, but we have a lead. It is dangerous, and risky, but we should hear back soon if it's going to give us the information we need."

"What lead? Who's the information coming from?" I demand, looking between him and Enzo .

"It's a credible source," is all Enzo says.

Nissa's voice begins rippling through my brain again.

"It's Caspien! Please. Help!"

"Varethiel, please!"

"Please hear me..."

The brokenness has me dropping down on my haunches. "NO!" I roar out as each panicked word breaks me further.

Enzo's communication device that connects him with Varethiel's vampire guards pulses and he turns away from us. I have never interacted with the Night Watch but have heard the rumors about how impressive they are. The vampires use their natural skills to guard the city through the night. I pray to the Goddess they can use those skills now to help us.

"Talk to me, Nissa! I'm Here! I'm Coming!" I'm running my hands through my hair as I try to get my message back to her.

Niko grabs my shoulders, and my focus is drawn back to his pale blue eyes, alight with determination.

"We have a location. We need to go." Enzo yells out the location just as thunder shakes the ground around us and the rain begins to pour down from the sky.

"Goddess, help me..." is the last thing I hear before we all disappear into smoke and water.

As soon as we materialize, Aiden grabs me before I can take off running into the building. Rain soaking us through, "I'll handle Caspien. You get your mate. Enzo and Niko can handle any unexpected threats and take care of the other girl. Everyone else, take the doors around the building! He does *not* get away." He yells the last part to the guardians and night watch who accompany us.

Even though I want to be the one to go after Caspien, every cell in my body is screaming out for Nissa. Every fiber of my being, craving to find her, hold her, be with her.

The cobblestones around us slowly begin to shake. We all look at one another for half a breath before we take off running.

"I'm coming."

CHAPTER
THIRTY-SEVEN
NISSA

Poisons and potions or not, I won't go down without a fight. I invoke every last flicker of magic that is left in my blood to fight. One last effort I pull from my fear in this moment, from my anger for Nova and my love for Cillian.

The foundation of the building shakes. The brittle and broken door slides off the top hinge in the tremor. It isn't strong, but it is just enough to give me hope... *until it doesn't.*

Everything stills, and one of Caspien's eyebrows lifts, humor dancing in his eyes. "Well, that was interesting." He chuckles. "Pathetic. But interesting. With how much I gave you, there's no way you should be able to access any of your magic." He studies my face, a momentary curiosity filling his eyes.

Thunder rumbles from outside the building, distracting him. He looks up at the ceiling with a villainous grin. "She didn't like when I killed Nova either."

I do everything I can to move while he is looking up but the best I can manage is getting a hand flat on the slick floor.

He must notice my efforts since he looks back at me and laughs, "Like I said, Pathetic. So, how should we do this? Should I kill your human friend first and make you watch?" He says it casually - playfully- like we are figuring out plans for the day. His eyes brighten, "We could wisp my brother! Let him listen to your screams!"

The rage that rushes through my body sends a tingle across my skin. Hope blooms in my chest that my magic is returning. I reach out to pull at the seed of power but it still lay dormant just out of reach. Buried by the effects of the forget-me-nots and whatever else he gave me.

The tingling intensifies anywhere my skin touches the stone floor, and a soft pulse begins beneath my palm. This time, I don't try to take from my element - I surrender to it. And in that surrender, I feel it respond. Not by giving, but by taking. The moss and algae that cling to the floor rise to meet me, drawing the poison from my body as if the earth itself is protecting one of its own.

Distracted, I don't even realize Caspien has stopped pacing. Pain erupts, white and searing, as fire chews through my ankle where he just grabbed me. I scream as the fire blazes through my veins. The putrid smell of burnt flesh fills the room with my cries, turning my stomach.

"Great, now that we are all listening," He says, voice simmering with sarcasm. "Like I was saying, Mother always said I am too reckless. So I guess I shouldn't risk involving a wisp."

My chest heaves erratically. The microorganisms below pulse harder, knitting my charred skin back together, leeching the toxins from my blood.

I am physically exhausted but haze filling my mind thins. Caspien is back to pacing, now ranting about Isolde's criticism of him. *I get that.* But when I roll to my back he pauses mid sentence.

"How did you-" he snarls, stomping over. I'm still weak. My heart is still pumping poison through me. But I can't pass up the opportunity he unknowingly gives me.

As soon as he is within reach I lunge. Seizing his legs and yank as hard as I can. A loud crack fills the room when his head smacks against the stone.

I roll away from him but freeze. A laugh, low and broken, crawls up his throat. *Not unconscious. Not even slowed.*

Looking over at him, a stream of blood drips from one of his ears. I didn't expect it to kill him but I had hoped it would at least knock him out for a breeze.

"That wasn't very nice." He seethes as he props himself on one elbow, blood sliding down his face, dripping into a puddle on the floor. His dead eyes locking on me.

With surprising speed he reaches out to grab me. I jerk backwards, sliding across the floor, scrambling to stand. The room tilts and spins, my vision blurring.

"Neither was killing my sister!" My voice splinters, echoing off stone. "Or kidnapping me, you lunatic!" My legs swaying like a sapling in one of Gaia's storms, roots too shallow to ground me.

He tilts his head like he is genuinely considering the accusation as he stands. "True but I never said I was a nice person, Nissa." He states, flashing me a bloody smile.

My body shakes, my muscles still half-frozen. I blink when, a subtle vibration whispers to me through the wall. Through the cracks a sprout, tiny and green, calls to me.

Caspien advances, "You're barely standing." He mocks, each step slow and deliberate. "I'm not sure what chance you think you have against me." Fear coils around me, each step like a wildfire driven towards the forest. But I remind myself that sometimes the blaze is what clears the way for new growth.

I bare my teeth at him, hoping the element of surprise will benefit me. I reach out my hand and *pull*. The tiny sprout transforms before my eyes into a vine, thick and spiked. Responding to my call, it snaps out, binding him around his waist and ankles.

The act drains me. My vision doubling. Sweat slicks my palms.

I close my eyes and focus on finding any roots to get me to the next room where I can get Ophe and rootwalk out of here. But it doesn't come. Even if I was able to find a root system to connect the two rooms, I'm too tired.

My bones ache, the tainted blood in my veins is sluggish, my muscles fighting against every movement.

Blinking my eyes open, the room blurs and slants. I rub my eyes to clear my vision.

"Very impressive," he says, drawing a blade. I glance between him and the door and my heart withers. He is too close to be able to make it out without him grabbing me.

Caspien slices through the fibrous flesh of the vine that is wrapped around his waist before leaning down. But instead of cutting his feet free, as I suspect, he slowly drags the knife over the flooring.

I flinch as the shriek of metal against stone slices through the silence in the room, flaring embers in its wake.

Calling the sparks to him, fire licks to his palm — igniting into a blinding flame.

His eyes bore into me through the flame as he burns my element away. "You, *princess*," he snarls through the firelight, "should not have access to your powers."

"Yeah?" My voice is a rasp. "Well, I'm the Queen now."

I am the Daughter of Gaia. The Goddess chose me. Not him. I may not understand why but she put me in this position but I'm not going to let some delusional, power hungry male stop me. Not like he did with Nova.

She deserves justice. Castara deserves justice.

I lunge to the side when he hurls a fireball in my direction, leaving a sear mark across the wall where I had just been. Embers rain down around us like dying stars.

Advancing towards me, his eyes flashing with murderous intent. They appear almost completely black, absent of the gleam that normally lights his eyes.

The tingling in my fingertips sync with my heartbeat. I plead to the stones. And they respond. A tremor shudders above him. Chunks of rock rain down — but he dissolves into smoke before they hit.

I curse as the sound of rock on rock rumble through the room. I jerk my head around for a moment but when I don't see him materialize, I crawl for the door. Climbing over cracked and broken rocks that are shattered across the floor from their impact.

I have to get Ophe and get us out of here.

My fingers barely brush the doorknob before an arm snakes around my throat, lifting me off my knees. Acrid smoke floods my lungs, clawing down my windpipe. I cough, choking. Desperate to expel it, but his grip seals off the air way as he drags me back.

"Uh uh uh," he whispers against my ear. The tone is soft, intimate, worst than a shout. My ribcage convulses against his hold, the smoke searing through my chest, trapped with nowhere to escape.

He flings my weakened body onto the mattress and I curl into myself in a coughing fit. Smoke and dust plume around me tainting the wind I am able to pull in.

My lungs burn, smoke still curling around me like a

serpent. He straddles me, binding my wrists. I buck, but my limbs feel weighted with lead.

I can't let him constrain me. The panic coursing through me fuels my energy. I *just* got my happy ending. There is a reason I am still here. *A divine reason.*

Searching out the edge of the mattress, I take my foot and slam it down onto the stones. Shards of rock explode from the wall, knocking him backwards. He groans, still partially on top of me as I try to push him off with my half bound hands.

As he sits up, his blood drips warm onto my skin. His eyes alight with murder. Baring his teeth, he rips a spike from his stomach.

I scramble backwards towards the wall but he wraps his burning hands around my ankle, yanking me back down onto the mattress.

"Caspien stop," I yell, my kick doing little more than taking his wind away.

His chuckle is a broken, simmering sound. He leans close, his words hot against my ear. "No," is all he says before he plunges the blade into my stomach.

Pain floods everything but I won't let it take me down. *Not yet.* The taste of iron, *and something else,* spreads thick across my tongue. "What... was on... that blade?" I sputter the words, blood spilling out of me.

In the next breath, my body is no longer mine to command. The taste of soil replaces the iron tang of blood and a floral scent fills my nostrils, offering me a momentarily reprieve from the pain that had taken over.

Suddenly my back arches off the mattress, as my magic erupts within me. A power I've never felt before taking root inside me, branching out through my blood. Exploding outward, unbidden.

A deep groan reverberates from the earth beneath. The

sound is low and primal, like the world itself is awakening from a deep sleep. The edges of my vision blur to black but through the haze I still see the room being torn apart.

Stones scream as roots spear through them, splitting the walls in jagged fractures. Vines burst through the cracks in a frenzy, writhing, coiling and spreading like veins across the walls. Dust and shards rain down, the stone beneath us shivering as though it is afraid.

Caspien staggers backwards, slipping to his knees. His head jerks up, eyes wide. Not from the pain but something sharper. *Fear*. His breath catches as the ground beneath him heaves and splits, threatening to swallow him whole.

And in that moment, before the black edges finally move in, he looks at me. Not as prey. Not as broken.

But as the Daughter of Gaia.

THIRTY-EIGHT

CILLIAN

Enzo leaves with Ophe. Niko and I follow shortly after with Nissa. Entering the castle with her tucked tightly in my arms, I'm escorted to the herbalists' wing of the castle. Ophe is alert now, and they're tending to a cut on the side of her head. Caspien must have hit her pretty hard.

Nissa is still bleeding from her stomach but the burn on her ankle has healed. She was awake when we found her but barely. The floor of the room she was being held in had collapsed, leaving only her and the mattress she was on supported.

As soon as she saw me, she gave into the darkness and hasn't woken since. I gently lay her limp body down on the empty cot next to Ophe's. Her friend immediately jumps down moving to Nissa's side, pulling the hair out of her face.

"Ophelia" Enzo snaps at her.

She shoots a look back at him that has the vampire pressing his lips tightly together. "How about you find her a blanket, *vampire?*"

If the human had magic, I believe she could have incinerated Enzo on the spot.

Stroking Nissa's face and taking in all the blood, Ophe looks up at me with her eyes full of guilt. "I'm so sorry. This is my fault—"

Before I'm able to respond, the door opens and Hazel walks into the room. Going to Nissa's bed, she lays some clothes at her feet. "I heard she may need some clean clothes. These are her sizes." She says as she checks my mate over.

Niko steps forward and hands Hazel the vial he found on the mattress next to Nissa. "I think she was given this. She isn't waking up and the wound on her stomach doesn't appear to be healing. Any idea what it is?"

As Niko briefs Hazel, I stand there, gasping Nissa's cold hand, feeling like I'm about to come out of my own skin.

When we first went into that room, I thought she was dead. I had never felt fear like I did in that moment. A shiver runs through my body at the memory of all the blood that surrounded her. The image of her head rolling to the side and her body going limp, crashes over me and sends my mind to worst case scenarios.

What if she doesn't wake up?

Hazel takes the vial in her hand. Removing the top, she smells it, runs a finger along the rim and rubs it between two fingers. While she examines it, Enzo approaches with a blanket and some gauze. He covers my mate's legs leaving the injury exposed for Hazel to examine.

"You are still bleeding." He turns to Ophe with the cotton pads, his voice low and threatening, intended only for her. "You won't do her any good if you're dead." He places a hand on her upper arm to pull her back to her bed.

Jerking out of his grasp, Ophe bites back, "It takes a lot

more than a hit to the head to kill me." She shoves him in the chest, and pushes him out of the way.

My eyebrows rise.

Enzo steps to the side with a slight glint in his eye as she actually does as she was told. Her eyes never leave Nissa even when she moves back to her cot for the herbalist to continue the exam. The vampire steps forward to apply pressure to the cut on her head.

The door opens again, and Aiden steps in, wearing a blood-soaked shirt. It isn't a small room, but it is quickly becoming crowded with all of us.

"How are they?" He appears calm, but beneath it, his normal unconcerned demeanor seems rattled as he appraises Nissa.

"I think she was given a potion that immobilizes the physical body,' Hazel says to the room, without looking up at anyone in particular. "Her mind would stay lucid but not be able to move—or fight."

A chill runs down my spine.

"I suspect he gave her more than this though," she adds, "if her powers were restricted."

"Why do you think her powers were restricted? She was fighting back." Ophe questions.

"With the level of power the queen possesses, there's no way he could have held her without binding her magic."

It matches my knowledge of Nissa's powers. "My guess," the witch continues, "he didn't anticipate how strong she was and didn't give her enough. *Of either.*"

"Is that why she isn't waking up then?" My voice shakes. There's no hiding my fear, and I don't care.

"My concern is her stab wound. The knife was probably coated in something and that could also explain why she isn't waking"—she is leaning over inspecting the opening in Nissa's abdomen. "I've seen this once before." A look passes between her and Aiden before she turns to the herbalist, instructing them to gather a list of materials for her.

Straightening, she faces me. "Or maybe her body is protecting her and has shut down temporarily. Without knowing what else he drugged her with, I can't know for sure. I'll run some additional tests. Either way, I would guess she'll be okay in a day or two once I take care of this." She says looking down at Nissa's stomach.

Some of the anxiety dissipates and I turn to Aiden. "Caspien?" I grit out.

He goes rigid at hearing the name. His cold eyes turn to me. "We will track him."

By the time we reached the room, the earth element had torn it apart. Stone lay in jagged shards, roots jutting through the wreckage, vines strangling the walls in a frenzy of green. Half the floor was missing *and so was my brother.*

THE NEXT MORNING, Hazel confirms that Nissa and Ophe are stable enough to travel even though she still has not woken. We return to Solevara with a hand written list of instructions for the royal herbalist to follow. Aiden asked me to send updates on how they are recovering.

For two days, there is nothing to send and I am going out of my mind. Like the eye of the storm I am motionless, never leaving Nissa's side. But within, I am chaos tearing myself apart.

I cling to the confidence that the witch gave me. *She will walk up. Just give her time.*

I hear a rustling fabric and lift my head from my hands. Ophe has kicked the sheets off again. She too hasn't left Nissa's side since we returned, but the girl is not peaceful when she sleeps.

I stand, pulling the sheets up over her body, tucking them between Nissa and a sleeping Cyndr who is curled into her side.

Settling back into my spot next to the bed, I look up and find her amethyst eyes blinking awake.

CHAPTER
THIRTY-NINE
NISSA

"They all knew," I croak out before Cillian can say a word.

Relief floods his face. My movements are slow, but I can actually move. And that's enough for me. I've been trapped in my own mind for days, and the moment the words are out of my mouth, I can feel my own relief at no longer being alone with what I learned.

Shifting the warm little dryrd to the side, I begin to throw my legs out of the bed. Cyndr looks up at me and sleepily nozzles his head into my hand happily.

Cillian's expression quickly morphs. "Stop. Lay down," he says, standing when I don't and offering hands out.

Ophe groans a little at the noise. I try to clear my throat as I reach for him. He responds immediately, grasping both of my elbows.

"I can't lay down," I manage as I try to stand, breathing heavy from even this small amount of movement after days of inactivity.

"Nissa, please." His eyes are imploring.

I drop back on the edge of the bed to catch the wind.

"What's going on?" Ophe's groggy voice fills the space as she stretches behind me.

I give a small smile at my friend, while Cillian exhales and drops back into the chair he's barely left since we arrived back home.

He takes both of my hands in his, and he drops his forehead to my wrists. "You're okay." His voice is quiet and broken.

"I am. I promise but Cillian— they all knew," I say again. I pull a hand free to stroke his head.

"Who knew what?" Ophe asks with indignation, ready to fight, as soon as she realizes I'm awake.

I laugh, then sober when I look back to my mate. I know he's been beside himself that I wasn't waking up, but I've also been trapped in my own torture. Unable to expose those that turned all of our lives upside down. Some who have stood in this very room, acting as if they care when their actions led to all of this. Their actions led to so many devastating repercussions, for my family, for Nova, for Cillian, for Castara as a whole. For me.

He says nothing for a moment longer, letting my nails run back and forth over his scalp, before raising his gaze to meet mine. "You need to rest," he says with determination in his eyes. He strokes my hand with his thumb.

"But—" I begin to protest.

He holds one of his hands. "Tell me what you know. Let me handle it while you recover."

Intensity boils in those beautiful eyes, and I know he would drown the worlds to make whatever I am talking about right. To protect me.

"The prophecy... they all knew. Your parents, my parents. They all knew."

I hear a small voice behind me. "Oh Nissa." Ophe's warm arms wrap around my shoulders.

Cillian stands and begins to pace, I link my fingers through one of her hands. Cyndr slips into my lap, offering his own version of comfort.

"Your mother is the reason my father left," I tell him. "Or they killed him." I shake my head, trying to untangle Caspien's claims. "Caspien was ranting. I don't know the details. He just claimed your mother *handled* it."

He stops, in the middle of the room. With the light hitting his face from the window, I can see the dark circles below his eyes. I heard him begging me to wake up, felt him next to me the entire time. I know he's exhausted, but the evidence makes my heart squeeze in my chest. And adding all this to his plate is not helping, but he has to know.

"My father was the only one who didn't agree with me being sent away. He wanted me to be Varethiel's queen."

He nods, then tips his head back, looking at the ceiling. "So you're saying," he bites out, his arms flexing as he lifts his hands to the back of his neck and linking his fingers together. "That my family may have killed your father and sent you away causing massive storms that have almost destroyed the entire energy system—all to maintain power over a weakened, destroyed world?" He lowers his head and is nodding by the end.

"There is more..."

He huffs out a sigh, dropping his arms. "Tell me."

"*He*"—I swallow—"killed Nova." My voice is quiet.

Cillian drops to his knees in front of me, his hands tightening around my free hand. "*Who* killed her?"

I look at him with big eyes, my lips pressed together tightly, tilting my head the smallest amount. It's silly to be scared of a name, but it feels like if I say it, he will appear, be summoned to this very room.

I swallow again, building the courage. But I don't have to.

"Caspien killed Nova," Cillian says slowly. It's a statement, not a question, but I confirm with a small nod.

"He thought she was me..." I say sadly.

He places a hand on my cheek. His lips brush mine gently. His thumb runs along my cheekbone for just a moment before he pulls away.

"They will all pay," he says, voice deadly calm. "You have my word, Queen. Though apparently the word of a Vaylor doesn't mean much."

Shoulders squared, he strides out the door.

CHAPTER

FORTY

NISSA

Three days later, Cillian storms into the Royal Guardians' command meeting. The wooden door groaning as it is thrown into the wall.

"Did you know?" he demands, his voice low. He doesn't even glance at anyone else as he marches across the floor and leans low into his best friend's face, hands fisted on Niko's desk.

Niko's eyes dart around the airy room before landing back on Cillian. "What the hell are you blowing on about?" he snaps back at him.

I should be paying more attention to the Guardian's reactions from my hiding space. But it is hard to pull my attention from the commanding energy that pulses around my mate.

His anger can be felt through the room, the weight of his rage pressing in like the depths of the sea, "Watch how you speak to me, *Lord Commander*," he snarls.

The tension around the room thicken as he uses Niko's title this way, pulling obvious rank. This is a king speaking to his subordinate, not friends.

Even the wind in the room seems to be holding its breath. The Guardian's glancing at one another, waiting to see their commander's response.

Some lounge on the cloud couches with their arms crossed over their chests. Others stand, watching Cillian and Niko with wide eyes. The males in this room have extensive inception mark that stretch high up up each of their necks. But none are quite as high as their leaders.

Niko's back straightens and he shifts in his seat. His eyes move around the room across his unit, taking in their watchful eyes.

Cillian ignores the other Guardians. They aren't important *yet*. But I keep a close eye on them. Each face has varying levels of shock painted across it. Some, maybe, even a hint of *fear*. Those are the ones that hold my attention the most.

"Were you part of the cover-up?" he demands. "Caspien confessed everything when he *kidnapped* Nissa. When he almost *killed* her!" I swallow, looking back at Cillian. My heart constricting. This anger is real. The pain of him almost losing me, palpable.

"She's well enough to talk?" Niko's eyebrows drop down low as if he's processing new information, fidgeting with a quill pen on his desk.

Cillian voice drops low but still audible to everyone around the room, "She remembers *everything* he told her."

Niko stands with this revelation, and Cillian pulls himself up from leaning over the desk. They hold each others gaze for a breath, the tension almost unbearable even to me.

"If all of you will excuse us." Niko's eyes are still fixed firmly on Cillian, but they have a new level of intensity. "*The king* and I have some security matters to discuss, privately."

From the root system that I occupy, I take in each of the

Guardian's faces as they stand to leave the room. Each one silently eyeing their commander and king.

Slowly they file out of the room, closing the door behind them. For multiple heartbeats, no one moves. Niko and Cillian still unmoving, watching one another over his desk.

I ease out of the root system that concealed me, materializing and collapse onto a floating couch that the top Guardian's just vacated. Niko finally cracks a smile and begins a slow clap. I quirk the corner of my mouth at Cillian as he turns towards me, rolling his eyes.

"*Lord Commander*, really?" Niko says his title with gusto, lifting an eyebrow at his best friend who has settled down next to me.

Cillian lets out a short laugh, pulling me close. "It felt right in the moment."

Niko's smile drops. "Did you see some of the looks on their faces? That was fear," he says.

Cillian nods soberly. "With luck it shouldn't be too long."

Niko leans down, pulling out a sphere filled with numerous sirilis guppies. It's taken days to gather them and get them here. We all watch them closely in fascination.

The tiny fish are an oddity, only found in the deepest parts of the ocean that separates Solevara and Varethiel. In the past, they were more readily available but the beasts that now plague the seas make it a perilous undertaking.

"Where did Hazel even get this many sirilises on such short notice?" Niko asks. He eyes the little fish that are needed to create the markings that run up his neck.

"I have no idea." Cillian wasn't happy about asking Aiden for the favor. He still isn't sure we can trust Varethiel's prince but we knew the witch could help with what we needed.

We fall silent when the mouthless fish begin to shimmer

and swim along the outside edges of their confinement. Suddenly, a dozen voices flood the room.

We flinch at the chaotic chorus of voices that flow from the sphere. But as the sirilis fall into a pattern, their scales shine brighter and begin to sift through the words, separating the conversations.

"Did you see how mad he was? I don't think I've ever seen Cillian like that." One voice fills the space between us.

"What do you think he confessed?"

"Who knows with everything that entitled prick did."

We glance at each other. "Just because they don't like him doesn't mean they were part of it," Niko says.

"Thank the Goddess the queen woke up. I was starting to think we lost them both."

"Mhmm," is all the relief about my life being spared is met with.

"Can you imagine the storms Gaia would have sent..."

We continue to listen to Guardian after Guardian discuss the day's gossip along with the show Cillian and Niko just put on for them.

Niko writes down a few names. Clearly some of the Guardians have realized, or been told, that the storms are connected to Nova and me. But there's no definitive evidence that any of them were involved in my kidnapping or any of the previous treachery.

As conversations begin to shift to drills and schedules, my heart sinks, losing hope in the plan.

"Maybe this was a bad idea—" I start but my voice breaks off as Niko holds up his hand.

A panicked voice echoes through the room.

"Your Highness..."

FORTY-ONE

NISSA

For the first time since we put our plan in place, I am out of our room without hiding. As we sit on the thrones on the Dias in the ballroom, I reach over and link my fingers through Cillian's. The room is decorated the way it should have been originally at our reception. The perfect mix of earth and water elements filling the space in honor of our bond.

With us diving straight into working on the elemental lands and then the kidnapping, we never had the Royal Procession—one that all Fae are welcome to attend, not just the Elite.

Typically this is a ceremonial procession through the streets of the Elite City but we decided to conclude it with a formal event at the castle. One where *everyone* was welcome. One that will show the Fae that things are about to change.

My new heartstone lay heavy between my breasts. The gold sewn into my dress shining in the lights of the room. My outfit complimenting Cillian's deep blue suit perfectly.

Butterflies fill my stomach for what is about to come but in the same breath, warmth blooms in my chest. Warmth at knowing I am exactly where I need to be. That we are taking the steps we need to, to revive our world.

A smile grows across my face as I watch every social level of Fae fill the royal ballroom. A solemn silence falls over the room, and Cillian squeezes my hand as his parents— the former king and queen—and Halcya are announced.

The Fae part to allow the three of them to approach the dais. Traditionally the former king and queen would sit to the new king's left. Receiving the respects given to the former monarchs.

The three of them hesitate when they reach the bottom of the steps and realize that their seats are missing. Isolde's eyes dart around the room quickly before landing back on us.

Cillian's father smiles softly up at us. "King Cillian, Queen Nissa." He gives a small bow that is not required of the former king to the new monarchs.

Isolde sneers in the direction of her counterpart, then says, "Cillian, where—"

He holds up a hand, silencing his mother. I fight back a smile of satisfaction, trying to keep my face tranquil. Her eyes go wide, but she has the sense to stop talking. A mottled red flushes her cheeks as she takes in those around her again.

"We have decided to use this celebration as the occasion for one of my first royal orders," Cillian proclaims to the room.

Confused eyes stare back at us.

"As all of you know, my mate, your queen was recently taken. In the wake of this, we have learned of a number of decisions and events that led to her kidnapping." He is addressing the room, but Isolde's mouth presses so tight that her lips are colorless. Her hands fisting the fabric of her burgundy dress in a silent tantrum.

Her mate, at her side, reaches for her hand. She pulls away from him.

"We have discovered," Cillian continues, "that my brother, the former prince, was responsible for Princess Nova's death."

Every Fae around the edges of the room begins talking in shock. Kiel jerks his head to Isolde, but she doesn't return his gaze, eyes locked on her son.

I share a look with Cillian. The shock on his father's face confirms it. He didn't know about Nova at least.

"Isolde Vaylor..." Cillian's voice is amplified by the wisps in the room. "As former Queen of Castara, we hold you responsible for the cover-up of the murder of the Daughter of Gaia, Princess Nova Navarro."

Isolde's mouth falls open, but she seems too stunned to speak. A few Guardians shift uneasily on their feet, some even taking steps backwards towards the doors. Before they can run, Guardians who Niko and Cillian have deemed trustworthy, along with a few back-ups from Varethiel, step forward through every doorway.

Chaos begins to break out.

"Furthermore"—Cillian holds his hand up, quieting everyone—"Isolde and Kiel Vaylor, High Priestess Halcya—you are all three being held accountable for the destruction and depletion of Castara's natural resources and energy. By concealing essential information and sending Nissa Navarro away from Solevara for so many years, you were the direct cause of the Goddess's attack on the elemental lands."

Halyca's hand is covering her bright red lips in shock. Her body frozen in place.

Kiel's ashen gaze moves between us and his mate who is fire personified. She looks like she wants to burn the world down around her. Which is ironic since she almost did with all of her deception.

Cries of anguish and shouts of outrage erupt from all those assembled. Everyone's powers have been directly impacted by the storms and they are realizing that those in front of them are directly responsible for that.

Guardians surround the three responsible and begin restraining them. Kiel has the decency to look guilty and is easily bound, but Isolde and Halcya struggle when the guardians approach. After so many years of lies, I guess I shouldn't be surprised.

"Son. Please, " Isolde calls out once she finds her voice again.

Son... I don't think I've ever heard her call Cillian that before.

Which breaks my heart a little more for him. How dare this manipulative female use her motherly bond to try and get out of the consequences of her own actions. Actions that impacted an entire world.

Cillian's voice rings out firm. "As Matriarch Queen, you will not be sentenced to death, but your magic will be bound, and you will be banished to the human world through the same portal where Princess Nova was killed."

Isolde, of all Fae, hates other species. To be sent to live out her immortal life in the human world, without her powers, basically as one of them, in her eyes death may be preferable.

"Out of mercy, your mate bond will be broken," Cillian continues, looking to his father. "Patriarch King Kiel, you will be imprisoned here until Gaia sees fit to return you to your element."

Kiel's shoulders drop in obvious relief, and he hangs his head. Isolde's stone facade doesn't react at all.

My eyebrows draw together. Breaking a mate bond is excruciating, mentally and physically. Yes, this is a mercy on Cillian's part, but true mates should be in a panic.

"High Priestess Halcya, you, along with any Guardians

suspected of being part of these cover-ups and conspiracies, will be confined and tried at a later date."

More pandemonium erupts, with Guardians restraining other Guardians suspected of misconduct. Niko takes a stance behind us, ensuring our safety. Niko and Cillian have planned well. Soon, the guilty are all being led away.

We both stand again. Cillian offers the remaining crowd a serene smile. Only I realize it's full of pain.

He explains to the Fae before us that we believe that by correcting the decisions of the former monarchs, Castara will be restored to its full potential. It will take a lot of work to rebuild, but we are committed to doing everything within our power to fix it all.

With the adrenaline leaving my body, I begin imagining the future. A future where the useless synthetic energy sources are removed from the Two Kingdoms. Where plants grow in thriving, healthy soil; fresh water flows freely; air blows naturally; and fire burns unassisted. Energy and magic will be restored.

Then something pulls at a memory. Something that Caspien said before giving me that potion...

When we sit back down, I whisper, "Are the storms starting back in Varethiel?"

FORTY-TWO

NISSA

B linking awake, I moan as I feel petal-like kisses moving down my stomach. Strong hands grip my hips under the sheets, holding me firmly to the bed.

Reaching the top of my underwear, he lifts his head from my abdomen to slip my underwear down my legs. Unfortunately for him, *and me*, Cyndr takes notice of the threat moving under the covers—and *attacks*.

Cillian yells out as claws penetrate through the sheets into the top of his head. My eyes go wide, and I jerk up to grab my miniature protector. Before I can pry his claws out, Cillian lifts up on his knees, still covered in the blankets, and Cyndr screeches, digging his claws in tighter. Pure pandemonium fills the room.

By the time I separate the two, I am in a full blooming laugh. With his hair in all directions from the sheets and the attack, Cillian gives me an outraged-filled look, like I have betrayed him. I laugh even harder.

Before I realize what is happening, he lunges for me, grabs my sides, and tickles me until tears are streaming down my cheeks. I scream between the laughter for Cyndr to get him. But now that he has identified the threat as a friend, he lazily curls up in the sun by the window, swishing his tail in the stream and ignoring my plea.

When Cillian finally relents, we are lying side by side, chests rising and falling rapidly. Random laughs bubble out of both of us.

Linking our hands, Cillian rolls his head to face me. "Are you going to see your mother today?" His expression is concerned.

It has been two days since they took everyone into custody. My mother had not arrived at the celebration yet, so she was apprehended from my childhood home. The same home where my father taught me to love and laugh, to dance and cherish those in your life. The home that now sits empty—my sister dead, my mother contained, and my father gone.

I take a deep breath and sit up, cross-legged next to Cillian. "Want to see a trick?"

He gives me a knowing smile but nods. Placing his hands behind his head, flexing his arms and putting them on full display for me. I smile at the ease of the moment and allow myself another few minutes before facing the question of my mother.

"Cyndr," I whisper, and a single eyelid opens to look at me. "Let's show him." I tilt my head towards Cillian and note the growing interest on his face. He sits up, watching closely.

Excited but in no rush to share his new trick, Cyndr stands and stretches his back. He sits back on his haunches, and I giggle at the confident look on his little face. He looks up at me and then to Cillian before his chest grows as he sucks in air. Cillian's eyes go wide when Cyndr blows out and a small burst of fire fills the space between us.

"Your fire!" Cillian laughs in excitement. "How did this

happen?" he asks as Cyndr jumps to his lap to receive his praise.

"As soon as you told me that he'd lost his fire, I began working on some different herbal concoctions I hoped would help. I took them to the library every day, and it seems to have worked."

Cyndr puffs up his chest again, now perched on Cillian's shoulder, and blows out another burst of fire. I smile, watching the two of them.

"I'm going to talk to her this afternoon," I say, finally acknowledging his question about my mother.

His smile fades for a moment before returning. He nods and we let it drop. He knows I'll come to him when I'm ready to talk about it.

～

I'VE PUT it off as long as I can. I slowly pull the wind into my chest as the Guardians pull the iron doors open for me. They watch me with sympathetic eyes as I stand there, staring into the dark hallway, unmoving.

When an uncomfortable amount of time has passed, they look at each other.

"Queen—"

I hold up my hand. They both dip their heads towards the floor and give me the time I need to build up the courage to get answers that I don't know if I want.

When I eventually cross the threshold, fae fire torches along the wall dimly come ablaze providing me with the needed light. I look past barred cell after barred cell before I find my mother in one halfway down the hall.

I stand there, firm as a tree trunk, rooted to the hallway's stones as she looks back through the bars at me. She looks older here, her thin body clothed in black, washing out her natural coloring.

"Nissa." My name comes out like a prayer on her lips. Like she isn't sure I'm really there.

I swallow hard.

When I don't respond, she stands and walks to the bars. She studies my face for a breeze and then returns her gaze to my eyes. "Do you want to know?" she asks.

I blink back the burning in my eyes.

"No excuses," she rushes out. "I'm as guilty as the others, but can I tell you why?"

I try to nod, but the movement won't come. "Is my father actually alive?" I have to know. I don't want any story or excuse until I know that truth.

A single tear slides down her cheek. "Yes. I can still feel him out there." She places fingers to her chest. "I don't know where. But somewhere—he lives."

I nod the smallest amount, and she stares at me for just a moment. "He loved—loves you and Nova so much. When the High Priestess told the four of us about the prophecy, you could see the pride in his eyes. It filled my heart so full, *until* I saw the horror on Isolde's face."

She looks to the ground. "I knew something was wrong. But Kiel decided immediately that you would be trained alongside Nova. It was Gaia's decree, so neither of them questioned Isolde when she said we should keep it quiet. They agreed with her logic about not telling Castara until the four of you were older." She shakes her head and looks up at me. "I should have spoken up then. I could see in her eyes that she did not like the prophecy. A mother's intuition maybe. And once we learned about Aiden... I knew she had no intention of letting him take half the kingdom from her children."

I take in her words. Isolde has been at the center of every-thing, in everyone's account. She manipulated everything.

"Then there was an accident..." Tears fill her eyes, and a line forms between my eyebrows. "You were hurt badly."

What accident? I don't remember this.

"Isolde had the images removed from your memory," she explains.

"Why?" It is the first word I've gotten out since she started.

"I think Caspien caused it. He was becoming violent even then." A look of confusion crosses her face. "You fell. To be honest I don't remember exactly what Isolde said happened. Just that it would be better for everyone if we sent you to the Homestead to recover."

And I never came back.

"Did you know he killed Nova?" The words rush from my mouth. My entire body shakes, waiting for the answer.

Her eyes go wild, "No! He wanted to be king more than anything. Killing Nova would make no sense. He *needed* her."

"But you warned me." I narrow my gaze on her.

She nods. "I agreed to send you away, but it was always to keep you safe. And as you got older, it was clear you hated it here and didn't care about being queen. And I saw just how dangerous Isolde could be. I was terrified when you started looking into Nova's death. The Vaylors were obviously covering something up. I just didn't know why. I didn't want you upsetting the wrong person. And Isolde is easily upset."

"So it was all out of *love*," I say, jaw tight.

Her eyes are sad, her shoulders dropping. "As I said, no excuses. I could have spoken up so many times, and I didn't out of fear. It was the wrong decision and impacted *every-thing*." The weight of the last word is heavy between us. "Once the storms started I didn't speak up. I didn't fight for you. Just because you were gone didn't change Gaia's plans and she made that clear. I will take whatever punishment you and the king decide. I deserve it. "

I take in her words and realization dawns on me.

Just because Nova is gone...

How could we have missed this? I know why the storms are starting back up in Varethriel.

CHAPTER

FORTY-THREE

NISSA

T he last time I was carried through the doors of the dark castle that looms over us my life had changed in so many different ways. Cillian has explained what happened that night and everything they did to help Ophe and me. I owe Aiden and his team, Hazel specifically, a debt of gratitude. Hopefully what we came for will suffice as a thank you.

We are led past the council room that we met in previously and are welcomed into a study that has a large sitting area carved from rhyolite rock in front of a warm, natural fae fire. Aiden is leaned back with his ankle over his knee, showing off more tattoos that creep up his exposed ankle.

Hazel and Enzo are seated in surrounding chairs. Enzo stands, looking behind us as we enter. Hazel remains sitting, smiling up at us politely.

Cillian grips Enzo's forearms in greeting and moves casually to sit on a couch for two across from Aiden. Caspien would have baulked at the fact that Aiden and Hazel didn't stand, but Cillian is unfazed.

We have spoken at great lengths about this meeting and

how we want to present ourselves. How we want to address Varethiel's current problem with the storms starting again. Another example of a stark difference from how Caspien would have handled things.

"What do we owe this pleasure?" Aiden's tone is even but tinged with suspicion. I can't blame him, his history with the Vaylor family would have me cautious too.

I speak up, my back straight and hands entwined in my lap, "Well, first, I wanted to thank all of you." I look between the three of them. I catch Aiden's eyes moving up and down my body intently. "Catch" is probably the wrong word, because he isn't hiding it or trying to be subtle. But like before, it doesn't feel sexual, it feels... protective, like he's checking for any injuries that remain.

"I'm glad to see you doing so well," Hazel says in her melodic voice, smiling at me. "The poison from the blade is powerful."

It seems sincere. I return her smile. "Thanks to all of you. Without your assistance in finding me, the medical help and" —I focus this on Hazel—"helping enchant the sirilis, it all could have been a lot harder—a lot *worse*."

"Right, well, anything else?" Aiden begins to stand, dismissing us.

I almost laugh at his impatience. He seems to not like wasting time. Or maybe he's just tired of dealing with the Vaylors.

"Actually yes," Cillian replies.

Aiden lets out a long breath before sitting back down. Hazel looks amused, but Enzo returns the uneasy look.

"We're aware that the storms seem to be starting here again. Since we believe we've discovered their cause, we think we have a way to stop them here as well." Cillian pauses.

"And what is that?" Aiden asks, seemingly bored with the line of conversation.

"We've discovered a prophecy that was hidden—" Cillian begins.

"Right, the mirrored princesses. What of it?" Aiden asks calmly. I had suspected he knew when we thought he was involved in Nova's death but the confirmation uproots me.

"You knew?" I blurt out. "But you never reached out to me, tried to connect with me. Bring me back. Well, not until..."

Cillian's hand wraps around mine, protectively. As if he feels like Aiden still has some type of right to me, even though the Goddess clearly made *us* mates.

He shrugs a shoulder. "I had no desire to make you my queen. I can rule without taking some female hostage—"

Hazel snorts a laugh, and we all turn towards her.

"As my queen," he finishes as he glares at her.

"Sorry." She laughs again, putting her hands up.

Enzo looks equally amused, while Aiden looks like he could burn them both alive on the spot. I wonder what they are going on about.

We all turn when we hear a commotion through the door to the hallway. Enzo quickly stands, but Hazel speaks up again. "No, I'll handle it."

"Probably a good idea," Aiden grumbles under his breath as she breezes out the door, closing it behind her.

"I don't care about some prophecy claiming I need a queen, mate, or whatever. I can rule my kingdom without all that." He shoots an intentional look at Cillian, staking claim to half the Two Kingdoms.

"That's actually why we're here," Cillian says.

Aiden raises a single eyebrow.

"As you clearly know, the Goddess intended for you to rule your kingdom." Cillian pauses.

The silence is thick in the room.

"Obviously the priestess got it wrong when they believed you were meant to be with Nissa. But we believe Gaia still wishes for you to rule even if Nova isn't..." He squeezes my hand. "We want to officially make you the King of Varethiel. Not just in title but you will have all the say, all the power over it—without Vaylor involvement."

It's Enzo's turn to laugh. "What's the catch?"

Aiden says nothing, watching us intently.

"No war? No arguments?" Enzo asks, more serious. "You want us to believe a Vaylor walked in here to just hand over half the world that you rule?"

"We don't want a war." Cillian focuses on Aiden. "We want what's best for the Fae across both kingdoms, no matter what king rules them. We don't know why but it is clear in the prophecy that our world needs you on the throne as well. The storms are starting back, but only here in Varethiel. We want to do whatever we need to make them stop."

Enzo looks at him like he's grown a second head. Aiden seems bored.

"It's true," I chime in. "We've already been working to restore the energy in our elemental lands."

"It won't matter if I rule over all of it," Cillian says, giving Aiden the same rationale he gave me outside of his office that day, "if we're all too weak to protect ourselves against an outside attack. We've stopped them in Solevara, but I don't believe they'll stop here until you're in full control. We can work together, rule as allies. I'm not my mother or brother. I don't care about power. I care about the Fae."

Again, Aiden just stares at us like he has better things to do.

Cillian stands. "We'll let you think over everything. I'll be in touch to discuss the logistics and what changes need to be implemented."

Aiden and Enzo follow Cillian's lead, standing to escort us out. Aiden reaches for the door to let us out.

I stop him before he steps through, "One last thing. How did you find me and Ophe? Who was the lead?" I search Aiden's face and catch a spark of something in his eyes.

"That information is—" He breaks off, looking into the hallway. He drops his head and rubs his eyes, mumbling something into the wind.

I can't hear what he says because the blood is rushing in my ears. Blinking, a hand pressed to my chest, I look past him into the hallway.

To a Fae who is supposed to be dead.

Nova is standing there, staring back at me.

EPILOGUE

I'm amazed at the difference in the sounds of Aquaria that surround us. The first time we came here together, the prominent sound was the dried mud cracking under our feet. Today the roar of distant waterfalls mixed with the subtle trickle of the streams nearby bring a smile to my face.

"How was your conversation with Nova?" Cillian asks, his fingers threaded through my own, warming me. I just got back from Varethriel and I still haven't shaken the slight chill that fills my bones from their snowy environment.

"Alive," I say, shaking my head. Still in shock even after hearing her story. It's been a week since I realized my twin sister was alive and still haven't wrapped my head around it. Cillian gives me a soft smile as he continues to lead me deeper into his elemental land.

The elemental lands have begun to thrive from our clean up efforts and from the lack of Gaia's storms in Solevara. I can't say the same about Varethriel though...

"Caspien did *try* to kill her but instead of finishing the job he threw her through the portal, assuming the poison in her system would finish her off," I explain what she told me.

"So how did she survive?" He asks. "How did she end up with *Aiden?*" Humor filling his voice with the prince's name.

"A human found her and did their best to heal her. It didn't work but Aiden came for her before..." I clear my throat when it cracks slightly. He squeezes my hand gently.

"Anyways, I guess Hazel has been keeping an eye on both of us since we were children and realized what happened. She is the one who healed Nova. That is how she knew how to help me. Nova was the *'one time'* they had seen the poison before." I let the words fall off when we stop at the edge of the water. A waterfall is crashing over the rocks to our left before settling into the reservoir at our feet.

I release the wind slowly, even though it isn't my element, being in Aquaria has my magic humming. I'm not sure if it is being back in a thriving natural element or if it is because of the bond Cillian and I have. Either way, I cherish it. There is still a lot of work to do but the change is evident. The power returning to Solevara is evident.

He wraps his arms around my waist, resting his head on top of mine. "So what is the plan now? Is she going to come home? Stay in Varethriel?"

"She said she wasn't ready to talk about the prophecy. She needs time to wrap her head around it and figure out what to do. I'm not sure what is going on with her and Aiden but she is not interested in coming here."

"You think something is going on with them?" He asks, surprise coating his voice. "That could help with the need to fulfill the prophecy..."

I don't really know. From her notebooks I know he drives her crazy and I still get that impression but something else was there. A spark in Nova's eyes that has been missing for a long time. Maybe it is just her having her freedom for the first time in her life. *Maybe it is him.*

I just hum in response.

"We agreed to wisp each other. I don't want to get my hopes up but she seems serious about staying in touch this time." We fall silent for a minute. His calm peace pours over my shaken soul like a river washing over parched soil. Filling me back up, *nourishing* me.

"Anyways... What did you want to show me?" I ask, looking up at him over my shoulder. His eyes shine down at me, a brilliant blue that makes my heart beat a little harder.

"Come on," Cillian takes my hand and leads me along the waters edge towards the waterfall. Mist tickles my face and arms as we approach. Cillian shifts behind me as the path narrows.

"Watch your step," he says loudly over the thunderous sound of the crashing water.

The rocks have become slick with algae from the damp surroundings and he places his hands on my hips to keep me steady. My magic rises up to meet him in response. I climb the naturally created steps, leading us closer to the cascading water.

I turn and look out over the bluff we stand on when the walkway abruptly ends with a deluge of water before us. The beauty takes my breath away.

The trees and plantlife around the reservoir are lush and green. Brilliant flowers paint the bushes and vines that line the blue and green hues of swirling water beside and below us.

"It is stunning," I whisper but he still hears me.

Grabbing my hand again we walk towards the wall of water and with a laugh he drags me under. I gasp as the chilled water soaks through my dress as I am pulled into a cave hidden beneath the waterfall.

The rumbling descent of the water echoes off the walls. Rays of light stream in through the crystal clear water creating rainbows across the walls of rock.

"You know you could have done that without getting me soaked!" I shriek, laughter quick to follow as I see that he is just as wet as I am. He runs his hand through his wet hair, pushing it back. His perfect smile fills his face as he looks back at me.

"Where is the fun in that?" he teases, eyeing my *now* almost sheer dress.

I give him a sly smile and rub my hands down the wet shirt that grips his chest. As I slowly trace my fingers down the ridges of his abdomen I feel his abs shuddering under my touch. When I reach the bottom of the shirt, I slowly untuck the linen garment. Looking up at him through my lashes, I move on to the clasp at his waist.

In one swift motion he pulls the fabric over his head and discards it to the side. His pants hang undone, loose around his hips as he looks at me with predatory intent. He wraps his arms around me, gripping my ass and lifting me up. I wrap my legs around his waist, his excitement pressing against me.

I slide my fingers into his wet hair, and our mouths find each other with growing urgency. Drowning in the moment, our connection to one another is the oxygen we need to survive but we are unable to get enough.

He breaks us apart, our chests heaving, and gently lays me across a rock that the waterfall has smoothed over the years. I swallow thickly as the light shines across his chiseled muscles, emphasizing each groove, like they are carved in stone. My eyes follow the vee that disappears into his pants. *He is perfect.*

His eyes glow darker as he runs his hands slowly up my body. He unclasps only the top buttons of my dress, freeing my breasts, allowing him immediate access. My nipples harden as the cool air and mist of the cave blow across my wet skin.

He licks his lips at the sight and leans down, giving them all of his attention. The heat of his mouth finds one while he rolls the other in between his fingers. With the perfect amount of pressure my back raises up off the rock in pure bliss. With an ache building between my legs, both my hands wrap around his neck to pull him closer as my body demands more of him.

"Cillian," I call out his name and it joins in the echo of the water around us.

His sultry chuckle vibrates through me causing me to moan in agonizing pleasure. He grinds into me and slowly begins kissing and sucking his way up my collarbone to my neck. His lips ghost across my ear, "Be patient, Lila. I promise I'll give you what you want."

His hand has left my heaving chest and his fingers are lightly skimming down my stomach causing a chain reaction of each nerve along the way to fire.

Gathering the wet skirt of my dress he pulls it up around my hips. When he reaches my soaked underwear the wind leaves my lungs in anticipation. He stares down at me with hooded eyes before, tracing my slit through the thin fabric.

I groan in frustration when he moves his hands to my thighs, causing his perfect smile to grow. His eyes swimming with mischief when he looks back up at my face.

"So eager." He teases as he walks his fingers back towards my center. "Is this what you want?"

My legs spread farther apart as he reaches the apex of my thighs. My eyes silently beg as my whole body trembles with anticipation.

He hooks his fingers into the fabric and pushes it to the side. He pulls a low moan from me as he slips one finger between my folds.

"*Yes!*" I cry out in pleasure as he slides a second finger inside, stretching me deliciously. I give myself over to him completely. This is what I need, and he knew that. I am lost to him. I was drowning in the tide of today's revelation, buried beneath its weight. And Cillian is both air and solid ground. *Breath and anchor.* Everything beyond my mate, beyond the echo of our entwined pleasure, dissolves into nothing.

His mouth swallows my moans as his thumb makes its way to my clit. Moving in synchronized movements to match the song that he is makes my body sing.

I am rapidly approaching a release but I don't want it to end this way.

As if reading my mind, he pulls his hands away, the promise of my approaching climax crashes around me like the waterfall at my back. His absence is immediately felt but my body and magic are still humming, wanting more than just his fingers inside of me. I move up onto my elbows, pouting as I watch him take a half step back.

A cunning smirk pulls across his face, as he slowly starts to pull my underwear down my legs and the water from above me begins to fall. I was so wrapped up in what we were doing that I hadn't even realized that he was controlling the water above us. The slow, pure flow of the waterfall between us is beginning to pick up. *It splits me in two.*

As soon the fabric separating us is gone, the water above me replaces where his thumb had been circling, hitting me in just the right place. My hips tilt and my arms give out beneath me. My head falling back with a cry of pleasure.

At that exact moment I feel him pushing against me asking for entrance, his hand on my hips under the water. With the water beating down on my sensitive clit, I scream out in ecstasy as he fills me so deep that I can't take any more. He slides back and stills when he is almost completely out but the water is unrelenting.

I can't form coherent words at this point. Needing him to move to match the other sensation assaulting my body, I hook my feet behind him and pull him back into me. He takes my cue and starts a determined rhythm pumping in and out of me.

Our moans swirl together like the waves meeting the shore, rolling together until the cave carries them away. With each thrust I feel my stomach twisting into a coil ready to explode. When his hand reaches through the water and gently rolls my nipple between his fingers, I *unravel*. The orgasm that rips through my body has my back come entirely off the rock before collapsing back.

Coming down from my high I'm overwhelmed with the extent of sensations. "Cillian, it's too much!" I whine, as I grab his hands and pull him forward enough to block the water falling from above with his body.

I feel him pull all the way out and easily flips me onto my stomach. Leaned over the rock he is back at my sex in seconds and pushes back in. The position makes me feel even more full than before. His thrusts become erratic as he gets closer to his own release.

He reaches around and begins circling my clit, taking me back to the edge with him. Our mating bond coursing through our blood, our magic emphasizing each sensation that we share.

I hear his strained words in my ear over the crashing waterfall, "I love you, Nissa."

And as we come together, it is not just with flesh, but with the divine certainty that we were always meant to be together. To find our way back to each other.

BONUS SCENE
ONE WEEK AGO

"If we had something of hers, I could do a locator spell. Maybe see if Cillian has anything of hers on him when he arrives?"

I appreciate Hazel's suggestion, but it's *far* from enough. "That will be too late! If Caspien really does have her, we can't wait another second." My attention is on Aiden. "We have to find her *now*," I plead.

"I'm doing everything I can, Nova. We have every guard awake and looking for her. We'll do the spell as soon as they're here. We'll find her," he says, attempting to reassure me.

The minutes are passing too fast. Nissa has been with *him* too long.

"What about me?" I throw my attention back to Hazel, trying to read her reaction. "We're twins! Can you use me?"

Her eyes are trained on Aiden.

I look back at him. "Please, you know what he's capable of."

He looks back at the petite witch, "Could it be done?"

"Well, yes... but I can't do it and hold the shield that's hiding her. I'll have to drop it, do the locator spell, and then put the shield back up. Nissa will immediately feel her. And if anyone is actively looking for Nova, then they'll be able to tell she's alive."

"Nova..." He looks back at me with weary eyes.

He is going to tell me no.

"Do it. Now!"

They share a worried look.

"What the hell are we waiting on?" I scream. "This is my sister! He *will* kill her and only the Goddess knows what else."

They still don't make a move.

I walk to Aiden, shoulders squared, and look directly into his smoke-filled eyes. "You claim I'm not a hostage here. So, this is *my* choice. We're doing the locator spell," I grit out, hoping my confidence sways him.

His jaw flexes in annoyance that this is when I've decided to stand up for myself.

"I'll still be here with all of your protection," I say.

He holds eye contact with me for just a moment before he nods and looks at Hazel. "Do it, quickly. I'll go wait on Cillian and his guards."

I take his hand in mine. "Thank you, Aiden."

He squeezes once. "Go find your sister." Looking over my shoulder to Hazel, he says, "Send me the information as soon as you get it."

And he walks out the door.

Thank you for stepping into Castara with me.

It means more than I can tell you. If you have a moment, leaving a review is one of the kindest ways to support an indie author.

Your words truly matter.

Amazon

GoodReads

StoryGraph

NEXT IN THE SERIES

The story is not done...

Book Two: Coming in 2026

Aiden's Story

❧

Book Three:

Ophelia's Story

GLOSSARY AND PRONUNCIATION GUIDE

Glossary

Gaia: (GUY-uh) *Fae Goddess*

The Mother of Nature, creator and caretaker of the fae realms, tied to elemental balance and the natural world.

Asteria: (a-STEER-ee-uh) *Witch Goddess*

Goddess of the stars, intuition, and celestial magic among witches.

Apollyon: (a-POL-ee-on) *Vampire God*

Ruler of the vampire realm

Elohim: (EL-oh-heem) *Human God*

Protector of humankind and the mortal world.

Castara: (kas-TAR-uh) *Fae World*

Ruled by Gaia, the Fae world of elemental magic and two Fae kingdoms

Pollara: (po-LAR-uh) *Witch World*

Ruled by Asteria, a world connected by arcane ley lines and deep celestial magic.

Alhena: (al-HEE-nuh) *Vampire World*

Ruled by Apollyon, home to vampire clans and ancient courts.

Solevara & Varthriel: (so-leh-VAR-uh & vuh-RETH-ee-el) *The two kingdoms of Castara*

Distinct fae lands shaped by elemental influences and ancient rulings.

Vaylor: (VAY-lor) *The first king of Castara*

Placed on the throne by Gaia. His bloodline continues to rule the Two Kingdoms.

Prophecy of the Dual Birth: *Fae prophecy that no queen may conceive until Castara requires a new heir.* On the birthdate of each crown prince, a Daughter of Gaia will also be born. Trained together from childhood, the pair will ascend to the throne on their shared majority date.

The Daughter of Gaia:*A female Fae child born on the same day as the crown prince.* Destined to be his betrothed and to rule beside him once both reach their majority and come into their magic.

Majority Date: *The date of maturity when a Fae gains their elemental powers.*

~

Solevara's Elemental Lands

Terrania (teh-RAY-nee-uh)
The elemental lands of the earth fae.

Dense forests, towering mountains, and the portal to the Human World.

Aeronia (air-OWN-ee-uh)
The elemental lands of the wind fae.

Crystal cliffs, strong currents, and the portal to the Witch World.

Ignaria (ig-NAR-ee-uh)

The elemental lands of the fire fae.

Volcanic terrain, rivers of molten lava, and the portal to the Vampire World.

Aquaria (uh-KWAIR-ee-uh)

The elemental lands of the water fae.

A realm of rivers, waterways, and abundant water sources. Primary location of trade routes to Varthriel.

Pronunciation Guide for Main Characters

Nissa — *NISS-uh*

Cillian — *KILL-ee-en*

Nova — *NO-vuh*

Caspien — *CASS-pee-en*

SPECIAL THANKS

To the team of individuals who helped me turn a literal dream into a real book.

- Developmental Editor: Karen Dale Harris
- Cover Artist: Seventhstar Art
- Map Artist: Talitha Cheeseman
- Myth & Legend Coffee Shop

About the Author

S.C. (Caitlin) Licata is the author of *The Mirrored Princess* and the forthcoming books in the series. She lives in Georgia with her husband and their two young children. When she isn't building worlds and sipping coffee, you can find her playing with her kids, reading under a heated blanket, gardening, or puzzling.

Despite her love for romance and fantasy, Caitlin never expected to write her own story—until she had a literal dream about Chapter 28. Three years later, *The Mirrored Princess* is her debut novel, with many more to come.

Find her on TikTok and Instagram
@licatabooks